The Journey Home

Willy Nywening

iUniverse, Inc.
Bloomington

THE JOURNEY HOME

Copyright © 2013 Willy Nywening.

All rights reserved. No part of this book may be used or reproduced by any means, graphic, electronic, or mechanical, including photocopying, recording, taping or by any information storage retrieval system without the written permission of the publisher except in the case of brief quotations embodied in critical articles and reviews.

iUniverse books may be ordered through booksellers or by contacting:

iUniverse
1663 Liberty Drive
Bloomington, IN 47403
www.iuniverse.com
1-800-Authors (1-800-288-4677)

Because of the dynamic nature of the Internet, any web addresses or links contained in this book may have changed since publication and may no longer be valid. The views expressed in this work are solely those of the author and do not necessarily reflect the views of the publisher, and the publisher hereby disclaims any responsibility for them.

Cover image © Willy Nywening

ISBN: 978-1-4759-8829-1 (sc)
ISBN: 978-1-4759-8828-4 (hc)
ISBN: 978-1-4759-8827-7 (e)

Library of Congress Control Number: 2013907655

Printed in the United States of America.

iUniverse rev. date: 5/22/2013

For Dick,
my love,
my home.

Acknowledgements

The Journey Home is entirely fiction. My father orphaned at seven, originally inspired the main character, Jamie. The way he lived his life taught me that we all have difficulties to overcome. How we choose to do that determines the course of our lives. Love makes all things possible.

Many people have helped me complete this book. To all those who provided support in so many meaningful, different ways, thank you. Your love and friendship have reminded me again and again of the importance of family and friends. In some way, each one of you has contributed to making this story come alive. Thank you for your insights and encouragement.

My mentor, friend and editor, Lorraine Jardine, deserves special mention. Her work in reviewing and editing and her unrelenting support empowered the completion of this book. I am indebted to her not only for her editing skills, but more importantly for her friendship. She was my constant; she took my hand and walked the journey home with me. Although her name is not on the cover, this book is also hers. Thank you, Lorraine for believing!

Special thanks to my granddaughters, Ella and Emma, for agreeing to appear on the cover.

The finest of all dwellings

An abode
      built on a foundation of love
      covered with a roof of understanding
      enclosed within walls of forgiveness

That becomes
      a niche in the heart
      an inner space of retreat
      detached from outside clutter

A refuge
      a tended garden
      cultivating colors of affection
      offering a sacred pledge
      that fuses the past to the present
      and reaches beyond distance
      gathering together its own

Is
Home

                                    willy nywening

1
The End of Childhood

He had never seen the nightgown she was wearing. Delicate lace covered her neck and extended from the sleeves to cover part of her hands. White satin ribbons tied in soft bows added an exquisite touch. The fabric was white cotton, starched and stiffened. Its beautiful simplicity unsettled him and he wondered why he had never noticed it before.

"Mama," he murmured. He yanked himself free of his sister's hand and rushed toward the box. "Mama, wake up."

"No, Jamie, no," she moaned, but it was too late.

He arched over the casket to embrace his mother. Her face was ashen and grey. The cold clammy feel of her skin snapped him to the reality of her death. His bright blue eyes darkened. The tears dammed up behind them threatened, yet refused to break loose. He took a breath and straightened himself. He knew his mother. He loved his mother. This was not his mother.

Her wedding ring was missing. Her hair was forced back from her face; no soft, stray curls framed it the way they did when she was busy working. Her mouth, taunt and dour, could not sing the sweet lullabies she had sung to soothe the hardness of life. Her long slender fingers were clasped in an unfamiliar, stern form. Like her face, they were the color of death. They were not the kind, soft hands that had cradled his face, had comforted and blessed him.

A severe hand planted itself on his shoulder. He stiffened, sensing its intent.

"Be a man now, Jamie. Let the others have a look." The words, like his hands, were firm and demanding. Any contradiction would be futile. Jamie complied only because he knew his mama would expect it.

"Sometimes we just go through the motions, Jamie. God understands and will make it up, someway, somehow," Uncle John declared in a judicious voice.

He heard Mama's voice whispering and he stepped back submissively. He would be good, but not for God – for her. He had watched her retreat so many times that now he was able to do what she had done, to withdraw within himself to a place of solace that allowed no trespassers. With his feelings securely fenced there, he could feel the comfort of her touch; he could permit himself to go through the motions.

He stepped back and stood silently next to his sister Martha and his Uncle John. The realization dawned on him that he had never before been a visitor in this room. Often he had helped Mama carry cleaning supplies here, but he had never had an official reason to be here. The room was always sterile and sealed. Only exclusive occasions allowed entry – the minister's visits, special guests, weddings and of course funerals. It occurred to him that his mother had spent countless hours cleaning and polishing here. At least it looks nice for her now, he thought. He wondered who would purify the room now that she was gone.

The drawn, heavy, velvet drapes gave the room a dark, somber feeling. He knew Mama had loved the sunshine and wouldn't have approved. He inspected his surroundings in the dim light. It looked smaller than he remembered. The furniture was sparse. Two high backed chairs were covered in dark fabrics that had once boasted a tapestry of colors. It was obvious that time had long since dulled the intricate patterns. He remembered sitting on the matching sofa once when Mama had played the piano. It was the central piece of furniture in the room. Polished mahogany housed the instrument. The ivory keys, yellow with age, had seldom been touched in the past years. The red book of Sunday School hymns was open to the last song she had played for him, "Amazing Grace." She had sung it with a sweet clear voice that made the words come alive. Now she was dead. The penetrating sound of the music echoed through his ears. The melody had turned rancid and bitter.

When he remembered pulling out one of the tufted buttons on the sofa, the worried look on her face came back to him. She had scolded him and quickly pushed it back, hoping it wouldn't be noticed, but it didn't look the same. He saw it now sticking up and wanted to yank it from its base. He longed to pull out all the buttons from their sockets and let them know that what was happening was unjust. Instead, he did what was expected, standing straight and tall.

Two slender white candles burned in buffed brass candlestick holders. They stood erect on the piano; the light flickered and glowed with little interest, like soldiers marching joylessly to the beat of a cheerless drummer. On a walnut table next to the sofa, the light of a small hurricane lamp flickered, casting obscure shadows on the wall. He watched it earnestly, trying to decode the strange language of light. It mesmerized him.

The simple, pine casket sat on the seats of two plain kitchen chairs in the middle of the darkened room, in front of the white stone fireplace. No fire had warmed its hearth for many seasons. The mantle was bare, except for a delicate china vase that stood alone and empty. It looked undressed; there were no flowers to adorn its white milky skin. His Mama loved flowers.

Wrapped in their best black finery, the visitors came forward to greet the family. They retreated and stood at arm's length, as if afraid to come in contact with the curse that had robbed Esther of her life. For two hours the family stood, receiving the well-intentioned mourners. Few spoke to him or to his sister, Martha, directly. They clicked their tongues and patted his head, muttering obligatory condolences that he neither required nor understood. Martha responded with polite thanks, but Jamie could only stare mutely from the hushed, inside place where he hid. He saw the scene as if watching it through a peephole in the wall. In the vignette that unfolded, he surveyed himself standing emotionless and rigid next to his sister. One fussing matron enticed him to expose his sorrow. She crushed him with hugs, wanting him to feel her sadness, wanting him to expose his grief. He veiled his misery in a façade of courage as she broke into a loud lament, protesting his apparent lack of feeling. He would always remember the smell of mothballs intertwined with perspiration.

Martha rescued him by gently pulling him away. She took his hand, "Jamie, it's time to say goodbye."

"Go Jamie," Aunt Lydia's voice spoke softly. "Pay your last respects to your mother."

Martha led him again to the head of the coffin. She bent over, kissed her mother goodbye and wept silently. Jamie touched her stone cold hand, remembering the last time she had held his face. He saw himself sitting on her bed; was it possible that it was only a day ago? She had cupped her hands around his face, had looked deep into his eyes to take her leave.

"Don't be sad for me, Jamie," she said. "It's time for me to go home to be with your father."

"No, Mama, don't leave us," he had cried.

"Jamie, remember to love God, to be good and to work hard. Promise me." The pleading in her voice made it impossible for him to refuse.

"Yes Mama, I promise," he said kissing her cheek, stroking her hair lightly.

"Martha," she whispered with her last breath, "take care of your brother."

The rest of the day was a blur in his memory. He retained only snippets of images from the funeral: the warmth of the spring sun hitting his face, the dandelions that bloomed in the cemetery and a robin that sang in the old maple tree as they lowered her casket into the ground. Later it occurred to him that they were the kinds of details she would have noticed. The things she would have pointed out to him as they went for a walk.

Martha tucked him into bed that night. She looked into his eyes, but they were blank. She knew he didn't hear the words she spoke to comfort him, so she wrapped him in her mother's shawl hoping that it would soothe his pain. There was no comfort for her either. She tried to rock him the way Esther had done, searching desperately for some solace for both their spirits.

Jamie could not tell her that her arms were like salve on his wounds, that the smell of his mother's essence bandaged the hole in his heart. He could not weep openly, afraid that the tears caged in his body would turn to screams. He breathed deeply, inhaling her lingering fragrance, feeling her closeness. There were so many unsaid things, so many unanswered questions and so many untold stories. In the silence, there was only the throbbing, wordless pain of emptiness.

The two frightened children huddled in the bed. They slept fitfully, hibernating like scared cubs fearful of the realities that daylight would bring. Even in sleep, they were afraid to let go of each other, perhaps sensing that the end of sleeping would also be the end of their childhood.

2
Closed Doors

Jamie had never met his father, James. He had gone off to war not knowing he was to have another child. Because his parents had been immigrants from Holland, he had felt the obligation to defend his motherland against the invaders. When word came that Hitler's forces had invaded the country, he had gone immediately to the recruiting office to sign up. His father had supported the decision, especially since his older brother was needed at home to run the farm. His mother cried when he told her what he was doing. Esther, his wife, had known somewhere deep inside herself that he would not return. Instinctively, they had known each other's fears. Lovingly, they camouflaged them with words and demonstrations of affection. That last night, they loved each other completely.

Three days a week, Esther went to the Red Cross to roll

bandages for the war effort. She wrapped fervently. With each one, she included a prayer that the bleached white cloth would bandage some young man's injury. She pleaded that the man would be safe, that he would live and come home to his family. Then selfishly, she prayed for James, beseeching God to return him to her. She wrapped desperately, petitioning Him that one of the sterilized cloths would protect her husband from the spiteful wounds of war.

When the white envelope edged in black came, she didn't open it. It lay on the kitchen table for a long time. She stroked it, smelled it and pressed it to the beating heart in her swollen belly. When the pains of labor began, she unsealed the envelope and delivered her grief in the screams of childbirth. The child tore her flesh as the anguish of her loss ripped open her heart. She delivered the pain, like the afterbirth of the infant. It lay on the floor bleeding. She could see it but feared touching it again, suspecting it would consume her. Reverently she wrapped it up and buried it in a hidden, private place, in the recesses of her soul. She resigned it there, determined she must be resolute; she must be all that her children would need. She would be enough for them.

She named him Jamie, for a father that he would never know except through her parables – stories of courage that she would weave into the fabric of their simple lives.

Her husband's brother, John, owned the austere cottage in which they lived. James had arranged with him to help work his land in exchange for the rent. Esther supplemented their income by doing laundry and baking bread for several townspeople. Shortly after the news of James' death, John and his wife Lydia visited Esther. She had anticipated it, knowing their sympathy would be pragmatic. She listened to their suggestions and understood their proposition completely.

She was to come and live in their larger house. In exchange for a place to live and food to eat, she would help Lydia with simple household chores. She would have her own rooms to manage and she would have the advantage of having a man to help with the children. John and Lydia were barren. Her children would be their surrogate children. It sounded ideal. Esther had no money, no income. There were no other options for her so she agreed to the arrangement. As Lydia pointed out, it would be good for the children.

At first, all went well. Two vacant rooms on the second floor of the old farmhouse were assigned to Esther. Martha slept in one and Esther and the infant shared the adjoining room. There was time to nurse her baby and nurture her children. The rooms were small; the furniture was meager, but the bond of love that blossomed there made it a garden of beauty and sanctuary. It was an oasis in a desert place. Esther sang and laughed, surrounding and protecting her children with the same selfless love she had bestowed on their father. The joy she found in loving them, kept the pain of her husband's loss buried beneath a counterfeit, bright pallet of reality. There, the ache could be obscured from well-meaning trespassers.

There was no way Esther could know that Lydia listened to her laughter, that she tiptoed to the door and eavesdropped, that she wept tears of jealousy. Ironically, Esther stayed walled up for fear of disturbing Lydia and John. She would have been happy to make them a part of her joy. If she had known Lydia stood outside the room, wanting what they had, she would gladly have invited her in.

Lydia was too vulnerable to ask for entrance. There was a crevice in her heart, a gaping hole she didn't know how to fill. Many times her hand was ready to knock, to enter into the world Esther created, but she was powerless to make the attempt. The tears she wept were those of frustration and helplessness; eventually, they watered the seeds of bitterness she had not known were there. Slowly, they began to grow.

She sought for a way to talk to John but he was unknowingly imprisoned in his own shame – regret that incarcerated his spirit and constructed a charade of counterfeit optimism. There was no one to whom Lydia could look for comfort or support. No one who could help her understand her feelings. No one who could help her displace the anguish of being barren. Out of weaknesses and ignorance, the hopelessness took root and sprouted.

One day she stopped listening at the door. The happiness there served only to expose her loneliness. She couldn't bear it and withdrew to muted silence behind other doors in the house. There, the germs of enmity flourished. Like a creeping weed, they grew ugly tentacles that choked her maternal instincts and smothered her innate kindness.

John saw only the surface happenings of the household. He was satisfied that their daily lives were methodical and orderly. He saw two women who listened and worked, who gave him the respect his manhood decreed. That was enough for him. He noticed a change in his wife, but surmised it was the normal moodiness women experience. It never occurred to him to question her about the subtle changes in her behavior or about the long periods of silence that reverberated through their bedroom. Feelings were a luxury that he had never known. He did not, could not, see the closed door. Even if he had been aware of it, he had no words to ask for entrance to her heart. Gradually they became two aliens existing side by side, frustrated and humiliated by caged up emotions they were unable to communicate.

He lived in a world that required hard work and order and a son to carry on the family name. Anything that didn't add to that commission was frivolous and unnecessary. Those were the rules that were entrenched in his stern upbringing. Mandated at birth, it was a predetermined design, a set pattern for living. It was a birthright, imposed by generational tradition and practice. Unknown to anyone, he would willingly have sold the inheritance. He would gladly have exchanged it for a life that included books, music, art and some time to enjoy the trivial amenities of life. Before his brother went to war, it seemed possible that an exchange of the birth order and its responsibilities might be possible. James loved farm life and might well have a son to carry on the family name. When his brother died, so did John's dreams for the future. It was a loss more personal than anyone could have imagined. He was incapable of sharing it even with his wife. As he ploughed the fields, he let go of the ideas and imagined his aspirations cut into a thousand bits of sand, thrown haplessly to the wind. For a time, he managed to meet the expectations imposed upon him.

Lydia developed headaches. They blinded her and forced her to retreat to her darkened room. The doctor did tests and prescribed pills but the pain grew relentlessly. At first, the women's guild came with pots of soup, but John needed a real meal at the end of the day. Gradually, Esther took over the household chores of cooking and cleaning. More and more, she confined Jamie to his playpen. While her mother was busy caring for Lydia, Martha regularly entertained her infant brother. To pacify him when he cried, she sat Jamie in an old red wagon she found in the shed and took him for long walks around the farm. It was often a futile effort; another sad child could not soothe him. It was his mother he needed and wanted.

Esther worked fiercely to be mother and father to her two young children during the small remnants of time she had to herself. She read to them and told them stories of their father. She painted him caring and heroic, telling them what he would have done had he not given his life for them. They grew up knowing him. Had their father walked through the door, they would have welcomed him and known who he was by his upraised eyebrow, his lopsided smile and his unkempt hair. They would have recognized his enormous hands, ones that would cup their faces, hold them and tell them he loved them. He would have swept the three of them up in muscular arms that would protect and comfort them. He would have rescued them and carried them instantly to another place and moment in time. Their father was visible like a mirage they saw in the distance. When the stories ended, he evaporated until the next tale. For a time, the visions lightened the heaviness of their daily lives.

The weight, of a dream that could never be, eventually became clumsy and awkward to carry. To lighten the burden of the self-imposed yoke, Esther's stories became about God. An omnipotent, Supreme Being, who like their absent father, would make all things well. There were times it made sense to the children. But as they watched their mother struggle to lift the overwhelming obstacles from their daily lives, there were also times they hated their father and their mother's God for abandoning them.

They were too young to understand that she concealed a hidden impediment of grief, stored in the inaccessible places of herself. They didn't know it grew heavier with age and that hiding it dragged her down into a pit of melancholy. They could not know she colored her anguish with laughter and caresses for them. As the years crept by, Jamie and Martha grew, despite the cold undercurrents surrounding them.

During the same time, Lydia became reclusive, withdrawing into a veiled, detached world of her own making. The pain in her heart grew with her headaches. Esther tended her as she did her children, with a patience and kindness that knew no limits. As she applied cold cloths to her forehead, she sang to her and read her love poems. Lydia's troubled spirit responded with periods of calmness. There were days, even weeks, when she felt normal; however, it didn't last. The emptiness of her existence extinguished the small measure of contentment. Then the headaches returned and once again, the house was in darkness. Especially during these times, it was important to be quiet for Lydia. When there was noise, the pounding in her head caused her to scream with anguish. She shouted at the children until they withered into silence. She bellowed commands to Esther who waited on her as an obedient, patient servant. When the episodes ended, their weight immediately expunged them from memory. Then she could go on until the next time.

In the five short years of his life, Jamie learned how to be good. Very early, he knew that obeying was a sure way to make his mother embrace him. She would tell him how special he was and how much she loved him. She would wrap him in her arms and kiss him tenderly.

"You are such a gift," she would whisper in his ear. "I love you as big as the sky."

Jamie looked at the sky when he was sad or afraid. When he needed to feel loved, he looked up. He knew.

The day of Martha's thirteenth birthday, Lydia needed Esther to go to town to buy the special tea she liked. There was regular tea, but it wouldn't do. Martha offered to go for her mother, but Esther insisted that she was to celebrate her birthday without having to do any chores. It was an unusually bitter cold, wet April day. Esther wrapped herself in her coat and shawl and set out for town. Normally, she didn't mind the thirty-minute walk; often she took Jamie and they made it an outing. Today it was too cold for him to go and she felt somewhat resentful that it was necessary to make the trip. Her free time was precious and she had wanted to spend it finishing a dress for Martha's birthday. On this one occasion, she had dared ask Lydia if it couldn't wait until the next day. The protests that followed quickly made her regret the request.

She walked hurriedly, her head bent to keep the cold wind from biting her face and freezing the tears to her cheeks. By the time she returned, she was tired and worn. Lydia reprimanded her for wanting to sit by the stove to warm up. Moreover, there was still the dress to finish and dinner to prepare.

Jamie knew she was bothered. He could see it in the way she set about doing normal things. He could sense her unusual feelings of frustration and bitterness. He only remembered a few times that she had behaved this way and he recognized that his best behavior cheered her and brought the smile he loved to her face. He followed behind her like a puppy wanting to please. To contain her tears, she scooped him up and held him close to her heart.

"My precious, blessed child," she whispered.

"What's blessed?" the naive child asked.

"You are my darling," she replied, "and so am I."

She set him down and ruffled his hair, "Let's make a cake for Martha, now."

He relaxed when he saw that the smile was back on her face. Now that they were baking a cake, he knew she felt better and everything would be fine.

Jamie had continued to sleep in his mother's room. It was during the next night that her deep, coarse coughing woke him. In the following days, she was not herself. She got up to tend to Lydia but needed to rest before preparing dinner. Lydia commented that she really was making too much of just a cold. Martha and Jamie were frightened; they had never seen their mother sick.

On the fifth day, the coughing worsened and Esther was bedridden, burning with fever. When John came in for lunch, he went to her room to see how she was feeling. He was alarmed as he felt her hot forehead and immediately drove to Strathroyal for the doctor. When Doctor Smit arrived and examined her, he prescribed mustard plasters and chicken soup.

"Pray that her fever will break tonight; she has pneumonia. She's very sick," he explained. "Penicillin may help but she should have had it sooner. Pray for a miracle." His face disclosed the seriousness of the situation. He admonished John for not calling him sooner.

Esther lay in the bed exhausted. She imagined she saw her darling James in the room. She shook her head to bring reality into focus, but there was too little stamina left in her frail body. When the doctor returned the next day, he listened to her chest and shook his head.

Martha and Jamie sat by her side. She told them to go to bed, but for the first time in their lives, they refused to obey. They talked to her and sang the songs she had sung for them so many times. Jamie had a strange foreboding; he didn't know what he was sensing, but he recognized the menacing gravity of it.

For two more days, they waited. Then she kissed her precious ones good-bye and spoke her final words to them. She saw her husband waiting. As she took her last breath, she smiled serenely and reached for the hand James held out to her. John knew Esther was gone and he gently took the children's hands and guided them out of the room, quickly closing the door behind them.

"She's resting now," he said. He felt powerless and unable to say that she was dead. The children didn't see the tears welled up in his eyes. The blame was his. He had asked too much of her and given too little, too late. He had failed her, just as he had failed his parents and his brother. Shame sat like a boulder on his shoulders. He tried shaking it off, but its intense heaviness weighed down his spirit. He was afraid the burden of it would crush him.

It was May 5, 1945. Dutch citizens rejoiced. Canadian soldiers victoriously rode through the streets of Holland. The war that had cost so many, so much, was finally over. For some, there was peace. Despite the internal gloom in the farmhouse, the sun had finally broken through the clouds. Esther was home with her beloved.

3
The Apple Tree

The day after Esther's funeral, the children awoke late. Martha thought it strange that no one had wakened them. She helped Jamie get washed and dressed. The cold chill of the day reminded them that they needed to go to the kitchen where it would be warm. Esther always cooked them porridge for breakfast. She said it would stick to their ribs and give them vigor for the day. Jamie didn't understand what vigor meant, but he knew it must be something good because he always felt satisfied and content afterwards. The smell of brown sugar and cinnamon was an everyday comfort for their senses and their spirits. This regular routine added a familiar reassurance to their sparse lives.

Neither one of them had given any thought about who would assume the role of cooking their meals. Martha wondered if she would still be going to school. They had journeyed to a new country and there were no road signs to show the way. Martha felt lost; she hoped for some direction to help them find passage to a meaningful existence in these new circumstances.

Much to their surprise, Lydia met them at the foot of the stairs.

"Your breakfast is on the table," she remarked. Her voice sounded brisk, but her eyes were kind.

"Thank you, Aunt Lydia," Martha replied. The siblings shared a look of disbelief that Lydia didn't see.

Jamie couldn't remember ever seeing her before lunch. He had often watched as his mother prepared her breakfast tray. It was always the same: one soft-boiled egg, two pieces of toast with lots of strawberry jam, (the special kind reserved for her alone) and a cup of tea that was brewed to just the right moment. Once the tray was prepared, Esther had to deliver it immediately because Lydia hated her food cold. He wondered who would make his aunt's breakfast now.

He marveled that Lydia had made their porridge, even though it didn't look or smell anything like his mama's sweet creamy mixture. There was only a hint of brown sugar and the cinnamon he loved was missing. The children sat silently eating the lumpy, dry cereal without complaint, instinctively knowing any criticism would not be appropriate or tolerated. Lydia fumbled around the sink and stove, trying to organize the preparation of her own meal. As they spooned up the last bits of their unsavory gruel, John entered the room.

"Well, good morning then children," he spoke in a deep assertive voice. "Isn't it great that your Aunt Lydia is feeling well this morning?"

"It's wonderful, Uncle John," Martha stammered softly.

"Well now, we'll have to talk about how we'll manage, won't we?"

"Yes, Uncle John," Martha and Jamie replied in unison. They knew nothing he said was debatable. The best they could hope for was that he wouldn't expect them to earn their keep completely.

"Martha, you'll have to keep going to school till next year. By then you'll be fourteen, old enough to do a full day's work. I'll think about whether there's any need for you to have any further education. Lydia will need you and perhaps a few widows from church could use you to help them from time to time. How does that sound?"

She wanted to answer his question with the protest that was screaming in her head. She wanted to tell him exactly how it sounded. Her mother had talked to her about going to college. She knew that somewhere there was a jar filled with pennies, nickels and even a few dimes and quarters, saved for that purpose. Just the idea of cleaning and waiting on old people made her uncomfortable. She remembered Widow Jansen, who sat next to them in church sometimes. She reeked of stale urine; just the thought of it made her feel nauseous. Tears threatened to burst forth, but she blocked them with a stubborn clenching of her teeth that pulled the muscles in her face to a rigid tautness, refusing to allow her feelings to show.

"Whatever you think, Uncle John," she answered obediently.

Jamie knew that something about what was unfolding before him was very wrong. He looked at Martha and saw the strain in her face and the white knuckles of her clenched fists. She must be tired, he thought.

Ignorant of Martha's true feeling about his proposal, he continued, "Good. Until next year then, you will be expected to help around the house. You know Aunt Lydia isn't well. She'll make you a list of what she needs you to do."

Jamie, you're really getting to be quite a big boy for five. We'll have to find a few more chores for you to do. Your mother really did baby you far too much. Don't worry; we'll have lots of time to sort that out. I'm sure you'll soon get used to doing your share of the work. Right, boy?" He slapped Jamie hard on the back.

Jamie knew that a response was expected, "Yes, Uncle John."

"Good, well then, things will be fine. It will be proper for you to stay home from school for a few days. You can help Aunt Lydia around the house. Next week you'll return to school and everything will be back to normal." As an afterthought, he added, "And you are not to sleep in the same room any longer. It really isn't right."

Lydia sat silently listening to the edicts. "Well, I'm feeling quite tired. You can tidy the kitchen and begin the chores. Martha, I'm sure you remember the things your mother did on washday." Her voice sounded unusually pleasant and confident and she even managed a smile. "Let's try not to dawdle. I'll be down later to give you a hand."

It occurred to Jamie this was the most he had ever heard her speak in one breath. He looked at her face and noticed the dark lines encircling her eyes. He'd never really studied her so closely – now he saw her severity. Her dull, brownish hair was pulled into a tight, characterless bun at the back of her neck. It was so different from the shiny golden hair that had always framed his mother's face. She wore a dreary, gray dress. Its only embellishment was the speckled remains of foodstuffs that had left interesting mosaic patterns on its front. He stared at them and wondered how many were remnants of meals prepared by his mother. For reasons that he would not understand for many years, he felt a deep sense of empathy for her. As he watched her, the realization surprised him.

"What are you gawking at Jamie?" Lydia quipped. "Close your mouth. You look like a dead fish." The tone in her voice was suddenly different. Lydia immediately regretted the strange comment when she saw the hurt look on Jamie's face. She was irritated with herself for being so abrupt.

Although Jamie was taken aback, he immediately complied. He looked past her out the window, to the old apple tree that was suddenly in bloom. He and his mother had watched it prepare to don its finery for weeks. He believed she could see it and wondered if she had made it happen from heaven. He wanted to touch and smell the blossoms. He wanted to believe that Mama lived. He imagined her as an angel, touching each limb gently, kissing it softly and then watching flowers burst out of their crusty cases to produce sweet blooms. The apple tree, Jamie thought, must be a sign. He didn't understand it, but he knew it nonetheless.

"Jamie, didn't you hear Aunt Lydia?" The sharp sound of Uncle John's voice jolted him back to the kitchen.

Unlike Martha, he couldn't hold back his tears. They dribbled down his face and hung on the end of his nose. Martha wrapped him in her arms and tried to lead him away. She recognized that escape was not an option.

"Jamie, I know you miss your mother. Unfortunately,

she's gone. Now you're going to have to learn to be a man. God knows what he's doing and you and Martha must accept your lot in life. Now dry those baby tears and let's get to the chores. Aunt Lydia needs to rest."

John didn't notice that there were tears in Lydia's eyes as well. She had removed herself from the conversation and was busily trying to smooth her crumpled dress. Had it not been for John's blunt remarks she might have found the courage to take Jamie in her arms and tell him she loved him and wanted now to be his mother. She longed to give in to the tender maternal feelings that were bubbling just beneath the surface. The moment quickly passed and suddenly her head began to pound. The pain made her catch hold of the chair and sink powerlessly into it.

"See what you've done!" John snapped at Jamie. "Martha, help your aunt upstairs. Jamie, you'll have to clean up the kitchen. I'm going into town to look after some business."

Martha glanced at Jamie and then set to helping Lydia up the stairs to her bedroom. She did exactly as her mother had done so many times. She put cold cloths on Lydia's brow and talked to her, encouraging her to think about the beauty of spring. Lydia envisaged that it was the sweet sound of Esther's voice and she quickly succumbed to the peace it brought. Regret that she had not appreciated Esther, washed over her. The events of the morning were more than her fragile emotions could process. She wanted it to be so different. For the first time, she resented John. She loathed the way he talked about her as if she wasn't in the room. She was annoyed about the way he bellowed orders to the children; furthermore, she realized he had not been her husband for a long, long time. She knew there was nothing she could do or even wanted to do to change it. It occurred to her that she was a hostage in her own house, in her own body.

Lydia began to realize that her beloved sister-in-law was no longer able to attend to her needs. Moreover, she believed Esther's death was her fault. Her selfishness had sent her friend out into the cold. With Esther gone, there was no one for her. She felt absolutely and utterly alone. Like her infertile womb, the landscape of her life seemed totally barren.

"Get out of my room," she screamed at Martha. "Leave me alone, just leave me alone!"

"But Aunt Lydia, you're..." Martha protested.

"Get out, I need to be alone," Lydia would not let her see the tears that were waiting to erupt.

Martha left the room, closing the door quietly. She sat curled up outside the entry, listening to the anguish that exploded from the stranger in the next room. She felt paralyzed, overwhelmed by emotion. She waited, determined to hold back her own feelings of desperation. For some time the sobbing persisted with the same intensity. Then, as suddenly as it had started, it stopped. She wondered if she should return to the room. Noiselessly she opened the door a crack and saw Lydia curled up on the bed, wrapped in her own arms. She appeared to be sleeping. She remembered that her mother always said things looked better after a good rest, so she gently closed the door. Her mind abruptly turned to Jamie. She'd completely forgotten that he was downstairs alone.

She rushed to find him. He'd done quite a good job tidying the kitchen. Martha smiled. Mama would be proud of him. She decided to finish the little clean-up details after she talked to him. She looked around but didn't see him;

since the outside door was ajar, she assumed he'd gone out to play.

"Jamie, where are you?" The air still had a chilly feel to it; she hoped he'd remembered to put on a coat.

"Jamie, where are you?" This time her voice was insistent.

He sat in the tree and watched her look about the yard, putting his hands over his mouth so she wouldn't hear his giggles. He had climbed the tree to feel his mother's nearness. By inhaling the scent of the blossoms, he could sense her touch. The view captivated him. He could see the fields, the trees, the barn and most importantly, the sky. Sitting there, he thought about his mother's last words. He had certainly worked hard this first real day of his life without her. He had tried to be good. He knew Mama would be pleased with the way he had eaten "the stuff" for breakfast. She had also asked him to love God. He wondered where God was, who he was and what he looked like. The only remark he remembered from the funeral, was the minister saying that his mother's death was "God's will." The idea that he was to love the God, who had taken his mother, agitated him. He'd always said his prayers, listened to the Bible stories she told him and believed her when she said God loved them. Without her there to explain the inconsistency, his understanding and beliefs were obscured and blurred by innocence.

"James, where are you?" He heard the annoyance in her voice. She had never before called him James. She was serious.

"Up here Martha," Jamie blurted out.

"Oh Jamie! Come down!"

"No, come and get me," he taunted.

It was more than Martha could bear. She crumpled to the ground and let go of the emotions that had built up during the last tedious days. For the first time she allowed herself to cry freely. Once the dam was broken, there was no way to hold back the pent-up tears. Fatigue swept over her. She sobbed like the helpless tired child she was.

Jamie immediately climbed down from the apple tree. Martha was his security; he knew that as long as he had her, he wouldn't be alone. To see her so deflated, terrified him.

"Martha, it's alright. I'm sorry. I'll never do it again, I promise. Hope to die," the words tumbled from his mouth as the boy held and rocked his dejected sister. For a moment, he was the big brother taking care of his little sister.

"Please Martha, don't cry," he pleaded, "don't cry."

"Don't hope to die, Jamie. Please don't hope to die," was all she could say.

The two frightened children sat on the ground, numb with grief. Childhood had banished them. Death stood guard at the door to its entrance. They were isolated from the naive world of innocence. There could be no return. The best they could hope for was a guardian angel who would take their hands and escort them through the callous adult world, into which life had cruelly shoved them.

Suddenly a soft spring rain began to fall.

"See," said Martha as she began to recover her composure, "God is crying with us Jamie. Everything's going to be alright."

Jamie couldn't imagine God crying, "Let's go inside, Martha. Can we make some hot chocolate? Do you know how?"

Martha knew. She took the hand of her little brother and they went inside together.

4
The Marker

After he had given the children his instructions, John got his car out of the barn and drove into the city. Although he didn't really know why, he had reservations about what he was planning. He hadn't mentioned it to Lydia, knowing she probably wouldn't approve. Even though she might have been jealous of the niceties Esther owned, she would never take anything that wasn't rightfully hers, even if she had been feeling better. She would surely have chided him. Some things she just didn't understand. He knew the sensibility of it; yet, he was uneasy about its necessity. After all, valuables ought not to be hoarded when they were needed for practical purposes. There were funeral expenses to be paid and a dignified stone was required to mark Esther's grave. The marker would also have the name of his brother who was buried somewhere overseas. John believed that

Christians required the place of their burial to be marked. Feeling very dutiful about attending to this detail eased his guilt and calmed his misgivings. He wanted, even needed, to believe Esther would understand.

In his pocket were the only earthly possessions Esther had treasured. After the funeral, he had gone into her room and taken the items from the small box on her dresser. In his pocket were a filigreed silver locket, with the pictures of Martha and Jamie, and the matching earrings. In small velvet bag was an exquisite cameo laced with a fine gold ribbon that had been handed down from Esther's mother. On his pinky was the wedding ring taken from Esther's finger. He thought his brother had been very frivolous. He couldn't afford the extravagance of fine jewelry and yet he had regularly lavished gifts on Esther as if she had been her namesake. There was definitely something very sinful about purchasing luxuries when he couldn't even afford to buy a proper house for his family. Well no matter, at least his brother's generosity would help with the expense of Esther's death. Perhaps it's providential, he thought sanctimoniously – God works in mysterious ways.

There was no pawnshop or jeweler in the small town of Strathroyal. It had only the essential business and services needed to maintain its inhabitants and the surrounding farms. Therefore, it was necessary to drive the extra hour to London. It was a beautiful spring day; he hadn't had the car out for a while, so it would do the vehicle good to make the excursion. He'd heard about a place that might give him a fair price for the gems. Although London was a large city, he found the shop in the center of town, not far from the main street.

The stale, musty smell hit his senses when he opened the door. It took a minute for his eyes to adjust to the dim light. Every space in the drab, dusty room contained a peculiar collection of gadgets. Old shoeboxes that dangled with numbered tags cluttered the counter. Odd pieces of furniture held an ill-sorted array of items. Accordions, guitars, radios and clocks were stacked on each other and crammed into every available space. A potpourri of objects was haphazardly heaped on flimsy shelves. Dark wooden cases with multiple small drawers lined the wall from floor to ceiling. A maze of small pathways made it possible to maneuver through the shop. John was aware of a strange odor that hung in the air, an odd haze that could not be seen or touched. He felt unsettled and self-conscious as he approached the bent over man behind the counter, engrossed in the numbers on a ledger page.

"Morning," the man grunted.

"Good morning." John eyed the trays of rings and assorted jewelry displayed under the glass. Everything was strewn together, treasure-chest fashion. There were no price tags visible.

"I'm looking to sell some jewelry," said John, producing the jewels from his coat pocket. "How much will you give me for these?"

The man fingered the silver and looked through an eyeglass at the cameo, "Twenty-five dollars for the lot."

"But I'm sure they're worth more than that," protested John.

"Not to me," he shrugged.

John looked into the man's eyes. Black indifference met his gaze. They glared at each other. John knew the items were worth several hundred dollars; he had anticipated getting at least fifty. Probably a Jew, he speculated. He considered looking for another pawnshop but he really shouldn't leave Lydia and the children alone for much longer. It didn't occur to him to leave with the items. This would have to do.

"Thirty-five. Can't let them go for less than thirty-five," wouldn't hurt to try John thought.

"Hmm? You think I'm a stingy Jew?" grumbled the man.

John could feel his face turning red. Maybe this had been a bad idea after all.

"Thirty. That's it. Take it or leave it."

Something about the number bothered him, but he didn't have time to sort it out. All he could say was, "Fine."

The deed was done. Feelings were an unaffordable luxury today.

The man counted out thirty one-dollar bills. John clenched them in his hand and stuffed them in his pocket. He did the required paperwork, muttered his thanks and quickly made his escape from the shop. Esther wouldn't get a very fancy stone; something simple would be more to her liking anyway. He tucked the claim check into a fold in his wallet. He was dubious about ever needing it again, but it eased his conscience knowing the sale might possibly be temporary.

He stopped in Strathroyal on his way home and ordered the tombstone at the mason's. The smallest stone would cost fifty dollars. There was room for Esther Jacobs, 1918 -1945, wife of James Jacobs. RIP. It was white and rather roughly cut but it would have to do. He felt fatigued and irritated after the long drive. It was time he was home. He wondered how Lydia had made out with the children. Life was going to be very different from now on.

At dinner two weeks later, John announced he had had a marker placed on Esther's grave. It would be proper for the family to put on their Sunday best to see it and say a prayer. He ignored the surprised look on Lydia's face. He hadn't told her what he'd done. The children listened passively, not knowing what to expect. John interpreted the silence as a sign of acceptance. Life had quickly settled into a somewhat reasonable routine, he mused. He was quite satisfied with himself.

Martha and Jamie hugged each other as they stared at the meager marker. There was a clumsy, awkward silence. In the nearby tree, Jamie thought he saw the same robin he'd noticed at the funeral. He listened to the bird's song as John piously said a prayer for his brother's and Esther's souls. Jamie thought it strange to hear his father's name mentioned. He wondered where his grave was or if he would ever see it. He imagined hearing his mother's voice telling him she was with his father. They were together. That awareness relieved him of the unanswerable questions.

Upon their arrival home, memory abducted each person in a singular way. Lydia was tired and went to rest. John escaped to the barn to do chores. Martha went to gather wild flowers and Jamie climbed up into the apple tree.

A sudden storm arose and thunder and lightning raged across the sky. Jamie covered his ears. He clung to the tree paralyzed, but at the same time, the explosions of light that ripped across the sky captivated him. Was this God speaking? Was he angry about something? He smiled at the idea and envisioned the old man waving his cane. The rain pelting his skin brought him back to the reality of his perch. He slithered down the trunk; the wet bark smudged his clothes with a grimy blemish. Martha was going to be as angry as God was.

Martha wasn't cross; she also came home dirty. When the storm came up, she had started to run for home and had fallen in the field, layering her clothes in muck. Both children came running to the door from different directions, each sharing what had befallen them. They had both ruined their Sunday clothes. Fortunately, Aunt Lydia wasn't in the kitchen. They hurried to their room to change into their pajamas.

Martha scolded Jamie for staying in the tree after the storm started, but he knew she wasn't angry by the way she hugged him. She said she'd wash their clothes later. Martha let him sleep in her room that night even though it threatened a reprimand from Uncle John. They talked about Mama and reminisced about special times with her. They recalled how she had told them stories of their father. They wondered about what their parents were doing in heaven. Jamie reminded himself that he must try harder to be good. His desperation to see them again would motivate his behavior for many years.

They looked at their parents' wedding picture set in the gold frame and decided to take turns having it in their rooms. Around it, they placed Esther's hair combs and her beautiful hankies, trimmed with lace. Martha salvaged an old candle and set in on a saucer. They decided they would light it on special days.

On the dresser in Martha's room, they put the album, in which Esther had carefully positioned their few photographs.

Jamie especially liked the one in which his mother was holding him. Martha was standing beside them. He gazed lovingly at the sweet smile on Mama's face. When Martha wasn't looking, he secretly slid the picture out of its spot and tucked it beneath his clothes in the dresser. He carefully opened the drawer that still held Esther's clothes. He held the garments, breathing in her familiar fragrance, remembering the last time he had seen her wear them. Touching her things made him feel close to her. Somehow, it made her death feel less raw.

The next week, John felt it was necessary to gather up Esther's remaining belongings. He had performed the same duty when his parents died. Although he found it a despicable task, he believed it was good way to bring closure to the past. He reasoned that getting rid of Esther's things would make it easier for the children to adjust to life without her.

It was the first time he had looked in Esther's room since he had pilfered her jewelry. He was dumbfounded at the makeshift memorial the children had created. His stern Protestant upbringing deemed it necessary to dismantle the shrine immediately. The children would not be able to move on with their lives by hanging onto the past. Quickly and haphazardly, he packed Esther's clothing and possessions in boxes.

He was surprised to find the jar of coins in the nightstand and wondered why Esther had hidden it away. Remorse abruptly tapped him on the shoulder; for a moment, he reconsidered taking it, but he quickly dismissed the thoughts. The money would help pay for the care of the children. He also argued with himself about removing the wedding picture, but decided it was best for now to put it away. Making a clean break would be simpler for everyone. Resentfully, he lugged the boxes up the attic stairs and stacked them next to the containers that held the token remnants of his youth. He didn't allow himself to feel the sadness licking at his memory. When he heard the children in the kitchen, he hurried downstairs.

"I've put your mother's things away," he informed them. "It's best not to dwell on the past. Life goes on. Martha, there's one more box that needs to go to the attic. It's not that heavy so you can carry it up. Be careful when opening the door at the top of the stairs."

Jamie glanced at his sister and rushed up the stairs. When he looked around, he saw his mother's smile had disappeared from the room. Once again, she was gone – dead – hidden in a deep dark place where she couldn't breathe.

5
The Attic

Martha was stunned into speechlessness. Resentment washed over her. Knowing Jamie would be devastated, made her want to go and console him immediately. Every night he had found some solace in his mother's keepsakes. Surely, Uncle John hadn't put everything away. She'd never been to the attic. Her mother had told her not to go there because often attics had bats nesting in the rafters. The story she had told her about one that had bitten her father made her shiver with fear.

"I'll do it right now," she blurted out.

"Fine," Uncle John responded. "And, Martha, don't coddle Jamie. He needs to grow up."

Martha rushed out of the kitchen without the usual, "Yes, Uncle John."

In his room, she found Jamie curled up on his bed, cuddling

his mother's shawl. He slept with it every night and kept it folded under his blanket. A quick look around confirmed that all other traces of their mother had vanished.

John reluctantly followed Martha upstairs. Perhaps asking her to go to the attic had been too much. Regret silently marched behind him. Lydia should be dealing with these things, he mused. He'd have to talk to her about making more effort.

"Martha, I'll help you with that box. I'll open the trap door. The ceilings up there slope, so watch your head." There was genuine kindness in his voice.

"Jamie, come and help us," Martha called to her brother vociferously. She hoped he would recognize the warning in her voice and conceal the shawl before John saw it. Jamie responded by getting up and pulling the blanket over his treasure. That fact escaped John as he led the way up the stairs to the attic.

"Stay down there. There's nothing for you to do here," he shouted to Jamie who was already standing at the bottom of the stairs.

The attic had a trap door that swung up sideways and clattered down. One of the hinges had broken so it was difficult to move. A single light bulb hung from the ceiling, casting a dim light that seemed to bounce off the rafters. Martha surveyed the contents and saw a plethora of things. Old doors and windows, a multitude of boxes, broken furniture, a large spinning wheel, a baby's cradle, a rusty steel bedspring and other assorted unidentifiable things were packed under the slopping beams. She was amazed and intrigued by this unexpected storeroom.

John pointed to the spot where he had stacked the other boxes. "Just put it over there with the rest, Martha."

When her eyes became accustomed to the light, she spotted a large stack of books piled high in a corner, not far from the trap door. It was impossible to read the titles and the books looked old and tattered. Water had seeped through the roof and saturated them, leaving the covers stained and the pages curled.

Reaching deep down inside herself, Martha summoned up the courage to ask Uncle John if she could take some books downstairs to read.

"They're pretty old and musty," he said. "Just take one or two at a time and put them back when you're finished. Some of them are Dutch books that belonged to your grandparents, so you won't be able to read them. Some of the old poetry books I used to read are there as well. Do you like poetry, Martha?"

Although she loved to read, she didn't know much about poetry. She replied honestly, "I haven't read much poetry, but I'd love to read some."

"Just be very careful when you're up here. I really need to clean up this place."

It occurred to Martha that he wasn't really talking to her as much as to himself.

"Thank you, Uncle John. I'll be very careful." It was difficult to hide the enthusiasm in her voice.

John's sudden thoughtfulness astonished him as much as it did Martha. It eased the guilt that he had been feeling. He thought he might pick up a book and take up reading again. He remembered how much he had loved it as a child. Years ago, he had even considered becoming a writer. It had been a secret ambition. He wondered if it was possible to salvage any of the aspirations of his youth.

For Martha, the unexpected luxury of a library left her feeling happier than she had been for a long time. Maybe I'll be able to find Mama's pictures for Jamie, she thought. At that moment, anything seemed possible.

A sudden sound burst the small bubble of bliss. It fluttered and drafted above her head. She looked up, startled. When she saw it flapping about, she let out a piercing scream and shook with fear.

John laughed, "It's only a bat, Martha."

To Martha, it was *not* only a bat. It was a nightmare.

"Bats carry rabies. Don't ever touch one," she heard her mother's voice saying.

The screech summoned a misplaced memory from John's youth. He heard the cries, the cries of his young brother, James. After a bat bit him, he had endured a painful series of injections to prevent rabies. His father had laughed it off and told him to stop his senseless sobbing. His mother had pampered and coddled James. John had long ago forgotten it, but now he felt the envy that had consumed him at the time.

"You're just like me," his father would say. "James is a *mama's boy*."

John had never wanted to be just like his father. He would have given anything to have his mother fuss over him. Eventually the hostility became a lesion that would not heal. Each time his father belittled James, he felt the scab being picked. It oozed puss and infected his relationship with his mother and his brother. He didn't want to be his father's son and he couldn't be his mother's little boy. Caught in their parents' competitive snare, the brothers were used as pawns to negotiate a pretentious brittle affection in the family.

The delight of the previous moment vanished; John, the irritated, confused youngster emerged and yelled at Martha, "You're just like your father!"

Panic swallowed Martha. She felt its suffocating wheeze, sucking the joy out of her. Gasping for breath, she groped her way down the attic stairway, past a puzzled Jamie. She flew down the next flight of stairs and out the kitchen door into the field. She gulped for air, trying to comprehend what had just happened. Her mother had often told her she was like her father. Mama considered it a blessing. Obviously, it was a curse to her uncle.

When Jamie caught up to her, he pulled her back from the brink of despair. He held her and told her he loved her. It was all she needed.

"I want us to go home," he whispered softly.

"Yes, Jamie, I know."

Eventually, they walked back to the house in a cloud of unified confusion.

In the attic, John sat very much alone. Like Martha, he didn't understand what had happened. In a single moment, everything had changed. Again. Just when he was beginning to feel some affection for the girl, his dead brother's ghost seemed to make a bond inaccessible. She was sweet and kind like her mother and he knew she didn't deserve the hostility he had just heaped on her. At the same moment, he realized his brother hadn't warranted it either. It shaped a fresh new bitterness about his life.

"I didn't deserve it either," he hollered at himself. He needed urgently to understand. He wanted desperately to talk to Martha, to hug her and explain; unfortunately, the sins of his father and mother were fetters he didn't know how to break. It was a defining moment. He felt totally disorientated, not knowing which path to take.

"Leave the past behind," he told himself. Slamming the trap door shut, he left the attitude of pleasure in the attic where it belonged. He carried a fresh resentment of his brother down the stairs.

It was a long, long time before either John or Martha went to the attic again.

6
With Heart and Mind and Soul

Slowly, the days passed and a familiar routine became established. Martha made breakfast for Jamie and herself; she learned to set everything ready the night before. She packed their lunches in the old square metal lunch pails. She felt too old to be carrying one to school, but Aunt Lydia said the idea of buying and throwing away paper bags was sinful. After school, Martha did tasks around the house and helped prepare dinner with Lydia. Jamie did chores in the barn and then laid the table for dinner. They shared the cleanup before Martha did her homework on the kitchen table. Much of the time, they were alone.

Lydia seemed to be better, but Martha noticed that somehow she was different. Her eyes were never the same after her strange, volatile outburst. At times, she sat and gazed into space and appeared oblivious to what was going on around her. If there had been any encouragement, Martha would have comforted her the way her mother had done. Because she feared another irate episode, she didn't initiate any further physical contact with her aunt. Years later, she wondered how their lives might have been different if she had followed her inclinations.

Martha often saw Lydia stare at John, but not really look at him. Once she even contradicted him when he told her to go and have a rest.

"I'll decide when to rest," Lydia had said in a voice unusually calculated and controlled.

John was startled and looked at her curiously. It seemed as if he saw something he thought was lost. He hesitated and almost asked her about it. That night she decided to sleep in another room. She told him it was because she was afraid she would wake him. She explained there were often times when she couldn't sleep and she didn't want to disturb him when she got up during the night. He readily agreed to the arrangement. There was no comfort or nicety for either of them in their marriage bed. Although he wondered at times if he was missing something, John believed that indulging in intimacy that couldn't produce any concrete benefits, was somehow vain and self-indulgent. He convinced himself that at least for now it would be fruitless, futile even, to extend their relationship to a level irrelevant to their essential needs. As long as she continued to know her place, could deal with the daily routines of the household and could cope with their two charges, he saw no reason to change anything about the way he managed their lives.

Overall, John believed that things were going quite well. The crops looked promising; the children appeared to be adjusting and generally doing what he instructed them to do. He had even begun to entertain the idea of finding a farm hand to help with the chores and the fall harvest. That would allow him a little more time to be involved in the church and maybe even in local politics. Recently there had been people who had urged him to consider running for town council in the fall. Others suggested he would make a model deacon at church. Both ideas appealed to his ego. He certainly knew enough about how things ran and had very exact ideas about how things should be. It would be nice if someone would listen to him for a change. The young people seemed to be taking over everywhere, wanting to change things that had worked well for years. He had read somewhere it was an aftermath of the war. As far as he was concerned, there wasn't enough respect for the old ways. The new loud rock and roll music becoming popular with the young people was a good example of the times. It was certainly a sign that things weren't getting better in the world. How could anyone who found that sort of heathen music ever amount to anything worthwhile?

The summer came and with it came school vacation. There was always work to do, but the long days also allowed time for playing in the sunshine. Martha and Jamie began to look tanned and healthy. Lydia took to sitting in the shade for long periods. Martha would bring her glasses of lemonade, which she sipped contentedly. There were times she even appeared cheerful. On especially good days, she would catch a stray ball, throw it to the children and smile. The desperate throbbing pain of their mother's loss began to soften and they felt a measure of contentment in each other's company.

Like her mother, Martha became a proficient housekeeper.

She spent the mornings making sure the house was organized and pristine. John made sure that there was adequate healthy food in the house and Martha learned to prepare stark but generally nutritious meals. Lydia supervised the routines and at times helped with less strenuous tasks. She regretted yelling at her and awkwardly attempted conversation and friendship. This confused Martha. She didn't understand her aunt's eccentric moods. She was always polite and obedient but was afraid to be warm in her interactions with Lydia, lest she say or do the wrong thing. The fear of rebuke built an emotional partition that neither Lydia nor Martha understood, or had the ability to bridge.

Jamie remained fascinated with the apple tree. He often climbed it and had silent imagined conversations there with his mother. He told her how he was trying to be what she wanted. Sometimes he tried to voice the questions he had about God. He wondered if God was ever in a good mood or if he ever laughed or told a joke. He pictured his mother sitting in God's office. Of course, God was a stern old man with a long white beard. He had many lists on his desk to keep track of all the sins of his people. He knew that in heaven, everything was made of gold. God surely must live in an enormous church. He couldn't quite picture a building made entirely of gold; nevertheless, he liked the idea that his Mama spread her wings on a perfect, golden chair. He had tried quizzing Martha about the details, but she didn't seem to have any answers either. Whenever he would speculate aloud to Martha about God, she would ask him about school or find some menial task for him to do.

One Sunday afternoon, after a long sermon about how God knew every evil thing anyone had ever done, he sat and told his Mama every bad thing he could remember doing since she had been gone. He felt true remorse and pleaded with her to ask God not to be angry with him. It troubled him to think he didn't truly love God as she had told him to do. Once, he bravely approached Uncle John with his concerns, while they were working in the barn.

"How can God see everything I do? What makes something bad? How do I know if I really love God?" were some of the things he asked his uncle.

The questions annoyed John because he didn't know the answers either. "You love the Lord your God with all your heart, mind and soul," had been the reply. "When you're older and learn the catechism, you'll understand it better."

Jamie speculated about what the catechism might be. He didn't know what a soul was, let alone how to use it to love. How to fit God into his heart was his biggest concern. He decided he had better put on a good show for everyone, since it seemed he was expected to know. He stopped asking questions and tried to figure it out himself. What he had known became the foundation for his understanding. He knew he loved his mother even though she was no longer there. His love for Martha was as real as the flowers that his mother had planted everywhere. He supposed love must be like the rain and the sun that kissed the earth and made things grow. He remembered the time his mother picked a bouquet of Queen Anne's Lace and put it on the kitchen table. Aunt Lydia had told her to throw it out because it was just wild carrot weeds. Mama had taken it to their bedroom and told him a story about it. He wished he could remember it now. He could only recall that the story was somehow related to her pretty hankies. It had brought a smile to both their faces.

When he saw flowers in bloom, he thought of his mother and honored her by appreciating the finery there. When they worked in the garden together, his mother would often say, "Jamie always remember to be thankful for the beauty and miracle of flowers." The saying remained with him and became a truth that took root in his life.

There was an acute awareness in him, that like the flowers she loved so much, his mother's love and Martha's love was tangible. He could accept it and even return it. It touched him. He could feel it in the same way he could feel the sunshine and spring showers. Moreover, he needed it as the earth needed rain. He knew without it, he would shrivel up and die like plants that burned in a summer drought. He hoped that when he learned the catechism, all his questions would have answers.

It frightened him that he didn't know how to love God or that he didn't know how to fit God into the events of his life. It terrified him to think he might even be angry with God for taking away his mother. He sat for long periods thinking about this and having imaginary conversations with her. He tried to keep in mind all the things she had told him. It bothered him that there were already things he couldn't remember. He hoped Mama didn't think forgetting what she had said meant he had forgotten her. Martha and even Lydia, often wondered why he would sit for such long stretches of time in the tree. He couldn't explain it to them, fearing a rebuke that would warp his distorted perspective.

As he contemplated these truths, Jamie noticed there were many worms in the apples. Uncle John said it cost too much money to spray the tree and they would just have to eat around them. At school, he'd heard maggots ate the dead. The image of his beautiful mother consumed by black ugly larvae repulsed him. He totally rejected this possibility and instead chose to believe she was a special angel with a halo and wings that were the most beautiful in all of heaven. Those who were her friends would come to her for advice. She would teach them about love. He even envisaged that God would come down from his throne, single her out and ask her for help. This surreal fantasy of heaven provided him with an ambiguous comfort. He feared sharing it with anyone, in case he was wrong and his illusions were shattered.

Jamie listened intently to try to discover the answers to his many questions. Because there were so few people to whom he could really talk, eventually he gave up looking for the answers. It seemed Uncle John expected him to know everything without being told. When he saw Aunt Lydia, she sat for hours at a time staring into space. Even Martha didn't seem to want to explain things to him the way his mother had done. She treated him like a child. Sometimes he wondered if she really knew much more than he did and if she really understood all the grownup talk. Once he had even said that to her. She cried. He couldn't bear it when she was sad, so he decided it was best not to ask any more questions.

Although it took them at least an hour, Martha and Jamie hiked to the cemetery once a week. Uncle John didn't approve, but didn't forbid their visits. Saturday morning after they had finished their chores, Martha packed sandwiches and water in an old vinegar bottle. Often they reminisced about their walks with their Mama. The weekly pilgrimage became an obligatory tribute that enabled them to deal with her loss.

They carried crimsoned colored rocks from the fields to outline a flowerbed. In it, they planted the wild flowers she loved. Eventually there were Black-eyed Susans, Queen Anne's Lace, Wild Snapdragons, Violets and even Dandelions were encouraged to produce their rich yellow blooms. On every visit, they carried water from the old pump for the plants. It became a picture perfect garden of lush greenery. It was a childish act of devotion that lovingly served to keep her alive in their memory. It became the most charming unique grave in the cemetery. They knew their efforts would have pleased her. Often when they were there, people remarked that underneath the blanket of blossoms must be a very special person.

When fall arrived and the flowers wilted, they both cried. Everything looked so lifeless.

"Just like her," Jamie observed casually.

Martha quickly contradicted him. "No Jamie! She's not really dead – she's in heaven."

"I know," he sighed, "but she's still dead."

7
Applesauce

Then Samson entered his life. John had decided he needed help on his farm. As a result, he hired Samson to do chores and to help with the harvest. Jamie was fascinated with him. He thought of the story that his mother had told him about the biblical Samson. He looked like a Samson. He was massive, standing six feet five inches tall, and had muscles that were larger than any Jamie had ever seen. His dark hair fell in curly locks around his face and his mysterious eyes glistened and smiled, especially when he laughed. Uncle John told him Samson was as strong as an ox, but also as dumb. Jamie believed only his mother and perhaps God were smarter than Samson was.

Samson had done farm work for most of his life. He was a migrant who seemed to enjoy moving from place to place. John fixed up a small room in the barn with a bed, a table and a chair. Since he knew how to take care of himself, he could live there without creating any mess or extra work in the house. He was welcome to eat his meals with the family in the kitchen.

On the day of his arrival, John introduced Jamie to the new farm hand. Samson extended his hand and Jamie shook it solemnly. Jamie noticed the gigantic fingers. He had never seen anyone so mammoth.

"Nice to meet you, Jamie," Samson stated seriously.

"Nice to meet you too, Samson," Jamie stammered.

Jamie watched Samson pick up large bales of hay and move them as if he was playing with blocks. He followed him around, enthralled by the man's strength and stamina. In the middle of the afternoon, he brought him a glass of Martha's fresh lemonade.

"Thank you," he said as he sat on a bale of hay to drink it.

Jamie hopped up next to him.

"How old are you Samson?" he queried.

"Dunno."

"Of course you do," laughed Jamie "everybody knows how old they are."

"Not me."

"Why don't you know? When's your birthday?" he persisted.

"Don't have one."

"Of course you do. Everyone has a birthday,"

"Not me," contradicted Samson.

"Maybe today's your birthday, Sam."

"Dunno."

"Maybe," Jamie looked long and intently at Samson. There was something very, very different about him.

"Do you have any friends Samson?"

"Nope, no friends," this question seemed to bother him. "You got any?"

"Just Peter in my class, but I don't see him in the summer holidays," Jamie explained.

They were both quiet.

"Maybe we could be friends," the child suggested boldly.

Samson's face broke into a smile. Jamie thought he had never seen a smile that big.

"We can be friends, Jamie," he said as, he gathered Jamie into his arms and hugged him.

"If we're friends, can you give me a piggyback ride, Samson?"

"After supper – got to do work now."

Jamie watched him work. He followed him around the farm like a puppy, rambling on about everything he knew. He bombarded Samson with the questions that he had about God, about life and about living. There were few answers, but Jamie took the nods and looks of encouragement as affirmation. Most importantly to Jamie, there were no admonitions. It didn't matter that Samson didn't provide any answers; what mattered was that for the first time since his mother's death, he had a dedicated audience. Although he wouldn't have been able to explain the approval, he knew his questions were legitimate. That was answer enough.

They became inseparable. Samson thrived on the attention. For him, it was the first time anyone has treated him as a grown-up. It was not the least bit important that

Jamie was a child who didn't understand his lack of intellect. Their respect was mutual. Without being aware of it, they gave each other a precious gift. Samson carried Jamie on his back and together they galloped about, exploring the mysteries of life. They were two innocent children finding joy for their spirits in the most unlikely of places. Like wild flowers nurtured and watered, they bloomed in each other's company.

Martha watched them. She was gratified – Jamie was sleeping better and the color had returned to his cheeks. She was also envious. Before Samson, Jamie had come to her for help, for comfort, for love. She missed the times they shared and felt very much alone. She became a woman that summer. Because her mother had prepared her, she wasn't afraid. Esther had told her they would celebrate. Now there was no one to tell. She knew Jamie wouldn't have understood, but he would have been pleased to know she was happy. They would have gone for a long walk and picked wild flowers. She felt badly for resenting Samson for denying her the simple pleasures she enjoyed with her brother.

There were many days Martha stood at the door of the attic hoping to find the courage to look for a book. Always, her fear of the bat bolted the door shut. She looked forward to returning to school. The idea that it might be her last year gnawed at her. She began to pray that Uncle John would let her continue to study. He hadn't said any more about it so there was still an ember of hope that he had changed his mind.

On a Saturday in the fall when Martha was busy helping Lydia, Jamie took Samson to the cemetery. Samson had listened to the stories Jamie told about his mother. He had nodded wisely when Jamie described his version of heaven.

"I'd like to see her special place, Jamie. Will you take me to the cemetery?" Samson asked.

As they walked, Jamie told his friend what he remembered about the funeral for his mother. Some of the details were blurred, but it didn't seem to matter since Samson didn't ask any questions. When they arrived, Samson took off his hat and stood reverently for a long time staring at Esther's grave. He traced his finger over the letters on the stone.

"What was her name, Jamie?' he asked meekly.

"Esther Jacobs."

"It's a pretty name. It's a nice place, Jamie," Samson whispered. There were tears in his eyes as he turned away from the child to hide his emotion. Wordlessly, Jamie understood and took his hand.

He recognized his friend's grief. "It's alright, Samson. She's in heaven with my dad, James Jacobs. His name is there too, 'cause he died in the war and we don't know where he's buried."

He hoped the words he had heard so often would reassure his friend. Instinctively he knew the companionship they shared, was a salve that could soothe his friend's pain. Samson smiled and then piggybacked him all the way home. He said the horse was tired and sometimes just needed to walk, so there was no galloping the way he usually did. They sauntered home in silence.

"Sometimes even horses need to just walk and think," he said to Jamie.

Jamie knew.

When they arrived at the barn, Jamie sat silently beside

Samson. Timidly he took the conversational lead. "Where are your parents, Samson?"

"Gone, like yours."

Jamie sensed and understood the sadness in Samson's voice so he quickly changed the subject. "So where do you live?"

Samson grinned. "Right here, silly."

"Yes, but where's your home? Where do you live when you're not here?"

It seemed to take a long time for his companion to answer. Eventually, he put his hand on his heart. "Jamie, my home is right here."

Although he was perplexed, it didn't seem right to question Samson further.

"It's past your bedtime, Jamie. Martha will be getting worried. You'd better go now."

As he walked to the house, Jamie heard the night sounds as he had never heard them before. Tree frogs were shrilling their searching songs. The wind was rustling rhythmically through the cornfields. The cricket melodies resonated through the air. He was intensely conscious of the veiled panorama that cloaked the darkness. He embraced the night and eavesdropped on its exchange. In a strange, unexpected way, it soothed him.

"Jamie, come inside." Martha's proverbial voice completed the concerto.

"Coming," he shouted.

When the apples ripened, most of them fell to the ground. They weren't much good for eating but Martha, Jamie and Samson gathered them anyway. The worms still bothered him but Martha said she'd cut them out. Esther had made apple pies, but that was beyond Martha's mastery so she carefully salvaged the edible parts and sliced them to make applesauce. Into a large pot, she stirred the apples and added a generous amount of sugar. Jamie remembered the smell of the cinnamon his mother had added. He insisted on putting it in himself and happily emptied the spice into the bubbling mixture. Even Lydia commented on how sweet the kitchen smelled. She remarked that maybe they could can some of it to enjoy in the winter.

Jamie proudly took a bowl of the thick dessert to the barn for Samson. "Martha made it just like Mama used to do," he said proudly. He knew his friend would understand the significance.

Samson could only say, "Good applesauce."

"Do you think they eat applesauce in heaven, Samson?" Jamie wondered.

"Of course," replied Samson confidently.

"Bet they put Mama in charge of making it."

Samson licked his bowl clean before he handed it back to Jamie. "That was delicious," was all he said as he gave the boy a big Samson hug.

As suddenly as he had appeared, Samson left. At breakfast a few weeks later, Uncle John announced that Samson had moved out early in the morning. The harvest was almost finished and he was no longer needed. Martha tried to stop Jamie from running out of the room, but he darted out the door like a frightened rabbit.

Jamie sat in the small space in the barn. This would always be Samson's room. The tears trickled down his face. He closed his eyes and pictured his good friend, Samson. He stored the image in a special spot close to the one that held Esther's fading likeness.

On the small side table beside the cot, Jamie saw the heart shaped stone they had found one day. He picked it up, stoked it lovingly and wondered why Samson had left it there. Had Samson forgotten it? He put it in his pocket and vowed that he would never forget.

The gloom allowed a new cynicism to circumvent Jamie's thoughts. Just like Mama, Samson was gone – dead – never coming back. It was the first time in his life he thought it might be better if there was no one to love. At least that way, he would avoid the emptiness that now wrapped itself around him. It was much too complicated for his young, naive mind to grasp.

For a brief moment, he thought about throwing the stone away. Curiously, as he rubbed it, he imagined hearing Samson's voice saying, "Hang on to it for me, Jamie. I'll be back to get it someday."

It was an alpha marker in the time span of his life. He longed to believe. He needed the stone. He tucked the keepsake in his shirt pocket – the one close to his heart. Pushing aside his pessimism, he chose to believe that Samson would return.

"Jamie, where are you?" Martha's voice interrupted his thoughts. "Let's go and find the barn cats."

"Coming, Martha." She was here. She was now.

8
Hagar

Life seemed good to John; it had started to have order and purpose. He determined he would become more involved in church work. He felt a sense of obligation to share his good fortune with the needy and the lost of the world. For the first time in his life, he felt a real sense of pride: he had done quite well for himself. His hard work was paying off, just the way his father had always told him it would. His life was becoming better than he had anticipated only a very short time ago. Letting go of his unreachable dreams for a different way of life had been a good idea. Perhaps he had misjudged his father's wisdom.

With his healthier mindset, John decided Martha could return to school for the time being. That also meant Lydia would need some help in the house. He thought she had improved over the summer. She seemed to have fewer headaches and he wanted to be sure that she didn't regress when Martha was in school. He had seen how much like her mother, Martha was. He also considered it might be beneficial for Lydia to have the company of another woman. Hagar, a strong, middle-aged spinster, who was known to be hard working and dependable, was hired. For two days a week, she would come to help Lydia manage the household and do the heavy cleaning.

When Hagar met Jamie, she knew him. She recognized the veneer of the quiet, pensive boy who sat angelically in church. Like him, she had mastered the art of pretense. Everyone knew the story of the orphaned children. Although her parents were not actually dead, she could relate implicitly to their loss. In her childhood, her parents, although alive, had never been in any way parental. Her story matched theirs in its despair. She had long ago learned that death could take diverse forms. It had occurred to her that the physical earthly detachment might be easier for a child to manage than a demise of rejection. She lied and told herself it no longer mattered. Her childhood was long gone. If there had ever been any good in her youth, the memories had been conscientiously abandoned. They were peeled off and left on the floor like soiled old garments that were not worth reclaiming.

After the death of her paternal grandmother, for whom she had cared, Hagar tended an old woman whose family could afford to pay for her care. They loved her enough to let her die among the things she possessed. Sadly, they hadn't loved her enough to provide the affection she really needed. Hagar became a surrogate caregiver, who like them, knew little of love.

Hagar understood about death. She had smelled its stench and touched its coldness. Only after her grandmother's death, did she learn the particulars that surrounded the leaving of her mother. She was five. Snippets of details were entrenched in her memory. One day she was there, the next day at breakfast her father stated she was gone. Nothing else was said. Grandma would move in and care for them. It was all for the best. If anyone asked, she was to say her mother had departed. The child could not grasp its true connotation; therefore, like the other enigmas of her young life, she accepted the anomaly without question. Because there had never been any familiarity between her parents, it didn't strike her as odd that her custody was reassigned to the old woman who had often looked after her as a child. The only peculiarity was her father's statement that there would be no crying. It didn't matter — Hagar was a child immune to crying. The luxury of sentiment was never promoted and very rarely expressed in her detached family unit.

Although her mother had taken care of her physical needs, she had deliberately withheld any direct, tangible semblance of love. She grew up untouched and alone. In the frequent visits with her grandmother, there was some formal show of affection. A kiss on the cheek began and ended each encounter. She learned quickly that children were to be seen and not heard. On each visit, she noiselessly disappeared into the background in fear of eliciting an outburst from the old woman. Often she played with an old cat who became her best friend and confidant.

The controlling matriarch ruled the dysfunctional family, like a black widow spider that mercilessly sucks life from its victims. Shortly after their immigration to Canada, her husband died. She was alone with her young son. Unaided in a man's world, she learned to survive through hard work. She lived in the keen expectation that someday her son would be successful. He would marry and bestow many grandchildren on her to continue the family name. She felt she deserved and was entitled to this legacy.

The son never met his mother's rigid expectations. Hagar was conceived in one lust-filled night of loneliness. The deed at the same time consummated and terminated her parents' physical bond. In front of the church, they bowed their heads and confessed the sin of adultery. In the community, many knew getting pregnant was the true sin. The marriage was compulsory. Societal cords, securely knotted by the woman who ruled their existence, bound the trapped parents and their child to the mandatory matrimonial arrangement.

They called her Nana. She ruled with an inhospitable, manipulative stance. Hagar's unnamed mother was always referred to as *the woman*. The woman had tempted her son. The woman had disgraced the family name. She had broken the fifth commandment. Her son had clearly been a helpless victim. The two conflicting females never spoke. Each was antagonized by the other's presence. Since he had no aptitude for independence, Hagar's father submissively tolerated the circumstances as his admission of guilt and the same time, his act of contrition.

Hagar grew up alone. Because she seldom spoke, Nana said she was a little retard. It was God's way of punishing her parents. The best they could hope for was that she could be trained to be obedient and useful. Very early in life, Nana taught her to do menial chores. She was good at them and that satisfied the old woman. Surprisingly, she was not a sad child and even smiled at the slightest acknowledgement. She knew nothing different and seemed to accept her fate without any sullenness.

When she was asked her name, she responded with, "Lilly Tard." For a time, this perpetuated the myth that she was indeed retarded.

Nana would laugh and say, "Her name is Hagar and she's a little retard."

There were brick walls of silence built in the house. Behind each partition was a person who lived in muted resentment. They hid, from each other and from themselves. The baby girl was fed, bathed and put to bed at the expected times. When awake, she sat in her playpen, played with a few meager toys and watched life through the bars. There was a stern pretence of harmony. When Hagar's mother could no longer endure the abuse, she packed a suitcase; with the household money she had secretly saved, she took the train to London.

Nana took over Hagar's life and easily fashioned her into her own perfect little servant; she took great pride in teaching the child useful mundane tasks. Because she was perceived to be retarded, school was never considered. Society approved of placing those who were deemed incompetent in an institution to live with their own kind. Thus, the community admired Nana and her father for not committing her and teaching her to be useful. When she was old enough, she spent her days cleaning the homes of the well-to-do in Strathroyal. Her father pocketed the money and used it for assorted, forbidden pleasures.

When Nana's health failed, Hagar tended her with a kind gentleness the old woman did not anticipate or appreciate and certainly did not deserve. When she passed, Hagar felt acutely alone. Her father was a phantom figure who materialized only when he wanted something from her. After her Nana's death, she found the courage to break free of him. She completely severed her connection and reliance on her deficient parent. Although she had no friends and trusted no one, she excelled at being a domestic. To the surprise of those who hired her, she surpassed their expectations. To their added amazement, she began to demand her pay in cash. She became a professional who was never short of work. It was the first time in her austere existence that she had the income and the opportunity to decide what to do with her life. In a small dingy apartment, she created her first home.

Eventually in her late twenties, she taught herself to read. The small local library provided the resources for the education she had been denied. She was happy to oblige when John wanted to hire her. She, like most in the town, was familiar with the family's circumstances and she was ready and willing to be the person they needed.

9

Pretense

In spite of her severe persona, Hagar had a benevolent heart. After the religious, dutiful tending of her grandmother, she filled the void in her life with the challenge of bringing order and consistency to those in need. There was purpose and meaning in the employment of older people in the church. Feeling appreciated was the only true contentment she had experienced in her deficient life. She thrived when tending disadvantaged households and gave selflessly of herself. Over the years, she earned an outstanding reputation for her honest hard work.

In some ways, life became somewhat easier for Martha when Hagar arrived. The strong, lean woman felt called to cultivate cleanliness. She was appalled at the apparent disarray of the house and became obsessed with purging and polishing every inch of it. No curtain was left unwashed; no corner was left untouched. While she cleaned, she sang in a boisterous, loud voice that would have made any choir director proud. Her repertoire consisted mostly of old hymns she had learned in the church choral group. Whenever she began a melody of songs, Lydia developed a headache and went to her room. In a calm, kind manner, Hagar supported her absence. It was obvious that Lydia was not capable of seeing to the needs of the home. She felt it much easier to engage in her sanitizing rituals when she was alone. Orderliness was sacred to her. When the children came home from school, she gave each child detailed instructions about how to maintain the immaculate appearance of the house.

In the same way her grandmother had scolded her, she chided Jamie if there were any signs of clutter. That her rebukes might upset him never occurred to her. She practiced what she had learned, caring for others in the only way knew. The reprimands were daunting to Jamie, yet there was something familiar about Hagar. Her eyes seemed to look beyond him, but he sensed her smile was genuine and it kept him from despising her ways.

Every room in the house, even the parlor, was turned out and thoroughly cleansed. Now that John was involved in church work, they should expect that the minister and other important people, would come calling more often. It would not be appropriate to entertain them in any other room. Jamie stood in the doorway and remembered the last time he had been there. He could picture it in his mind's eye. Hagar was right, the room smelled stale and foul. He didn't want to enter. She said it needed ammonia to destroy the smell of death. Jamie thought it needed flowers like the ones his mother used to place there. Sadly, he knew it was winter and the flowers were also dead.

The sense of routine and stability Hagar brought into the house gratified John. He was very happy with the apparent harmony and structure Hagar brought. He found it odd and didn't understand why Lydia seemed to be getting worse instead of better. She had much less to do. Even though she had more opportunity to rest, her headaches were again more frequent and she was spending more time alone in her room. The doctor explained it as an extraordinary kind of emotional illness. It would take more than medicine to cure his wife. He suggested that patience, time and love were the best treatment. Since John didn't have much of either, he was more than pleased that Hagar agreed to come five days a week to maintain cleanliness and order. He dreaded the weekends when he needed to have more interactions with Lydia and the children. It seemed to take forever to get them all to church and back.

Hagar cheerfully tended Lydia the same way she had looked after her Nana. The more Hagar did, the less Lydia seemed capable of doing. Slowly she assumed the role of surrogate matron of the house. She now believed her purpose in life was to care for this brave, burdened man and his family who were dealing with such unfortunate circumstances. Her admiration for him knew no bounds. She marveled at his patience with his brooding wife. Although she felt some compassion for Lydia, Hagar thought she needed to stop feeling sorry for herself and be grateful for her many blessings. It served no purpose to be miserable and it was certainly not Christian to ignore one's husband, as Lydia did. Although she never voiced the opinion, she believed good husbands should discipline their flawed, lethargic wives. Silently she scoffed at the doctor's words of advice. All Lydia really needed was to be made aware of her matrimonial responsibilities. Hagar was very cognizant of her own status and deliberately refrained from voicing her views to John. Despite her feelings toward Lydia, she continued to tend her with a spirit of respect and consideration. She was keenly aware that if Lydia recovered, she might have to look for other employment.

Martha and Jamie cringed when her bellowing voice reverberated through the house. They considered her the commander general who trumpeted her orders. She required that they take responsibility for numerous chores. The children didn't mind the drudgery – they were used to working hard and doing more than their share. Still they found the steady scrutiny of their performance tedious and disheartening. If Hagar had been able to recognize her impact, she might have cared for the family in a different way. In spite of her abrupt ways, there was no malice in her heart. Indeed, she felt gratified that her help was needed and valued.

John was pleased. In spite all the perceived trials heaped upon him, things were going well. The house was well kept, the way it used to be and the children were more restrained and passive. Even Lydia, despite her illness, was easier to live with. He decided it was time to be of service to his community. When the minister came to see Lydia, John would often visit with him afterwards. When Rev. Sluis casually suggested the church was in need of devout men like John, he unreservedly agreed to answer the call.

Going to church had always been an important Sunday ritual for the family, but now it took on a new significance.

As a leader, John had to sit in a front pew with his family. He took great pride in displaying them. They all dressed for the occasion in their best clothes, those reserved only for wearing on the Sabbath. Often when he greeted people at the end of the service, they would make remarks about how good he was to his brother's family. To take in the poor orphans and treat them as his own children was surely a very Christian thing to do. It was a shame that his wife was not well, but how fortunate that Hagar had been able to move in and take charge. John accepted the compliments as a sign that he was doing all the right things. He was very proud of his standing and position.

The new role often demanded he attend church meetings and that he visit the sick and the widows. These calls he conducted with a dignified aloofness. He soon became known for the wise platitudes he offered as comfort to those who were less fortunate. Always when he arrived home, Hagar would brew him a fresh cup of tea and serve him the oatmeal cookies he liked. As winter began, there were times that it was more convenient for her to stay at the house rather than have John drive her home in the snow. Eventually, John decided that during the winter, at least, Hagar should live with the family. John appreciated the way she listened to him, encouraged him and applauded his good deeds. Often he wondered how they had ever managed without her. He speculated about how different his life would be if Lydia would just try a little harder to be more like Hagar.

Lydia sensed what was happening in her home. When Hagar began the reorganization of her domain, she felt as powerless as an infant plunked thoughtlessly in the confines of a playpen. There were times she attempted to assert her authority. She had spoken timidly to Hagar regarding some minor domestic matters. Hager didn't question her requests, but her response to the woman of the house quickly drove her back to the enclosure of her silent room.

Always Hagar said in a patronizing voice, "Lydia, I'm so glad you're feeling better! Soon you won't need me here at all. John will be so pleased to know that you'll be your old self again soon."

Even though there was no spiteful intent, remarks like these estranged Lydia. Although there had been days that she saw some light in her world, the thought of having to manage the household was too daunting, so she mutely surrendered to the housekeeper's authority. The certainty that she would have to explain the situation to John brought forth immediate apologies to Hagar and a retreat to her safe space. She was terrified Hagar would leave and she would be alone to cope with the household. Her headache would last for days. In her solitude, Lydia listened and watched. She had a sense that the children were turning into frightened puppies. She felt real pain for them and wanted to gather them up in her arms. Sadly, she realized that it was now too late to be their mother. Then she would wrap her arms around herself and sit in her rocking chair looking out the window.

She was ashamed of what she had become. Regret gnawed at her. She grieved for the children that she did not have. She repented of the villainous way she had treated Esther. She resented, even hated, John for his condescending attitude toward her. She was envious of the peace Esther had in death. She began to regard herself as deceased, coffined within the restraints of barriers she had no power to displace.

She knew she was breathing, but she was dead to feeling love and dead to living. More and more she felt suffocated, like a cursed walking corpse whose essence was being meticulously smothered. Daily her resistance to putting forth even the smallest effort was eroded. On good days she managed a prayer for release to a God she feared. On the other days, the devil was able to steal more and more of her peace of mind.

Martha's grief had eased during the warm summer days. Although she had worked far beyond what was reasonable for her age, she had still had time to benefit from the wonders of the outdoors. She had designed a routine that allowed her the time and space that she craved. That changed when Hagar took charge of the house and repeated the pattern of her own upbringing. She treated Martha as a young servant who needed constant reminders of her duties and responsibilities. Hagar believed when children were praised, they could become vain and insolent. It was always necessary to remind them of their place. Because that had been her experience, it never occurred to her there might be a different way to grow up.

Martha was obedient and respectful at school and at home. She excelled in her schoolwork and continued to be diligent in helping in the household. Unfortunately, there was no joy in her life. There were no friends allowed in the house. Her only comfort was Jamie. She nurtured and cared for him, attempting to shelter him from the domination that surrounded them. She disguised her feelings by patiently lavishing attention and affection on the only person she loved. They were two children alone and lost in their adult world.

Unlike Martha, Jamie didn't do well in school. He found it tedious to sit for long periods. He missed the open fields and freedom of Samson's room. Often he lapsed into thoughts that took him far beyond the classroom walls. Then the teacher put him in the corner for not paying attention. Although it was humiliating, he found a strange sense of comfort there. He envisioned it to be his apple tree. There he could contemplate life's ambiguities in silence, without worrying about the impression he was creating. His peers ridiculed him, especially when he wore the dreaded dunce cap. He pretended not to care.

Thoughts of what Samson had said consoled him. "They don't know as much as they think they do, Jamie," had been Samson's motto. Now Jamie knew what he meant. Samson was right. Lovingly he rubbed the stone that was always in his pocket.

Jamie tried diligently to read and do sums, but the numbers and letters were often misplaced. The teacher rapped him on the knuckles with her ruler and scolded him for being careless. Although Martha helped him in the evenings with his unfinished schoolwork, mastery of even the basic skills eluded him. The teacher said he just had to pay more attention and try harder. He struggled and tried tenaciously for his mother, knowing it would make her happy. He longed to know how to read as she had. Accomplishments were rare. Eventually he dreaded going to school. Ultimately, he became the teacher's evaluation of him. Trying became pointless and he stopped.

He discerned a change in Martha's mood. She denied it when he questioned her about it, but he knew she was different. Although she seemed detached and distant, he knew she loved him because she hugged and kissed him more than he remembered. Jamie longed to talk to someone. So many questions needed asking. Often he would sneak away to the barn and have imaginary conversations with Samson. For a time, the make-believe discussions provided some reassurance that someone understood. Eventually the pretense became more complicated than the reality. Finally, he solemnly promised to continue their talks when his friend returned. He said good-bye to Samson, knowing he would understand.

10
Alone

Jamie didn't remember the exact day that his mother's shawl no longer comforted him. One cold night as he wrapped himself in it, he realized her essence had dulled beyond recognition. It alarmed him and he closed his eyes hoping to squeeze and savor some last vestige of her presence, but it was gone. The thing now smelled stale and sour. He tried to envision her face and feel the tender touch of her hands. Now he saw and felt only emptiness.

"Mama!" he shrieked.

Martha waited for the next cry, knowing when it came she would go to his room to cuddle and comfort him. During the last few months, his screams had become less frequent and she believed he was sleeping much better. She was thankful that he often slept through the night without waking. She waited but there was no second cry and she felt reassured that he'd gone back to sleep. It was the first time Martha had disregarded her brother's cries and had not gone to pacify him. She would never be able to free herself from this regret-filled burden.

When there was no vision of his mother and Martha didn't appear, Jamie was panic-stricken. If the memory was lost and Martha didn't come to soothe him, he was alone. Oblivious to reason, believing he must find her, he crept out of bed. Guardedly he opened the door, slipped down the stairs, out the kitchen door into the cold night. He ran in his pajamas, clutching her shawl. He had to find his Mama.

Oblivious to what he was doing, he ran and ran. Like a startled abandoned puppy, he attempted to find the solitary scent that would lead to home. He knew where to find it. The familiar flowerbed with its limp remains was not difficult to locate, even with the light covering of snow. The trees stood as sentinels, tall and sparse, without their coats of greenery. Like guards, always at attention, they watched over her resting place.

Exhausted, he flung himself on her grave. He could feel her there beneath him. The frosty air swept over him as he prostrated himself face down on the ground. He imagined her face in the box below. He wanted to feel and caress her soft hair and smell her sweetness. He recalled touching her that last time. Remembering the bitter iciness of her flesh sent shivers through his heart. He pictured the spring day they had put her in the earth. Each detail was again vivid and alive in his memory, but she was not. He couldn't reach her. She was gone. He lay on her grave and sobbed. The tears froze to his face. The frigid air dulled his senses.

The trees swayed their branches, encouraging the wind

to howl. On his visits, Jamie had often acknowledged them. They knew him. They loved him. Now in a futile effort they tried to rouse him, tried to let him know he wasn't alone. When his tears were exhausted, Jamie drifted into a cold numb state of unconsciousness. His young frail body had no defense against the elements. Feeling nothing brought a strange sense of comfort and he let it wash over him as he drifted into the blackness, trying to reach his Mama.

Martha was always the first to rise. Her routine was to get up, wash and get dressed. Then she would get Jamie up and they would go downstairs for breakfast. Often Hagar would meet them in the kitchen. When Martha realized Jamie wasn't in his bed, she supposed he had gone to the kitchen without her. Maybe he had slept through the night and woken up early, she thought. She vaguely remembered his lone cry and hurried to the kitchen to find him.

"Hagar, is Jamie here?" she questioned.

"I haven't seen him yet. Isn't he in his room?"

"No, maybe he's gone to the barn; I'll go and find him." Martha was starting to feel a strange sense of foreboding.

She hurried to the barn, expecting that he would be in Samson's room. She called for him and searched all his favorite hiding places. When she realized he wasn't there, an alarming apprehension set in.

Uncle John was in the barn doing chores. "I haven't seen him. He's probably in the house somewhere, Martha."

He's probably in the kitchen with Hagar by now, she mused, shivering. Not finding him there, she quizzed Hagar, "Where could he be, Hagar?" It was a plea more than a question.

Hagar heard the apprehension in Martha's voice. "He's

probably playing his hiding game, Martha. I'll help you look for him," she said kindly.

The search of the house was futile. When they returned to the kitchen, Martha was in a full state of alarm. She knew Jamie must have a good reason for disappearing without telling her. She refused to listen to Hagar's reassuring words that he couldn't be far.

"He's not in the house or the barn, so he must be outside. I'm going to look for him." Martha was now frantic.

She went to the closet for her coat and boots and immediately saw Jamie's coat was still on its hook. His boots stood neatly beneath them. Running to the barn without her coat, had left her chilled. The wind was cold and raw and she prayed he hadn't gone out and fallen in the field somewhere. She ran into the field, calling his name repeatedly. Terror grabbed at her throat, straining her voice and sending shivers of angst through her body.

John came in from the barn. He was looking forward to a hot cup of tea. He was tired. He had arrived home late from a meeting and had been up very early to do the chores. He thought it strange that he could hear Martha calling for Jamie. What has that boy done now, he wondered.

"Uncle John, Jamie is missing." Martha blurted out as she met him at the kitchen door.

"Jamie! Jamie!" he bellowed. "He's probably hiding somewhere, Martha."

"No, Uncle John, we've looked for an hour. Please, we have to go and look for him," she pleaded. "He doesn't even have his coat on. He'll freeze."

John was annoyed. This was no way to start the day. "Where have you looked, Martha?"

"Everywhere – the house, the barn, the fields. He's gone, something has happened to him," she could no longer control the tears. Her sobbing became uncontrollable.

"Enough Martha! We'll find him," he replied irritably. "First, I need to go into the house." He longed for the tea that would be waiting for him.

Hagar tried earnestly to reassure Martha. "Don't worry child, your uncle will find him." Despite the optimism, fear was beginning to seep from her words.

The commotion in the house awoke Lydia. She made her way to the kitchen in her nightgown. As Esther had done, Hagar usually brought her a breakfast tray. She liked to start her day slowly and silently. Because of the unusual noise and stress in the house, a headache was already beginning to make itself known.

As John went back to the barn to get the car, he was already rehearsing the scolding Jamie would receive when he found him. With the windows open, he drove aimlessly calling for the boy. Only the sound of barking watchdogs answered. John began to worry; it really wasn't like Jamie to go running off. Gradually his annoyance turned to apprehension. Turning around, he headed home, telling himself that the child was probably there by now.

Martha came running out to meet him; he could see by her distressed manner that Jamie hadn't been found. She waved at him to stop but he spun the car around and headed to town. He drove dejectedly to the police station and reported that Jamie was missing. The desk officer shook his head as he listened, "Kids today are so different."

"Yes, yes, but he's a good boy. Very unlike him to run off," insisted John urgently.

"Don't worry, we'll find him, Mr. Jacobs."

John's fears were not suppressed. The anger he had felt morphed to a lament. Now he prayed, really prayed for the boy. He asked God to protect Jamie wherever he was. He even prayed he would have another chance to be Jamie's father.

As he drove home, he saw the sun on the horizon. Despite his anxiety, the splendor of it astounded him. The beauty foreshadowed hope; conversely, his heavy heart felt only despair.

The Gift

Peter, Strathroyal's retired gravedigger, got up early. Like John, he also saw the brilliant colors splashed across the sky to welcome the morning. It would be a fine day for the funeral of his friend, Nelly Van.

Although it had been an unusually early spring, a late snowstorm had abducted the warmth and left a blanket of snow that concealed the promise of spring. Today was cold and crisp; as the sun crept up, it burnished the land with temperate, comforting rays. Reminiscent of summer, it permeated the countryside with optimism. The resurrection of spring was certain and this brilliant day gave the assurance that it could soon be anticipated. The trees looked bare but hidden buds made them mothers-in-waiting. The life within stirred as a subtle reminder that gave birth to the confidence they could endure this short winter interlude. They had only to wait to embrace another genesis.

Peter dressed in his only suit. Since the task of digging the grave, would take him all morning, there would not be time to come home and change his clothes for the interment. His worn overalls would cover his Sunday ensemble. He deemed it appropriate to be well dressed for the celebration of Nelly's life. She would be delighted that the earth was receiving her in style. She was a good Christian woman, who had nothing to fear from the hereafter. She had lived a long healthy life; an attentive family cherished her; the community esteemed her. He liked to think the earth knew such things and rewarded the deserving with a special day to receive them into its bosom. He stood in the warmth of the rising sun and determined that today was such a day. He aspired to a similar day for his own requiem. Then his life would surely have credence.

Officially, Peter had given up working, but he still helped when he was asked. The community had thanked him and given him a beautiful gold watch for all his years of service. For fifty years, he had dug their graves. The work was his profession. He had labored solemnly over each tomb. He knew them all and considered the lives they had lived as he scooped the dirt to prepare their final resting place. Often he predicted who would be at the funeral and what they would say. He considered it a sacred trust to be part of returning them to the earth from which they came.

While others had scoffed at his ideas about machines entering the earth, Nelly had understood and honored his beliefs with her request that he dig for her. Last summer at the church social, she had approached him. A slight, frail woman, she had asked him to prepare her grave. It was her final gift to him; now he would return it with the love and respect she had offered to each person she knew. He felt privileged. Ceremoniously, he would prepare her resting place. No machine would dig. She would rest knowing peace. It bordered on sacrilege when the arms of the beast reached into the earth and tore callously at its flesh, like a violation that blasphemed the order of creation. Surely, God felt dishonored when such an invasive device traumatized the land.

He sighed – not many understood. They sneered at him behind his back. He knew, but he was beyond bothered. Life was changing, but as long as he lived, some sacred things would stay the same. It grieved him to think there might not be someone to dig for him. He brooded over it. No time to think on that now, he chided himself. Today, he would honor Nelly. He gathered up his tools, climbed into the old truck and drove to the cemetery.

Nelly would lie beside her husband. Peter had prepared his grave twenty years ago. She would rest well there. He knew that she had many suitors after her husband's death. She told him once that her life was complete and she was content to wait to be with her beloved. She would not marry again. He smiled when he remembered the conversation.

"If I married again, how would I know which one to be with in heaven?" she had quipped. "It wouldn't be fair to make a choice."

He had deliberated this concept in his mind many times. Why were such practical elements of heaven never discussed? It really didn't matter much to him. He had chosen not to get married. There had been many opportunities; nevertheless, he had been satisfied to remain alone. Now as he took his shovel from the back of the truck, he could picture Nelly reunited with her bridegroom. It all felt very right and good to know she was home with him again.

The ritual of marking the spot was always the same. After a brief moment of meditation, a prayer that the departed would have peace, he paced out the site, dug the edges and began to hollow out the hole. He was thankful that although the soil was cold and hard, there had been a good early thaw and most of the frost was out of the earth. Still, it was hard work and would take him the entire morning. It disturbed him that his aging body didn't respond the way it had years ago.

He looked across the graveyard. This place was hallowed ground. He glanced around, remembering the many he had helped lay to rest. As he took a last look, his eyes saw a curious mound on Esther Jacob's grave. What could be laying there? It was too large to be something her children had left. He had watched them tend her spot, had shared their grief from a distance; he had marveled at the garden they had planted for her. Strange he thought, I'll have to go and look later. Better get on with the digging now.

He delved into his labor. His old spade knew what to do. Short quick dips aptly began to extract the soil. Suddenly, he put the shovel down. The uneasiness about what he had seen refused to leave. He felt troubled and needed to investigate. Snow crunched under his feet as he marched to the young woman's grave. His pace quicken to a run, as the object came into focus. It was a youngster, shrouded in a shawl. He uncovered the face and knew the child. He listened for breathing and heard none. Why was the boy here? Had he been here long? Taking off his coat, he gently wrapped the limp, cold body in it. Since the boy appeared lifeless, he didn't think there was anything he could do. For a brief instant, he stood holding Jamie. His family must be frantic with worry, he thought. Even though the boy was dead, he knew the Jacobs family needed to know immediately.

"Take him to the doctor," Nelly's voice was distinct and urgent.

"But he's gone," his mind protested.

"Peter, take care of the child," Nelly repeated urgently.

Although he was confused, he trusted what he had heard and bolted towards his truck and laid the bundled child on the seat next to him. The old vehicle had never known such speed. It was only a few miles to the town. He prayed the doctor would be at home.

The doctor's office was in his house on the main street of Strathroyal. He pounded on the front door. Mrs. Smit peered through the window and quickly opened the door.

"It's Jamie Jacobs – I think he's dead," Peter stammered.

"Lay him on the sofa," ordered Mrs. Smit, "I'll get the doctor."

Doctor Smit was still dressed in his housecoat. The ends of his stereoscope were already in his ears. He tore away the child's pajama shirt and listened.

"Thank God, he's still alive," the doctor announced as he listened. "What happened? Where did you find him?"

Peter offered a quick explanation.

"Mary, telephone the police; I'm taking the boy to the hospital in London. Peter, can you come with me? We have to keep him warm." It wasn't really a question; the doctor knew that Peter would do whatever was necessary to save the child's life.

They drove without speaking. Peter sat in the back seat with the boy on his lap; he was engrossed in rubbing Jamie's body, trying to return some warmth to it. It took only thirty minutes to reach Victoria Hospital in London. Peter marveled that the trip was made so quickly, even with the doctor's fancy car.

In the waiting room, he paced like an expectant father, anxious to hear the news. When Doctor Smit came out of the emergency room, he was smiling.

"He's coming round, Peter. He's going to live," he said. "He owes his life to you. If you hadn't found him, he surely would have died."

"It's a miracle. It was Nelly who saved his life," was all Peter could say.

"He'll have to stay for a few days at least, but we'd better get back to town. John and Lydia must be sick with worry. We'll stop by the farm and let them know what's happened."

As they drove home, Peter realized it would soon be time for Nelly's funeral. He would return now and dig her grave. If he hurried, there might still be time to finish. He wondered what the mourners would think if they came to the cemetery and the grave wasn't ready. He knew he had Nelly's blessing and decided the rest didn't matter.

Thoughts of Jamie filled Peter's mind. Poor child must have been very distraught to go to sleep there in the cold. Good thing Nelly had died; good thing he had gone to look. Surely, John and Lydia had not done anything to provoke the boy. He believed them to be good folks, a little strange both of them, but to take in their brother's children was certainly a true act of charity.

Upon arriving at the farm, Dr. Smit and Peter discovered the police had already been there to inform John and Lydia that Jamie had been found. John had driven around for hours; Martha had walked the fields until she could walk no more and had eventually collapsed on Samson's bed in the barn. She knew this was a place of comfort for Jamie and hoped he would return there.

For the first time, Hagar had dared to reprimand Lydia. "If you tried a little harder to be a mother to the boy, he probably wouldn't have run off."

The cruel words echoed the conviction of Lydia's own heart. She should have done better. After the scolding, she retreated to her room and poised herself in the rocking chair in front of the window. Staring out, she saw a strange, grassy lane winding its way to nowhere. Odd that I've never seen it before, she thought. It looked inviting; perhaps, she thought this is the way to peace. She left her body sitting in the chair and effortlessly let her mind start down the path. From nowhere, a door stood ajar. It hung from a frame that was unattached and strangely affixed only to the foliage in the field. Through it, far down the way, she imagined she saw someone beckoning her. Who could it be, she wondered and how could the entrance stand there by itself, not held to anything? She felt the doorway inviting her to pass through it. It seemed to whisper her name. Stepping into the void on the other side, she felt the pleasant warm air on her face. The green field was dotted with bright flowers. It felt friendly and welcoming. She smiled and looked ahead. She heard her name again. Looking back, behind the door, she saw herself sitting rigid at the window. John was there, beside her chair, shaking her, calling her name. Suddenly another voice came from far away, beyond where she stood. It sounded like her mother, or was it Esther singing her lullabies?

She hesitated only for a moment. The voice in the remote, faraway place was sweet and alluring, unlike John's demanding holler behind her. Her longing was desperate. John's outline paled and grew distant. He would be fine; he didn't need her anymore. There was no reason to return. Carefully she closed the door and locked it with the key that was in the latch and clutched it tightly in her hand. Finally, she felt free to run.

John was alarmed. Lydia's eyes were open, but she appeared not to see him or hear him. He shook her and called her name urgently. She stared out of the window and seemed not to be aware of his presence. Thank goodness, the doctor was still here. Hagar was busy making him a cup of tea in the kitchen. He wondered about having him look at her. This was unusually strange, even for Lydia. Better to do it now, than have to run into town later. Maybe he could give her something to settle her down. It had after all been a long exhausting morning for all of them.

"Doctor, could you look at Lydia while you're here. She doesn't seem to be well. I think it's all been too much for her." John was embarrassed that his needy wife required the doctor's attention again.

"What seems to be the matter with her, John?" Doctor Smit questioned.

He was well acquainted with Lydia's headaches and spells. He had tried to explain what Lydia required, but John couldn't grasp the idea that she was lonely and craved some affection. He wondered what had happened of late. When he had last seen her, she had seemed so much better. He shook his head as John led the way to Lydia's room. She had not moved.

"Let me take a look at her, John. You go and have your tea," he ordered.

The words he spoke to her were kind and gentle. He held her hand and whispered her name. He discerned that she didn't see or hear him. He had seen these symptoms during the war in men who had been shell-shocked. He speculated about just how far away she was. He slapped her face hard, hoping that she would react. He wanted her to be within reach of physical pain; he had seen it work as a summons to return to the present. She teetered in the chair, but there was no response. He knew that she probably could not acknowledge his presence. It is a sad day for this house he thought – first the boy and now Lydia. He sighed deeply, patted her hand and told her that he would see to her care. He left the room, rehearsing the edict he must give John.

When the doctor explained that Lydia required intensive care and needed to be admitted to the psychiatric hospital in London, John put his head in his hands and wept unashamedly. How was it possible that in one day, the order in his life had been so abruptly and completely disrupted? He was angry with himself and with all of them. He should have put more restrictions on the children and his wife. Maybe if Jamie hadn't run off, Lydia wouldn't have snapped. Martha was at fault too. She should have watched her brother more closely. He had been so good to them. Why did he have to suffer this way? He wallowed in a bottomless well of self-pity, staggering on its slippery slope.

Hagar saw his anguish and put her hand on his shoulder. "It's not your fault, John. You couldn't have done more for them."

"Well, doctor, if it's got to be done, the sooner the better." He wiped the tears from his face with his dirty, red handkerchief. "Can we go right now?"

Peter had waited outside the house. He felt awkward being privy to the family discussion occurring with the doctor. Martha met him, as she was coming from the barn.

"Peter, what are you doing here? Do you know where Jamie is?" she blurted out.

The pain in her voice and her face, touched Peter,

"Don't worry Martha. We took him to the hospital but he'll be fine," he whispered.

He described how he had found Jamie that morning.

"I should have known he'd go there. He's alright Peter, really?"

"Yes, Martha, he's going to be fine. He may have to be in the hospital for a few days, but then he'll be home, good as new."

Martha recalled Jamie's cries overnight and suddenly remorse, shame and fatigue overwhelmed her. She fell into Peter's arms and cried. The weeping racked her body. Poor, poor girl, thought Peter. She's just a child herself and already so much to bear. He held her close, rocking her until the crying abated to long loud sobs that slowly diminished.

Wrapped in a blanket, they led Lydia to the car. She neither spoke nor protested. The doctor held her right hand. He thought it strange that the other hand was tightly clenched, almost as if she were making a fist. Somewhere there's something of her left, he told himself.

Martha was unaware of what had happened in the house.

"Uncle John, when can we go and see Jamie?" she questioned impatiently.

"Selfish child, can't you see that Aunt Lydia isn't well? It's all been too much for her. Doctor Smit is taking her to the sanatorium in London." There was no tenderness in his voice. "Jamie will have to wait."

Doctor Smit seized the opportunity to rescue Martha. "John, how be I drive Lydia in my car? Martha can sit in the back with her and keep her calm. You can take Peter to the cemetery and then meet us in London. Then you could check in on Jamie while you're in the city."

John was relieved he wouldn't have to deal with Lydia all the way into the city. "That's very good of you, Doctor Smit. I'm sorry to put you to so much trouble."

"No trouble at all John. Glad that I can help," he replied. "Are we ready to go then?"

Peter gave Martha a tender hug. Bless you, Doctor Smit he mused. And bless you Nelly for your gift.

12
The Reader's Digest

Martha was overwhelmed by the luxury of the doctor's car. It was a pure blue color, like a brilliant summer sky. The new Pontiac coupe was bigger and more comfortable than any car she had ever seen or imagined. The seats were plush velvet that felt richly luxurious. She sat in the back seat with Aunt Lydia. She looked into her eyes and saw the emptiness there. What would Mama say she wondered? She held Lydia's limp hand. Doctor Smit watched her in the rear view mirror. He attempted to explain Lydia's state was a way for her to escape the reality of her existence. Martha wanted to understand, but she found it very confusing. She understood about rejection, about pain and about loneliness. She wondered why Lydia could think that she had nothing for which to live.

Martha remembered the times she had felt some

tenderness for her aunt and the times she had disliked her for her detachment. Now that she saw how lost Lydia was and saw a glimpse of the weighty melancholy, she felt a deep compassion for her. She believed her mother would have been able to help her. Martha wished she felt capable of it too. All the way to the city, she rubbed Lydia's hand, praying she would know she was loved despite all that had happened. She repented of the times she had resented her aunt. She should have tried harder to understand.

If only she had tried harder. If only Jamie had not run off. She smiled, in spite of herself, remembering her mother's wisdom about "if only." She could hear Esther saying, "If only I had a crystal ball, I wouldn't make any mistakes."

It had taken her a long time to understand the saying. Esther had explained it to her repeatedly. She held Lydia's hand a little tighter. Don't worry Aunt Lydia, she thought; I love you. She surprised herself with the realization.

As Lydia wandered down her endless, empty road, she was aware of a ray of sunshine that kissed her skin and warmed her heart. She looked up into it and saw the semblance of a face. It was someone familiar but the details were camouflaged, clouded and vague in the light. Maybe later she would stop to look more closely. For now, she had to keep moving; the voice in the distance was urgently calling her name.

Martha had often dreamed about going to London. She had been there only once with her mother and some of her friends. It was years ago and she remembered little of it. She had heard from classmates at school that it was a splendid city. There were high buildings, stores, cars and parks with children's rides. Now as she watched the scenery, she marveled at the enormous countryside. She knew her world was small, but the predictability of it provided safety from the unknown. Someday she told herself; someday I'll see the city. Jamie and I will see it together.

The thought of Jamie lying in a hospital bed jolted her back to the reality of the situation. Why had he gone out so late at night to the cemetery? Why had he stayed there? She knew he would be anxious in the hospital by himself. He didn't like unfamiliar places or people. Doctor Smit told her he would take her to see Jamie after they had tended to Aunt Lydia. Martha was exhausted; the droning of the wheels and the rhythmic motion of the car lulled her to sleep.

Good, thought the doctor, the child needs a pause from the adult burdens that are much too large for her to carry. He gently woke her when they arrived at the hospital.

Lydia was carefully placed in a wheelchair and taken inside. Martha thought it very peculiar that most of the windows had bars on them. It troubled her. She contemplated that it looked more like a jail than a hospital. She had misgivings about leaving Aunt Lydia here. Perhaps, Doctor Smit would explain it again later.

She sat in the waiting room fascinated by the stacks of magazines on every table. *The Reader's Digest*, she knew and loved. On occasion, Lydia had received copies from the women who came to visit. Martha was enthralled with the stories of far-away places and people. She passionately devoured each book. There was another world beyond the confines of Strathroyal. Sitting alone she promised herself that someday that world would be hers to find. It was the first time in her life that she had really coveted something for her future. She positioned the seed in a deep hidden place in her mind, determined someday to nourish it.

When Uncle John arrived an hour later, he was abrupt and harsh when he found Martha in the waiting room. "Where's the doctor," he quizzed her. "What's happened with Lydia?"

"I don't know, Uncle John. Doctor Smit told me to wait here." Martha replied.

John inquired at the nurses' desk and was told where to find his wife. He could go and see her. He left Martha without bothering to explain where he was going. She waited patiently for another hour until the doctor and John emerged from the hall. Martha immediately saw the nervous tension that held him. Raw ropes of fear tautly pulled him together. His teeth were clenched and deep lines furrowed his forehead; he was the cold, ashen color of death. She knew he was beyond anxious.

"Is she going to be alright?" Martha's concern was genuine.

"No, of course she isn't," he retorted quickly, "she's in an insane asylum."

"Now, now John, you know the doctors said that with care and treatment a lot can be done. Let's try and remain positive, shall we?" Doctor Smit said.

Martha thought there was an edge of brusqueness in his voice.

"Well, I guess we'll go and see Jamie, Martha," John answered. "We'd better get moving. It's getting late and Hagar will have dinner waiting."

He thanked the doctor for his time and told him he would pick up his bill the next day.

Doctor Smit watched them leave. He wondered which of the two had the more difficult road to travel. Both of them are so alone and scared, he mused. Surely, there must be some way for them to bridge their alienation. He shook his head – it had been a long day. There would be a room full of patients waiting to see him. He too would have dinner waiting. His wife knew how to be a wife. Lydia should get to know her, he thought.

They drove to Victoria Hospital in silence. John murmured brash comments to himself. Martha didn't understand what he was saying, but she did recognize that his disposition was one she had never witnessed before. It unnerved her; she was not used to hearing vulgarity from him. She recalled how often he had denounced those who used profanity and concluded he must be feeling very, very bothered about Aunt Lydia.

John was aware that Martha was studying him. He was indignant. Lydia had not wasted any love on the children. She hadn't known how to mother them. He didn't understand it. She had wanted children desperately. When the specialist had told them they would never have any of their own, she had cried for days. He remembered how she had moped around the house as if she'd lost her best friend. She suggested once that they adopt children, but he hadn't liked the idea of raising someone else's offspring. There was no guarantee they wouldn't have some problems later in life that could create all sorts of inconvenience. Lydia had been so sullen about his refusal that he had seriously thought about reconsidering the idea.

When Esther came to live with them, it seemed to be a fitting solution for both families' dilemmas. John believed it was an answer to Lydia's prayers. At first, she had been eager to welcome the two children who were already through that horrible infancy stage. He had considered it very odd that his wife had not seemed more excited; she had not behaved at all, as he had expected she would. There were complaints about the noise and the clutter the children created. Lydia grumbled that Esther slighted her and didn't want her to be part of the children's lives. Her constant criticism annoyed him. After a time he felt things were going quite well, especially when Esther began to care for his ailing wife. Esther's death was most unfortunate, but the circumstances had certainly turned into quite a suitable arrangement when Hagar had arrived to help them. Once again, his life and everything in it was collapsing into chaos.

He was angry. Everything he had worked so hard to achieve was now threatened by Jamie's escapade and Lydia's condition. It was certainly going to be very problematic. First, it would be awkward and bothersome to have to explain it to the gossipy old women at church. He hoped they wouldn't resume their do-good missions with pots of the watered-down soup, offered in the past when Lydia had been unwell. Soup seemed to be their solution to life's problems.

The thought of soup also unexpectedly induced recollections of his mother. She had made soup that was satisfying and tasty. He hadn't thought of his parents since his visit to the attic with Martha. His only sibling, James, was born when he was five years old. His father always said his mother spoiled him. He had predicted James would never become a real man. He was too soft spoken and emotional. Father had no patience for crying boys. When he disciplined James, the child would cry and run to his mother for comfort and sympathy.

"Stop coddling the boy," he had heard him say to his mother. "You don't see John acting like such a baby."

He had taken this as permission to antagonize his younger brother. The memories of the relentless teasing troubled him. He knew he had been vicious and violent in his attacks. The physical torment had not affected him as much as the verbal beatings he had inflicted. It made him miserable when he recalled how James had cried when he had called him names and told him his father didn't love him. At times, his mother would reproach him to keep the peace; occasionally, even his father would agree that he had gone too far.

John recognized he had always been more spirited than James had been. He was proud of the approval his father had bestowed on him for this trait; even so, there were also snippets of envy. His mother had loved James; John had been pushed to become his father's son. This created an overt rivalry between the brothers. They were constantly searching for approval from opposing parents. James never attained his father's respect; John never realized his mother's love. Although they had never discussed it, John believed James must have known it as well. After Hitler's invasion of Holland, James told them he was going to fight for the motherland; John was certain he was really enlisting to gain his father's approval. When his brother died, his mother had been heartbroken and passed away soon after. Without her, his father couldn't cope. Although he had not actually voiced the idea, John suspected his father blamed James for his mother's death. Soon after her death, he suffered a massive, paralyzing stroke. John saw him as a wounded animal that needed to be freed from its suffering. When he died, John was grateful for the release it provided for both of them.

Seared into his heart were his father's last words, "John, make sure you look after your brother's children. Young Jamie must carry on our name. Teach him to be like his father."

His father's words had stunned John. Why, at the end, was James the one that mattered? Once again, he felt second best. His father's acceptance and love had always been unwavering. He could always count on this one reality. These final words had once again ignited a deep jealousy of his dead brother. Because John had no heir, his father had branded him as inadequate.

John spent endless hours trying to understand why his father had given his blessing to his brother and not to him. He had been all that his father wanted. Many times, he had denied his own nature and desires; he had molded his thinking to shape the ideas his father held. He had married the girl his parents had suggested. For his father's approval, he had become a farmer instead of going to school. When his brother died, he secretly yearned for the honor death brought.

On the day his father died, John vowed to prove them wrong. He would take control of his life and make it one that others would look to as an example of integrity and honor. He promised himself that in the future, things would be different; he would never again be second best.

John felt cheated by his brother's death and his wife's infertility; the idea festered in a deep lesion in his soul. Although he was not aware of it for many years, it was often the compass that gave direction to his life.

John parked the car and sat staring out the window. He had always done what was expected. He had made it happen the way he had planned. The townspeople admired him as a leader in their community. They respected him for taking in his brother's children. There was enough money to be secure. There had been a few difficulties along the way, but he had persevered in the face of adversity and had become successful. He believed that even his father would have been proud of the way he had shaped his life.

Now on this bright day, it was all turned around. He realized he had let himself be bound. He had performed but not really lived his own life. It seemed he was always trying to gain approval by living out the expectations of others. He felt trapped, like a pigeon in a coop, unable to escape and fly away. The thought made him more and more despondent.

"This time, I'm going to be free to find my own way," he declared emphatically; then added sarcastically, "Well father, what do you think of me now?"

"I'm sorry, Uncle John I didn't hear you," Martha stammered.

"You weren't meant to, Martha." He got out of the car and slammed the door.

Martha followed him into the hospital, ecstatic that she would see Jamie. She wished Uncle John would move a little faster.

13

Summer Wine

The recollection of wrapping himself in the shawl awakened Jamie's memory. He rummaged for it now, but his hands could not locate its familiar touch. Thrashing about, he became frantic – it was gone. A soft, warm touch stroked his cheek. When he opened his eyes, he saw the smiling face of an angel. She was clothed in white; a starched coronet adorned her hair. It was his mother; he must be in heaven!

"Hello Jamie," the voice breathed.

It was not his mother's voice. He closed his eyes and drifted back to sleep. If he wasn't in heaven, he didn't want to wake up.

The voice persisted, "Jamie, wake up now."

Again, he felt his face being embraced.

This time he saw his mother and reached out to her, "Mama, Mama," he cried.

"Jamie, it's not time for you yet. Now go – love God, be good, work hard. You promised Jamie." They were his mother's words, murmured in the soft caress of her voice.

"I'm scared Mama, don't leave," he pleaded.

Again, his mind became obscured in darkness.

"Jamie, Jamie, wake up, please." He also knew this voice.

"Martha?" he whispered.

"Yes Jamie, it's me. Now wake up please. Open your eyes. You're in the hospital," the relief in her voice was apparent.

"Mama was here, Martha. I saw her and she talked to me."

Martha's tears fell on his face as she pressed her cheek next to his. Was it possible that he had been at heaven's door? It didn't matter. He was back now and she would care for him. She would restore his laughter.

John watched the children with a sense of covetousness. He felt wholly detached from their love. They were alone but at least they had each other. He had no one to comfort him, to share his loss. Bitterness swaddled his vision. The encumbrance of his guardianship tugged at his heart. Hostility smothered the compassion that resided somewhere deep inside him. They weren't really his children. They were nothing to him but a cross to bear, a burden to carry up the solitary road of his life. Yet they were everything he knew. Everything he had been taught. Everything he could be. Even so, it wasn't enough. He was not enough for them, for Lydia, or even for himself.

Frozen in the moment, he considered his options. Discerning the fork in the road, brought to mind a poem he had read once. Something about two roads diverging and a man taking the one less traveled. He yearned to see down the path to the future. On one side were the familiar road signs his parents and his culture had posted for him to follow. On the other side were his cravings and aspirations signed in the language of desire. It was clear that the two alternatives could never merge. Like the poet, he didn't delude himself into thinking that he would ever be able to return to this place, this crossroad. Taking the road less traveled would mean casting off most of what he'd been taught and much of what he believed. He stood silent, completely engrossed by in the enormity of the decision. The baggage of responsibility weighed heavy on his shoulders. Although he knew the answer, he wondered if it was courage or cowardice to leave it sitting there. It would mean taking an enticing forbidden road, paved with the uncertainty of autonomy. There would be no guideposts and it would be easy to get lost on the unfamiliar pathway.

"Listen to the doctors and nurses, Jamie. They want you to stay for a day or two. We'll be back when you can come home." It was a brisk statement that signaled it was time to leave. "Come along, Martha," he added.

Jamie cried for Martha to stay. She ran back to give him one more hug. As they left, the angel in white came back to comfort him.

They drove home in silence. John tried to repress the unusual hunger he felt. The desire to be free gnawed at his gut. He feared the allure of independence might devour him. The determination to follow his fantasies was difficult to resist. The scent of alternatives titillated his senses. Its sweetness tantalized his thoughts. Unfamiliar desires stirred somewhere in a deep shadowy place. Long ago, he had concealed them behind the expected conventions of his father. Now, the facade he had created threatened to crumble. He questioned if he could endure the niceties he had practiced all these years. The fear of condemnation had constantly chaperoned his activities. If he took the alternative path, would he be strong enough to endure the certain denouncement of his peers? He was convinced there was only one way to know. He promised himself that tonight he would decide which road to travel.

As John had predicted, Hagar had prepared dinner. The familiar smell of her beef stew, his favorite food, greeted him as they entered the house. It appeased his drained spirit. At least, there was one good thing left, he thought.

Hagar warmly welcomed John, "You must be very tired, John. How is Lydia? Would you like a glass of summer wine? It might help you to relax."

"That's exactly what I need," he managed a smile. "Lydia is gone." He relayed the events of the day to her in a passive narrative.

For an instant, their eyes met. Unexpectedly, they both saw something they could not fathom.

Martha's voice brought them back to the kitchen. "Shall I set the table, Hagar?"

"Yes, please do. Don't forget to wipe the plates first," Hagar responded.

Martha didn't understand why the plates needed cleaning before they were placed on the table. Hagar said it was something refined people did. It was something Lydia had refused to do and they had argued about it. They assigned the job to Martha, who always did as she was told. She wiped them thoroughly before positioning them on the table. She made sure to place the forks and knives in the right place so Hagar would have no reason to criticize. She sensed something unusual was happening around her. A curious mood hung in the kitchen. It was an unconventional sentiment that could be detected, but was too vague to be identified or exposed. Perhaps, Martha thought, I'm just tired and worried about Jamie. When the meal started without the customary saying of grace, she knew it was not an imagined sensation.

Hagar recognized the mood as well. It didn't alarm or even unsettle her because she understood it. Her training as a servant included meeting the assorted, sometimes even the distorted needs of her employers. She had tried to question her father about certain strange requests they made. He instructed her to be a good girl and do as she was told. There were books in the library that taught her what she needed to know.

Unconsciously, Hagar had known it might happen from the day she had arrived. She had noticed the clues everywhere. She saw the estranged couple as two inhabitants living in the same house, but existing in different spheres. There was no unity, no connection. It had been pathetic to witness. She had tried her best to remain detached, aware that part of her role was to wait, knowing she would serve John at the preordained time. Destiny would unfold the obvious. It was like the fermenting of fruit, ripening to wine. Decay would bring a new taste, an unexpected indulgence. She filled John's glass, aware he was gulping the sweet nectar much too quickly.

John's senses were soon dulled. Exhausted from the

tensions of the day, he left the table wordlessly and went to his room. There was a chill in the air. His bed felt cold and damp. His inebriated state soothed him into a dull slumber. Tomorrow, he told himself, he would decide.

Martha was tired. The awkward silence of the ride home and the dinner table had drained her. It was a struggle for her to engage in Hagar's shallow prattle. In an empathic moment, Hagar realized the child also needed comforting. She attempted this by spewing forth perceived platitudes about life pasted in her impoverished emotional memory:

"In the end, it's all for the best."

"Good things come to those who wait patiently."

"We really don't need to fret. All things work together for good, to those who love Him,"

Hagar made the pronouncements with great satisfaction, fully believing and expecting that the empty words would console the discouraged child.

Instead, they angered Martha. The God of her mother did not retaliate, did not create injury; it would have been futile to protest. She realized how hard it must have been for Aunt Lydia when Hagar had insisted on being right. She was beginning to understand why her aunt had crumbled under the censure of this eccentric woman.

Martha also recognized that Hagar was attempting to be gracious. She found it strange that Hagar seemed so cheerful and optimistic. For Martha, the little bit of stability in their lives had completely deteriorated. She knew she had not always appreciated Aunt Lydia, but now she was beginning to know the depth of her suffering. Uncle John was behaving in a very odd way. She had never before felt him scrutinize her the way he had done in the car; she had never seen him drink so much wine. She wanted to assume that it was the stress of the day's events; still, his behavior was very unsettling. She needed to sleep. Tomorrow would be better. She prayed it would be familiar.

In the morning, John awoke conscious of the wine he had consumed. A deep dark pain filled his skull. He had slept fitfully. Today there were grave decisions to be made. The aroma of fresh brewed coffee beckoned him to the kitchen. Breakfast was waiting. John didn't seem to remember it was Sunday. The usual ritual of preparing for and going to church was neglected. When Martha came into the room in her Sunday dress, he realized they would be missed at the morning service.

"Aren't we going to church, Uncle John?" she asked innocently.

"No, Martha, we are not going to church."

"Martha, don't be bothering your uncle. He has a lot to think about today. Run along and find something to do," Hagar instructed her.

Martha couldn't remember a time that they hadn't been to church on Sunday morning. She went to her room to read a library book, again. It was hard to concentrate when there was so much to think about. She longed to see Jamie – maybe Uncle John would take her to visit him later. His strange behavior bothered her. She felt the strain of the turmoil of the last two days and her eyes brimmed over with tears of frustrated despair.

In a small town, news travels fast. The minister heard about Lydia and Jamie after church. He also noted that John and his family were absent. In the afternoon, Rev. Sluis came to see John. They sat in the parlor with the door closed.

Hagar dutifully postured herself in the kitchen. Martha stayed in her room. She was perplexed about the visit. Uncle John's voice levitated to the second floor. Martha didn't understand why he sounded so angry. Of course, she felt pity for him, but she was also embarrassed that he would be so conspicuously disrespectful; raising one's voice to the minister was never sanctioned.

Rev. Sluis emerged from the room alone. He looked distressed and unnaturally distracted. The look he accorded Hagar was reserved and aloof.

"I hope you're not part of John's plan, Hagar," he stated briskly.

The dismayed look on her face, gave him hope that John had devised his own course of action. He hoped and prayed that she would not be part of his mindless folly. Perchance, Hagar was as much a victim here as the children. It would be best for her to move out of the house immediately. Her reputation and good character could certainly be salvaged at this point. Perhaps if John realized that his rash behavior would ostracize him from the community, he would come to his senses.

"Is something wrong with John, Reverend?"

"Yes, Hagar, something is very wrong with John. I think the last few days have taken quite a toll on him. It appears that he's tired of playing by the rules. He says his whole life he's done what others wanted him to do. He believes it has brought him nothing but grief and now he's going to start doing what he wants. I don't understand it. He doesn't think he can care for Martha and Jamie and he wants me to find homes for them, at least until Lydia recovers. He says the responsibility of their care has been too much for Lydia and for him. What's going on with John? Has he said anything to you about this, Hagar?" The annoyance in the man's voice was obvious.

Hagar could feel herself turning crimson. She was awkwardly aware of the sensations that had passed between them the night before; however, nothing was said and nothing had happened that was improper. Although her mind whispered not guilty, her heart knew she was guilty of imagined possibilities.

"No, Reverend. He was upset last night when he came home after seeing Lydia and Jamie in the hospital, but he didn't say anything about his plans," she stammered truthfully.

The color of her face bothered him. He wondered why she was feeling so self-conscience. His intuition told him there was probably more.

"Well Hagar, I'd suggest you pack your things and move back home. No good can come of you staying here."

"But John needs someone to take care of him," she protested. "We can't just abandon him."

"It seems that's exactly what he plans to do with the children. I don't understand it. His father and mother would turn over in their graves if they knew what he's planning to do. Hagar, you can't be part of this wickedness."

The minister slumped into a chair. It really was unthinkable that John could so abruptly be throwing away everything he believed. He'd never seen a man so determined to pursue so egocentric a quest. He looked at Hagar again. John had been certain that she wouldn't desert him. How had he known? Was it already too late? He didn't want to believe she would take part in this immorality, but the look on her face made him question his instincts.

"Hagar, John will surely spend eternity in hell if he forsakes the children and Lydia. His responsibility is to care for them and to love them. You can have no part of this," his voice was solemn. He was acquainted with the temptation of tasting forbidden fruit. He had savored its sweetness and been ensnared in the consequences of consuming it.

Hagar's decisive moment faced her. She looked squarely at the features of defiance. How was it possible for everything to be so different in one day? Could she really give up everything she believed? Never in her life had she done anything rebellious. Like John, she had always stayed the course. She was still a virgin in many ways. She had a deep, pervading reverence for hell. Fear gripped her. It held her tightly as she considered the possibility of spending eternity there. The kernels of awareness planted last night had begun to sprout. Now, seeing the growth, she vacillated about whether to uproot them. She looked into the preacher's admonishing face. Is that what the face of God will look like if I stay with John, she wondered? What an absurd thing to be thinking, she told herself. It made her smile, despite the anxiety she was feeling.

"Reverend, John's terribly upset over what's happened. Maybe he just needs a day or two to let everything settle. He's always been such a God-fearing man. I just can't believe that he would do anything foolish," the words tumbled out with feigned naturalness. The voice inside her head whispered — and what about me? What foolish things am I capable of doing?

If the minister would just leave, she would have a chance to talk to John. Then she could clear away the clouds from her mind and try to understand exactly what was happening.

"Maybe you're right, Hagar," he told her. "Try and talk to him. I'll be back later today."

She nodded in affirmation, "John also needs to be loved," she whispered somewhat surprised at her own thoughts. "Moreover, so do I," she added to herself.

Thomas Sluis looked deep into her eyes; there was a tone of displeasure in his voice. "Yes Hagar, but remember your responsibility to this family. You know the right thing to do."

"Yes, Rev. Sluis," she responded meekly, "I know I'm here to serve the family."

He looked around the kitchen. It would be hard for Martha and Jamie to leave this place. He was incredulous about what John intended to do. He knew life wasn't easy, but Martha and Jamie were John's family. Surely, there was a sense of stability and security for them here. They'd been through so much already in their young lives. He had no idea where he would find families to look after them. Most of the church families had children of their own or they were older couples who were finished raising children. His two children no longer lived at home and he certainly wouldn't be eager to take on such an onerous responsibly at this point in his life.

John had told him that he was through with the church and through looking after others. He wanted to be released from his duties. He'd had enough of the rules, the regulations and the expectations. He was determined to unshackle himself from everything to which he was bound. He was tired of trying to live up to his departed father's expectations. He wanted to make his own rules and start enjoying life. The preacher shook his head. John had seemed possessed. Of course, he'd seen it before, but never to this frenzied extent. He didn't know what had snapped, but it was clear that he was single-minded in his intention to break all ties with his life as it presently existed. He thought that perhaps in some way John was more delusional than Lydia.

God, whatever will become of them? It was a question and a prayer. This was definitely one of those times that he didn't relish the responsibilities of being a minister. He left the house without saying good-bye. I'd like to disown him, he thought. Such a hypocrite! He considered John's selfishness a horrific sin.

John stood at the window behind the curtains and watched him go. He felt numb with exhaustion. For the first time in his life, he didn't know what to expect. Didn't know where his reckless actions would take him. The lecture from the preacher was just what he had expected. Perhaps if he had tried to understand, even a little, I might have been swayed, John reasoned. The self-righteous attitude the preacher had taken soured his thinking and cemented his resolve. I'm entitled to some happiness of my own. I've always followed the rules – always did what was expected. I've had enough! This is going to be my time!

Deliberately he shut off his conscience and went to find Hagar. A glass of summer wine would settle his nerves.

14

Sunday Sermons

The manse was an old house built long ago by affluent trades' people. Its days of splendor were long past but it still stood tall and proud beside the church. The yellow brick was weathered and polished with age. The purchase of the house had been a considerable tribute to the preacher of the Presbyterian Church. The parishioners maintained that their shepherd deserved the best. The man who tended their souls should be endowed with some earthly comfort and opulence.

Only one of the three tall chimneys, which stretched to the sky, was used now that the house had been modernized. An up-to-date octopus furnace, with long appendages that reached through the basement, heated the house. Black smoke rose upward to the sky when the coal burned. Some folks thought it was a most appropriate symbol. They saw it as incense rising from the tabernacle, carrying their prayers to heaven.

The house was spacious and bulky for the small family. Four of the six bedrooms were not ordinarily occupied. In Strathroyal, the only hotel adjoined the local tavern. It was not deemed proper for notable out-of-town visitors to stay in such a questionable establishment. Because there was space to spare, prominent visitors were often invited to stay at the manse. This added to the prestigious status of the dwelling.

Constance Sluis felt the house was much too massive and elegant for their small, simple family. She was a quiet introspective, modest woman who took pride in tasteful, basic pleasures. It required a great deal of time and effort to keep the house in an appropriate burnished state. Because visitors were often unanticipated, she maintained order and cleanliness at all times. Even though she enjoyed the house, a home that was less pretentious and ornate would have made her just as happy.

She tended the gardens as she did her children and her house, tenderly and patiently. Like a mother hen, she always put them first. In the summer, lush greenery sprang up against the walls. Each season a different variety of flowers boasted of their gardener's dedication by producing the most exquisite blooms. Weeds were never allowed to take root and the soil was attentively watered and turned. Eventually, the house and the yard were regarded as one of the town's most valued treasures.

While she worked in her garden, people often stopped to visit. Like the minister, his wife was expected to be attentive and comforting to any person in need. When older members of the congregation were taking walks, they regularly sat down in the wooden lawn chairs to rest. It was common for Mrs. Sluis to offer a cool glass of lemonade to a stranger who lingered to admire the gardens, or to rest in the easy chairs on the lawn. Her genuine respect for life in any form caused her to be a truly loved woman.

The couple had two children, Emily and Daniel, twins who were twenty-five years old. Their birth had been exhausting and premature. The doctor said it was nothing short of miraculous that the mother and her infants had survived. Because of the complicated birth, Constance was never able to bear more children. At first, this reality caused her great sadness, but eventually she was gratified to have two healthy babies. Mothering her children had given her a sense of fulfillment. To compensate for not being able to have more children, she nurtured other forms of life. People appreciated a unique sense of safety and comfort when they were with her. Plants and animals thrived when she tended them. This talent made her life rich and full.

It had turned chilly by the time Thomas Sluis returned home that Sunday afternoon. Constance sensed immediately that he was very distraught. She knew he was agitated in the way he closed the front door. He didn't offer his normal greeting when he came into the kitchen. She folded him in her arms and let her love circle his tired heart. They needed no words. When he sat down at the kitchen table, she poured him a cup of tea. He sipped it slowly, holding the cup between his hands to let the warmth penetrate his cold palms. Candidly, he told her the story. She sat and listened without interruption. When he was finished, they looked at each other.

"Poor, little darlings," she breathed as she got up to comfort him again.

She was amazed to see tears filling his eyes. Even though he often dealt with difficult situations and became very involved with his parishioners, he usually concealed his feelings from her. She rocked him tenderly. He kissed her cheek and gently cupped her face in his hands.

"You are everything to me, my love," was all he could whisper.

She held him tenderly, loving him for what he was and could be, "We need to think about the children. The answer lies with us, Thomas."

He nodded knowingly, but he didn't discern what she was implying. He felt a strange sense of shame for his friend, John. Surely, he would come to his senses. They sat together and prayed the burdens might be lifted from the Jacobs' family. She held him close; her tears fell for him. When one of his flock was hurting, the only thing she could do was reassure him and love him. Sometimes she questioned whether he was too involved in the lives of his parishioners. Once she had suggested if he were more detached, he might be able to facilitate more healing for the hurting. It was the only time he had ever raised his voice to her. He seemed to take pleasure in bearing the burdens of his sheep on his shoulders. Without complaint, he carried their crosses.

Abruptly the telephone interrupted the moment. Thomas went to the hall to answer it. Constance knew by the tone in his voice, that it was a parishioner needing help. She closed the kitchen door to let him tend to his profession. It was forebodingly quiet as she sat and tried to understand her complex husband.

Her mind tried to sort out the details. She accepted there had always been a part of Thomas she didn't understand. There was a piece of himself he had never been able to share. She supposed his compulsive involvement with his flock was in part an aftereffect of the war. He had volunteered for duty and returned home a different man. After spending two years consoling the wounded overseas, he constantly grieved the squandering of human life. The stories he told of mutilated men clinging to hope with their dying breath, plagued his conscience. Repeatedly, she assured him he had survived to minister to those left behind, to rebuild a better world. In his head, he confirmed her words, but in his heart, he carried the maimed victims of war. She reasoned his life had become its own battlefield of sorts.

She didn't know Thomas fought demons that threatened to ravish righteousness. There was no tolerance for wastefulness of any kind. When he witnessed recklessness that mocked the goodness of God or did not validate the capacity for good in the human spirit, he vocalized the failures in prolific homilies about corruption and its consequences. He preached hell was a real place that imprisoned honest, well-meaning people who had squandered their potential to do good. The passion with which he painted the horrors of the inferno even sent shivers up Constance's spine.

Always after such a session with his church, he wanted affirmation from her. He needed to believe he had proclaimed words that mattered. She was unable to convey the truth. He sensed the fear that tainted her sincerity. He comforted her with reassurances that his words were not meant to trouble her. He pontificated they were aimed at well-intentioned Pharisees who trampled on the faith of the righteous. It concerned her deeply. There were times she imagined in some way, he was speaking of himself. She believed somewhere under the polished veneer, there was a piece of him she didn't know. There was a part of himself he was unable or unwilling to share. While she didn't allow herself to dwell on these thoughts, she supposed deep inside him was a festering lesion she couldn't touch. This knowledge both concerned and frightened her.

Before he had gone to war, she had tried unsuccessfully to expose the darkness she was sure was hidden somewhere in a place she couldn't reach. When he came home, it was obvious the atrociousness of war clouded his outlook. For a time she didn't see the mania. Now it was slowly surfacing again. She was unable to identify it, but she recognized it in slight gestures. It was in the way he gazed out the window, in the way he talked in his sleep and some days even the way he held her. We will talk about it when the injuries of war have healed, she told herself.

This wisdom carried with it, its own forms of reproof. When he confided his fears and shortcomings, she thought she was committing treason for thinking critically of his words. He shared intimate accounts of the lives of people she knew and respected. Often he told her things she didn't need or want to know. It was burdensome to push the details from her thoughts as she talked to Mrs. Johnson. The poor woman didn't know her husband had been unfaithful. Thomas had asked her discreetly to help the misfortunate woman to be a better wife. He surmised it must be at least partly her shortcomings, which made her husband sidetrack his matrimonial vows.

She repeatedly asked him not to divulge so much detail

to her, but his need to have her listen was almost desperate. At times, he needed to entrust the confessions he heard with someone. Why he did this was beyond her. She couldn't offer him the release or absolution he wanted. Because she had no real authority to liberate him, the stories eventually began shaping an obstacle in their relationship. She knew, brick by brick, a wall was building between them. She believed that Thomas was aware of it as well. Neither one was able to find the tools or to muster up the boldness to tear it down. It grieved her deeply.

The garden provided Constance a reprieve from the sting of her unspoken thoughts. During the day when her house was in order, she withdrew to the flowerbeds. There she could think and talk. There she was able to articulate her fears and bury them deep in the earth. She gave up her perceived worries as she communed with nature. Like pulled weeds, she was able to root out the ideas and let them go. She reflected a great deal about heaven, even imagined herself talking to the groundskeeper there. Especially after listening to one of Thomas' fire and brimstone Sunday sermons, she found solace in the tranquility of the garden. The flowers, the birds, even the weeds, stimulated a peacefulness no sermon had ever been able to offer. She trusted the creator understood the authentic reasons for her dedication to the earth. She committed her wordless feelings into the gardener's hands, believing the enigma that tormented her would remain hidden in this sanctuary. She was distressed; she wanted to understand, to expose and to control her secret fears.

When the soil was left to sleep for the winter, the kitchen took its place. There she worked with the same commitment creating delicious delicacies for Christmas giving. Every member of the congregation received a plate of sweets. They marveled at how she illuminated the true meaning of the season. As soon as fall arrived, she started her special fruitcake.

During the special times, she missed the sound of children the most. Before the twins had left for school, the manse was regularly filled with their friends. The young people knew it was always a welcoming place. Often, laughter and the resonance of friendship filled the house. The cheerful chatter of young voices echoed through her mind.

"Mama, can we have some cocoa?" Daniel would ask as he greeted her with a kiss.

Her reply had always been the same, "Of course, darling, I'll put the kettle on."

Although they had been typical, vivacious siblings, there had never been any competition between the children. Emily and Daniel were best friends. They shared much more than a birthday. They seemed innately to grasp how to value and appreciate individuality and diversity in all God's creation. Constance and Thomas were acutely aware of this special phenomenon. They were grateful for the true sense of harmony in their household.

Constance loved her children and appreciated the people they had become. They had their own lives. She hated that they weren't with her, but she was very proud of them for being strong and independent. Daniel was going to university in Toronto to become a doctor. Emily had finished teachers' college. Her life's dream was to be with children. She had left for an overseas teaching position in an orphanage in Kenya. Once a week, they received a letter detailing the work in the mission. Constance read each one repeatedly. Then she stored them in a special box to be savored again and again when she most felt her daughter's absence.

Since her children had left the nest, there was a persistent, stubborn void, which snubbed her efforts to fill it. She tried not to dwell on in it; nonetheless, it was often extremely disconcerting. Although she missed them dreadfully, she stoically occupied herself tending the household and the constant duties as the minister's wife.

Thomas, finished with his telephone call, went to his office to work. Constance sat at the kitchen table, alone. She remembered Esther. They had met in church many times. The reserved nature of the widow made her difficult to know, but it had been easy to see her children were everything to her. She realized she felt pangs of guilt when she encountered women whose husbands had not returned from the war. Esther had appeared remote when she was in church and seldom attended any special functions during the week since she was busy looking after her children. Her death had been a shock to everyone in the community; somehow, it was softened because the children would be well provided for by their aunt and uncle. The awareness that they would be orphaned once again, prompted her to imagine the prospect of new children in the house. It was a desire she had let go of long ago. Now the possibility of mothering again, coaxed back the yearning.

Thomas left his study expecting to find Constance in the kitchen preparing dinner. Instead, he found her still sitting in the darkened room. It was unlike her to be so quiet and reflective.

"Constance is something wrong?" he asked as he put his arms around her.

"I can't stop thinking about Jamie and Martha."

"And what are you thinking, my love?" Before the words were out of his mouth, he knew exactly what she was thinking. Every day he was aware of the emptiness that existed in her daily routine without their children at home. He smiled remembering the stray pets lovingly nursed back to health by his angelic wife. He should have known what her response to the homeless children would be. He wasn't sure that he liked the idea that had obviously mushroomed in her heart.

"They need a home, Thomas," she said simply.

"Well, maybe we could look after one of them," he protested feebly.

"They need a home, Thomas. Furthermore, they need to be together." There was a reproachful tone in her voice. She seldom spoke to him this way. A feeling of some resentment crept into his mind. They never made decisions without discussing them at length. There would be a significant adjustment for the family if Jamie and Martha came to live with them. To oppose her would be futile, but still he resented her single-mindedness.

"Constance, we always talk about important decisions," he reprimanded, somewhat impatiently.

"Of course, Thomas, I'm sorry," she replied meekly. For a moment, she had forgotten that he needed to support the commitment. She understood how important it was for him to believe he was in charge. Thomas held firmly to the conviction that the he was the head of the family.

Thomas appraised his wife's earnest confidence. Her charity was tangible; it was authentic and completely selfless. She exemplified and practiced the sermons he preached.

He felt humbled knowing his own desires were usually much more self-centered. He wouldn't be able to refuse her. Moreover, it would certainly make them look good in the church community.

"It's a big decision, Constance. I considered the possibility myself," he lied, "but I really thought it would be too much to ask of you." He told himself this was partly true. "We could try it on a trial basis to see how it goes. We're not getting younger ourselves, Constance. If you truly want to do this, we could try to arrange it with John. It probably won't be long before things are back to normal there."

"Thank you, Thomas, for thinking of my well-being," she smiled and continued, "You know I'm only forty-four. Women are still having children at my age. I'm sure we won't have any regrets. It's getting late; I'd better start dinner."

She tried hard to appear composed but it was awkward to contain the excitement building beneath the surface. She was a caged bird set free to sing and fly again.

After the meal she hurriedly prepared, Thomas drove to see John. He hoped things would be more stable and John might have come to his senses. When he arrived, he thought he imagined the sweet aroma of homemade wine hanging in the kitchen air. John was brisk and direct. He had definitely decided that the children would have to go until Lydia was well enough to look after them. He would pay for their room and board as a matter of principle and honor. If the minister wanted to be responsible for their care, he had no objections. Of course, he wanted them to be well cared for and he had no doubt they would receive the best from Mrs. Sluis. Martha was already in bed. She could pack her things tomorrow after school and Rev. Sluis could come and pick her up then. He agreed that the minister would collect Jamie from the hospital when he was ready to come home.

John spoke to the minister in a hurried, detached fashion. The Reverend Thomas Sluis was not accustomed to being treated with any manifestation of disrespect; it irritated him that John spoke with such a lack of decorum. This was a certainly a different person than the deacon he knew and respected. John would not answer any of the questions Thomas posed. He stated curtly that his life was going to change. Furthermore, the alterations he was making would not be including any involvement in the Church. This revelation was made as Thomas was escorted to the door. Although it concerned him, Thomas didn't believe John would follow through on this stupidity. He credited the latest stress in the man's life with the foolhardiness he heard.

Martha secretly listened to the exchange from the upstairs landing. She felt abandoned and defeated. If only she were a few years older, she could look after Jamie by herself. The prospect of living with an unrelated family frightened her. Although she remembered that her mother had liked Mrs. Sluis, her only knowledge of the minister was listening to him in church. He always seemed so pessimistic. For every situation there seemed to be a commandment. She wondered how many rules there would be in his house. Moreover, how would she ever explain it all to Jamie? She shut her eyes tightly, praying sleep would end the nightmare. Sleep eluded her. When she got up in the morning, she knew it was not a dream.

When he arrived home, Thomas didn't tell Constance that John had made him feel like he was arranging the purchase of livestock. Nor did he mention the strange statements and cold detachment in John's voice. There was no need to alarm her. He was still reasonably sure this foolishness would pass as soon as Lydia recovered. He thought somewhere out of this mess, he could draft a compelling sermon about the consequences of neglecting one's responsibilities. It didn't occur to him that John wouldn't be interested in hearing any more Sunday sermons, especially ones about an angry, vengeful God who would no doubt condemn the actions he was contemplating.

Constance was surprised and pleased that the arrangements had fallen into place so quickly. She had already started making a list of things that needed doing to make the children feel welcome. She was eager to receive them into her home and embrace them to her heart. First, she must write a letter to her darling twins. Then, she would go to work and prepare her home for her new family.

15
The Emigration

Although Jamie recovered quickly, he slept erratically and heard the muted sounds of the hospital. The second night, he recognized the pitch of despair in a child's plaintive cry in the next bed. Silently, he slipped out from under his sterile sheets and crept to the infant's crib. He patted the baby's back and whispered soothing words in her ear. Slowly, almost reluctantly, the whimpering subsided into delayed sobs. The rhythmic sucking of a thumb replaced the lament. There were two other young patients in the room; they stirred and moaned at regular intervals. Jamie shushed them softly.

When he heard the nurse come in the room and check each bed, his tightly closed eyes feigned sleep. She shone a flashlight in his face. The angel in white smiled – she knew. She stroked his head until his breathing was rhythmic and deep. Unnoticed from the doorway, she had monitored his comforting gestures and marveled at the boy's empathic ability. His simple act of compassion embossed itself on her heart; she would never forget. He has a gift, she thought, an extraordinarily special gift.

"Dear God," she prayed wordlessly, "take care of this little one."

Fear, like a shadow, had stalked Jamie since his mother's death. In the glow of love, it faded to partial obscurity. In the darkness of uncertainty, it paced close beside him, looming over him like a menacing bully. Later that night, as he lay awake again, it stood before him shaking its loathsome finger in his face. It shouted possible repercussions at him. The sound reverberated through his body. It emerged in the face of Uncle John's bellowing reprimands for his behavior. Then it paled in the light of Martha's image surrounding him, illuminating his spirit and chasing the demon away. The terror he felt, shouted and echoed in his heart. Finally, the glimmer of dawn creeping into the room in the early morning hours muffled the echo and lulled him into an unsettled slumber.

The engaging smell of porridge tickled his nostrils; for a fleeting moment, he sensed his mother's presence in the sweetness. The room's background clatter instantly scattered the presumption. Opening his eyes, he saw the breakfast tray and the reality of his circumstances; he returned to full consciousness.

"Hi, Jamie, let's get up and eat some breakfast. You're going to need the strength. I think you're going home today," the attendant voiced cheerily.

Martha, I will see Martha. The thoughts of her were the

overshadowed by misgivings of how he would be dealt with at home. He didn't understand and only vaguely remembered running into the night to his mother's grave. He recalled the bitter chill in the air. It was an icy raw cold like the feel of her hand that awful day they put her in the ground. She was probably angry; it had been a bad thing to do. He accepted there would be a severe reprimand. The confidence that Martha would be there to embrace him would make what awaited bearable. He smiled at the nurse. It was the first optimistic sign she had seen. Her anxiety for him lessened. Despite whatever was distressing the child, he wanted to go home.

When Martha came home from school, she noticed boxes and bags sitting by the kitchen door. Hagar was busy puttering about.

"Martha," her tone was solemn, "Uncle John asked me to pack your clothes. You're going to be staying with the minister and his wife for a little while until your Aunt Lydia is feeling better. Uncle John just has too much to deal with right now."

"But, I...." she stammered. Fatigue and denial had overshadowed the memory of the previous evening.

"No buts, child; it's all settled." There was harshness, but also an uncharacteristic kindness in her voice; it unsettled Martha even more. She didn't hear Hagar's parting comment, "I'm sorry, child. You're a good girl."

Martha hurried to her room. The bedclothes, as well as her meager possessions, were all stripped away. The bureau, which held her few keepsakes, was bare. The room looked sparse and desolate. She sat on the drab gray-striped mattress and gazed about the room. The struggle of staying optimistic was too much. She felt as empty as the room. The void sucked her into a vacuum of numbness. Mechanically, she opened the drawers and closed them again. Daily existence here was tedious at times, but at least they knew what to expect and they had learned how to cope. Thoughts of Rev. Sluis and his reproachful sermons flooded her mind. A dull ache cloaked her perspective. If only she were a little older. Tears threatened to expose her vulnerability, but she would not allow them to fall. She had to be strong for Jamie. She packaged her emotions deep inside herself and returned to the kitchen.

When Hagar saw her, she felt immediate regret for the girl's desperate situation. It was clear, even to her, that the child was in pain. For the first time, she wholly connected with this friendless, lonesome girl. It reflected her own barren background. She understood. For the briefest of moments, she contemplated giving Martha a hug; however, the feeling slipped away as John suddenly entered the kitchen.

Uncle John greeted her, "Well, Martha, behave yourself. Make sure Jamie minds Mrs. Sluis. Once Aunt Lydia returns home, we'll see what happens. You have to understand that it has just all been too much for me. I need some time."

"Yes, Uncle John," was the only response she could muster.

The melancholy in the farmhouse was totally contradicted in the big house on Front Street. The excitement there was palpable. Constance woke early. The arrival of the children demanded careful preparation. She chose the two brightest rooms next to each other on the second floor. Although each one was spotless and scantily decorated, the wallpaper was somewhat discolored and dreary. She'd find some cheerful pictures to brighten the space. She scoured the attic for the boxes of old toys and lovingly placed them around the rooms. She hoped that they would greet the children and dispel some of the drabness. Someday, she had expected her grandchildren would enjoy playing with Emily and Daniel's toys. Even though Thomas had told her to give them away or to throw them out, she had secretly lugged them to the attic while he was working. She reminded herself to mail the letters she had written the twins; but for now, they would have to wait. She longed to sit, recall and savor the images of her darlings, but time was precious. She couldn't indulge in the tranquil mementos of the past; today was a momentous occasion, a prerogative to create another set of unique memoirs. Today was the future. She was elated by the possibilities. She felt as she did when watching and waiting for bright crocuses to nuzzle their way through the snow. She would create a new beginning; it would be a renaissance for the children and for her.

She was resolute. They would feel welcome. There was urgency and a sense of mission as she readied their home. Constance's expectancy was the sweet taste mothering created for her. The sterile austerity that had knotted her emotions would be unraveled. She could be whole once again.

Thomas watched his wife. She seemed consumed by her task. He was somewhat distressed by the elaborate preparations she was making. He admonished her to take care with her feelings. The children, after all, would only be with them on a temporary basis. She ignored his chiding – would hear none of it. He knew her behavior was completely selfless; this understanding appeased his agitation. He really couldn't chastise her for being an angel of mercy. Even so, her excitement disturbed him.

The Journey Home

On his way to the farm to collect Martha, Thomas tried to confront his annoyance. The uncertainty of the circumstances intruded on his objectivity. He feared Constance would bestow far too much attention on the children. She would become attached to them and be crushed when they had to leave. If John suddenly changed his mind and wanted them home, she would be devastated. Unwillingly he felt resentment toward them, even though he understood her altruistic ideals. He reasoned it was because she was a woman who was not able to bear as many children as she would have liked. Even so, in his heart he knew that it was more than that. Jealousy licked at his conscience. Like a tempting sweet morsel, it lured him to taste and indulge in the snare. Sampling the sweetness left a bitter aftertaste, one he promptly spit out. Even so, it lingered in his senses and disturbed his cleric mind set.

There was no pride in the knowledge that his fiery sermons were often decreed at his own self-pronounced deficiencies. The sin of pride was a fiend that sat on his shoulder and whispered seductive sensations in his ear. It took more than, "Get thee behind me Satan," to startle the demon into oblivion. In the secret recesses of his heart, he was envious of his wife's authentic humility; she was the most selfless person he had ever met. He understood that his distress was the shame he carried about himself. In an attempt to rid himself of it, he stepped hard on the gas pedal. The old car sputtered in protest. Thomas steered strenuously to avoid the children walking on the road. They must be coming home from school, he thought. He shook his head and raised a silent prayer for forgiveness.

Martha stood waiting anxiously. She peered out though

the kitchen window and saw the old black Chevrolet coming up the lane to the house. Uncle John picked up the boxes and carried them to the waiting car.

"No need to have the preacher come in. I expect he'll want to get to the city as quickly as possible to pick up Jamie." John spoke in a tone that lacked sentiment. "Good-bye Martha. Remember to do your share. I expect we'll be talking to you soon." It was best not to feel anything. Just do the deed and move on, he told himself.

Despite her emptiness, Martha wanted to hug him, to tell him that she would miss him, but he immediately moved away from her, waving to Rev. Sluis as he hurried back into the house. There would be no warm farewells. Again, tears threatened to expose Martha's feelings, but she clenched her teeth firmly, picked up the brown shopping bags with her clothes and politely greeted Rev. Sluis.

Thomas greeted Martha warmly. He sensed her apprehension and tried to reassure her with conversation about Jamie, school and the weather. He wasn't very good at it and although she was polite, she didn't appear to be very interested in talking to him. As he watched her fidget with her mittens, he surmised she was probably preoccupied with thoughts of Jamie. In a peculiar way, he empathized with her. The uncertainty of her situation must be very disconcerting for a young girl. He envisioned his own precious Emily, alone and afraid and a flood of affection swept over him. Constance was right. These children needed a home. He was proud of her. He would do his part. He straightened himself in the driver's seat, relieved that the vile presence that had been tainting his outlook had abated.

Martha was conscious of the inspection. It made her feel

awkward and nervous. Her desire to see Jamie and to know he was well was uppermost in her mind. There had been little time to reflect on how they would adjust to the new living arrangement. Again, she fought the tears that welled up. It reassured her to know that Mrs. Sluis was friendly and pleasant. Her mother had liked her and spoken of her as a friend; yet to expect her to be anything like her own mama was more than Martha even dared contemplate. Her understanding of women had certainly grown since she had known Aunt Lydia and Hagar and now she was suspicious of a situation that seemed so ambiguous. The uncertainty and the dread of being exploited once again, made her shrivel up and want to crawl inside herself. She wouldn't let it happen. Her love and concern for Jamie was the only certainty that mattered; she had to be strong for him.

While he sat in the hospital waiting, Jamie thought of Samson and the times they had shared. He wondered where he was and what he was doing. Someday when he was older, he would find him again. In his mind's eye, he went to the apple tree. There in its safety, the unspoken grief that crowded his being could be compacted away. He pictured his mama rocking him, singing his favorite lullaby. Her manner had changed again. At this moment, more of the details of her face blurred into the celestial features of those who had cared for him in the last two days. She wore a long flowing white gown; her voice floated in the air and she spoke of heaven. She had the smile of the angel in white, the one who had watched over him during the dark night.

When Martha and Rev. Sluis entered the room, Jamie was poised in the chair beside his bed. He sprang into Martha's arms and let her embrace him. He tasted the refuge of her love and could not hold back the tears. They flowed silently from his eyes.

"This is my sister," he announced with great pride to his roommates.

The siblings' love was a proclamation that showed not only in their faces but also in their demeanor. The sun had come from behind the clouds and painted a bright rainbow across their young faces.

"It's time to go, Jamie," Martha stated. She was relieved that he sought no explanation for the minister's presence. There would be time to elaborate in the car on the way home. She devotedly wrapped Jamie in her arms, intensely aware he was her only comfort – he was her home.

On the way to Strathroyal, Martha and Jamie sat in the back seat. Martha explained to her brother where they were going. Jamie was very quiet, trying to understand. He felt very sad to hear about Aunt Lydia and sincerely hoped he wasn't the cause of her illness. Although her detached, curious manner frightened him, he didn't dislike her. He even felt a strange connection to her. Martha made it sound reasonable that Uncle John needed to look after Aunt Lydia; she made the move sound temporary. She even said they would be going to the same school. The minister seemed a lot like Uncle John and that thought was unsettling; still, Mrs. Sluis often smiled at him in church, so he concluded it would be fine as long as Martha was there. Knowing that he had created quite a fuss by running off, he waited anxiously for the reprimand he knew he deserved.

"Promise me you won't ever run away again," was all Martha said.

The look on her face made his response instant, "I

promise, Martha, cross my heart and hope to die." He had expected a stern lecture. Perhaps, he mused, it will come later.

"No Jamie, never hope to die!" She always said the same thing when he repeated this pledge.

He gently reached over and reassured her with a hug.

Martha was relieved her brother seemed so accepting of their new living arrangements. She yearned for someone to soften the reality for her as well.

Thomas watched and listened silently to the children's exchange. He marveled at Martha's obvious maturity but also wondered what she was hiding behind the controlled demeanor. Her mother would be proud of her, he thought. As he validated his decision to take in the orphans, he was proud of himself.

Constance waited impatiently. She paced, fussed and rearranged the children's bedrooms examining them for evidence of the comfort and cheer she wanted them to see reflected there. She cooked and baked, wondering what foods they liked.

"Well, here we are," announced Thomas as he parked the car in front of the house. "Come along children; Mrs. Sluis will be waiting for us."

An enticing aroma welcomed the refugees as they entered the house. It was a pure, sweet omen; it delighted their senses and awakened their longing.

Martha looked at her brother. "I think it's apple pie Jamie, like Mama used to make," was all she could say.

"What's the matter, Martha? Why are you crying?" Jamie whispered to his sister as they stood in the doorway.

16
Advent

"Hush, Jamie," Martha ordered in a tone that was unfamiliar to him. Even though she knew his question was one of concern, the artificial annoyance allowed her to hold back the emotions that were threatening to rupture. The welcoming, unanticipated smell threatened to break down her stanch composure.

Constance feigned ignorance of the friction and greeted them warmly.

"I'm so pleased to see you, Martha and James."

Oh no, she's going to call me James; he hated being James. It sounded much too grownup. When he was called James, he thought of his lost father. Martha noticed it as well. She hoped Mrs. Sluis wouldn't mind calling him Jamie when she knew him better. Perhaps she would try to explain it to her tomorrow.

Constance sensed their discomfort and fought to control the excitement she felt in seeing them. The ride home had seemed long and quiet. Thomas scrutinized the reception; supper smelled good and he was hungry. The awareness that his home life was going to be quite different began to agitate him again.

Constance hung up the children's coats and led them to the kitchen. She could almost see the apprehension that clung to them, like the mist of a summer's dew that clings to plants. The sunshine of love will evaporate their fear, she told herself. It will just take a little time. I'll have to be patient. I'll just have to love them enough.

On the kitchen table were two parcels, brightly wrapped in flowered paper. She picked them up and cautiously, yet gently hugged Martha and then Jamie.

"We hope you'll be happy with us, children. Martha, I know that you've just had a birthday. We hope you'll have many more. James, there's a little something to welcome you to our home."

Martha's face turned white. Uncle John didn't believe much in celebrating birthdays. He considered it frivolous and egocentric. On her birthday, Hagar had been kind and even given her a kiss on the cheek. The rest of the day had been very ordinary. The remembrance of her last year's birthday was entrenched in her memory. Again, it paraded across her mind and Martha could feel her composure beginning to crumble. She saw her mother after she had trekked to town to get Aunt Lydia's tea. She had offered to go, but Esther had refused. The guilt that had followed Martha since her mother's death now crept out of the crypt where she had tried to bury it. Now that it was exhumed, it glared at her laughing and shouting, "See, I'm still here!"

Jamie was quick to tear the paper off his gift. His eyes opened wide when he saw his new Teddy bear. It had brown fur with leather paws. The eyes were dark and glassy. He had never seen such a beautiful toy. "Thank-you, Mrs. Sluis," was all he could manage to say as he cuddled his new friend. "What's in yours, Martha?" he asked his sister excitedly.

Martha was overwhelmed by the display of thoughtfulness and was finding it difficult to remain composed. During the last year, she had learned ways to shield herself from the harsh realities of her life. Strangely, she had no defense for kindness and it left her feeling vulnerable and exposed.

Annoyance licked at Thomas' awareness. Constance had probably been snooping again while she dusted in his office. He had left the children's baptismal records on his desk, which is how she must have known when their birthdays were. It really was an intrusion on his space. He made a mental note to discuss this with her later. Obviously, today would not be a discreet time. Having gifts for the children was not something he had anticipated; moreover, it was certainly not something he would have encouraged.

"Oh, Martha, can I help you unwrap yours?" Jamie bubbled eagerly.

"Go ahead and open it, Martha," remarked Reverend Sluis as he looked sternly at his wife. Constance avoided making eye contact; she had known he wouldn't approve. When he scolded her about it, she would tell him it was something she'd done at the last minute while he was in London. Humbly asking for forgiveness would pacify him. Usually that was easier than asking permission.

Martha tried, but it was no use. Her fingers trembled. Deep in herself, the tempest that had been brewing could no longer be contained. Every time the clouds had threatened to burst, she had stoically refused to acknowledge the pain and had pushed it away. Now, nature had to have its way. Martha could no longer manage the sentiments, stacked up like so many storm clouds, since Esther's death. The wall of defense came tumbling down as she sensed the woman's compassion and love. It swept her away in a cyclonic gale. Like the summer heat that erupts in the explosion of a thunderstorm, her body began to rack and heave with loudly uncontrollable sobbing. Tears erupted from a body saturated and now finally overloaded with the strain and fatigue of carrying the masked grief.

Jamie was taken aback. As he reached to hug her, his own tears fell silently. He knew and felt her torment. Without words, he tried to comfort her, but it wasn't enough. Martha's denial had completely disintegrated. She tried to push him away.

"It's OK, Martha. Please don't cry." The abrupt reversal of their roles paralyzed him into numbness. What would he do if he couldn't count on his big sister? He clutched his new bear and felt guilty for being happy with it while his sister was so upset.

Constance had never witnessed children in such agony. Immediately, instinctively she swaddled both of them her in her arms. Martha recoiled at her touch, fearing a reprimand. The unexpected contact of caring and reassurance further demolished her resistance and the weeping continued with an intensity that threatened to break Constance's heart. Martha's entire body heaved and shook with the weeping.

The dam that had held back the year of silent sadness had ruptured, exposing the vulnerable psyche of a little girl whose childhood innocence had been selflessly sacrificed to protect her precious sibling.

Thomas was disturbed over the outburst, but a pleading look from his spouse astutely led him to suggest to Jamie that they go to the car to bring in their belongings. Even though he felt compassion for the children, he detected his misgivings about this arrangement lingering in his mind. It troubled him to look at Jamie. He demanded that his imaginings stop as he tousled the boy's hair. At the touch, Thomas' hand trembled.

"She'll be fine, Jamie. Just let Mrs. Sluis look after her," he said kindly.

Constance half-led, half-carried Martha to her bedroom. Gently positioning the troubled child on her lap, she sat in the rocking chair where she had nursed and nurtured her babies. She rocked and sang old lullabies, gently stroking Martha's hair. An hour passed and finally the sobbing subsided and then ceased.

"Everything is going to be better now, Martha," she whispered lovingly.

Martha heard but did not respond. Her eyes were heavy with fatigue. Constance understood she was completely exhausted from the purging. She prayed sleep would restore her strength. She dressed the child in a silky nightgown Thomas had given her for her birthday. She put a cold, wet cloth on her eyes to soothe them. Martha surrendered to her caregiver. Constance sat on the side of the bed until she was sure the child was sleeping. Gently she placed a kiss on her forehead and tucked the quilt under her chin. She left the room drained of her usual optimistic energy. She was also spent. It was going to be harder than anticipated. Despite her fatigue, she was more determined than ever to make a home for the orphans. She discerned that Martha's anguish was deeply rooted. It agitated her to know that the children were hurting. Whatever it took, she would make it right. She would make it work!

His sister's behavior unsettled Jamie. He had eaten in silence with the minister. The food was tasty but he had no appetite. Somehow, without Martha at the table, it didn't seem right to enjoy the mouth-watering apple pie. When Constance finally came down, she assured him Martha was fine and just needed to sleep. She coaxed him to try the pie. Although he ate with a sense of obligation, its sweet delicate taste was familiar and brought some feelings of assurance to the tired, wounded youngster.

After dinner, Rev. Sluis suggested they go for a stroll so Jamie could explore his new surroundings. The minister walked him around the house and the block, pointing out significant landmarks of the neighborhood. He mentioned that Marty, who was about the same age as Jamie, lived a few doors down the street. Jamie tried to think of some questions to ask, but all he could do was listen in polite, innocent silence. The possibility of a new friend excited him.

When it was time for bed, he peeked in to see Martha, kissed her and told her he loved her. Constance told him that because his room was right next to hers, he would hear her if she needed him. It had been a long day for Jamie, so he let Mrs. Sluis take care of him. It felt good to be pampered and coddled. He let himself be the little boy that had long ago grown up and vanished. The clean sheets had a warm, fresh, welcoming smell. Sleep came easily. He dreamt of his mother. She sat beside him and sang the old songs. She wrapped him in her shawl. He slept.

    Although the room was still dark, Martha knew it must be day. She lay in the comfort of the soft bed trying to comprehend what had happened the previous night. It was so quiet. Somewhere there was a clock ticking. Her eyes made out the furniture in the room. There was a dresser with an ornate flute-like mirror. An old wicker rocker stood in the corner. Beside the bed was a night table that matched the decorative sleigh bed in which she lay. The birthday present lay on the night table next to the lamp. Her hand went to it and caressed the paper. How she wished she could package up the past year and then unwrap it to find some joy to remember and savor. She saw a bookcase with neatly ordered books. The thought of being able to read them brought a smile to her face. Although the room was not luxurious, she could feel its solace and security. As she looked around, she imagined the walls speaking words of comfort. She could feel the happy memories the room held. She closed her eyes and let the welcoming warmth enclose her. This time, sleep was a safe haven.

    When the awareness of hunger dawned, Martha realized she had not eaten since lunch the day before. Embarrassment and regret about the outburst of the previous evening, made her hesitant to get up. The behavior was so far outside her norm that she was unable to understand its significance. She was sure Uncle John would not be pleased when he heard about it. She'd have to make sure she worked hard to earn forgiveness from the minister and his wife. The routine of penance had become a regular, familiar habit: apologize profusely, work hard to make amends, then retreat into silent submission. It had proved to be the most effective strategy with Lydia and Hagar. She had learned from experience that this compliance was the easiest way to deal with the required dictates of her last residence.

Associations with other girls her age had been discouraged at Uncle John's house. She didn't make friends easily. Because she appeared disinterested and never reciprocated with an invitation to have friends over, the other girls stopped including her altogether. Martha missed companionship of people her own age, but she found looking after Jamie and helping around the house kept her busy enough. When she had time to herself, isolation was comforting and friendly. During the past year, solitude had become her best friend. With it there were no demands, no rejection, no expectations but the ones she set for herself. There she could sojourn to her dreams and aspirations without ridicule or humiliation. Only when she was alone did the loneliness leave her. Her silent hidden world became her apple tree. She had discovered she could find this unexposed place within herself whenever and wherever the cruel realities of life threatened to overcome her.

In her attempt to find dignity, she had begun to write down things she would have told her mother if she were alive. There were personal feelings and ideas she had, the kinds of details young girls share with their mothers. It had provided a protected quiet way to occupy her time. When she was scribing her thoughts, she didn't feel quite so alone. One day, Hagar had come into her room while she was writing and had demanded to see what she was doing. When Martha tried to explain, Hagar had become provoked. She ripped up the notebook, saying that it was wicked to try to communicate with the dead. She was severely admonished to pray for forgiveness. It didn't make any sense to Martha; she felt no need of forgiveness. What could be so wrong in wanting her mother to know what she was feeling? Instead of praying for a pardon, she prayed she wouldn't be caught again. After that incident, she was careful to hide her new notebook under the mattress of her bed. Now she regretfully remembered that in her hurried exit from the house, she had left it there.

Martha had trouble praying. The only thing she really wanted was to have her mother back. Since that would never happen, she found it hard to talk to the God of her mother. She was angry; he was responsible for the misery in their lives. If he really loved her, as her mother had taught her, why had he taken her away? He could have had Aunt Lydia instead – she had no one to miss her except Uncle John and he didn't really seem to care much about anyone. Martha doubted he even missed her very much. It was all very confusing to her. In spite of her annoyance, Martha was afraid to give up praying altogether. It was after all, something her mother had taught her. Maybe when she got used to Reverend Sluis, he could explain it to her. Even Jamie had commented quietly in the drive home that he didn't seem so bad.

As she lay in the bed, she savored the sweet taste of privacy. From somewhere in the distance, she was aware of Jamie coming into the room. Selfishly, she chose not to open her eyes.

"It's going to be alright here," he whispered in her ear, "Wake up soon, Martha. I want to tell you about my new friend."

She envied his obvious enthusiasm and willingness to adjust so quickly. Perhaps, she speculated, it was because he was so much younger. The prospect of having to start working after this school year, loomed ominously. Uncle John had said there was no reason for girls to study. Her mother's dreams of college for her daughter would not materialize. He hadn't said any more about it, but the fear of it hung over her head nonetheless.

Martha was mindful of her silky nightgown, but had no memory of putting it on. Carefully she removed it, folded it neatly and put it on the bed. It was one of the prettiest things she had ever worn. Her eyes swept around the room, examining every detail. The boxes with her clothes and things were sitting in the corner of the room next to the large wardrobe. She hadn't heard anyone bringing them in. It was strange that no one had awakened her. Surely, there were chores she would be expected to do.

She found her present again. It was so pretty that opening it seemed wasteful somehow. She wanted to enjoy the sweetness of anticipation, like a chocolate slowing melting in her mouth. The instilled obligation of duty, scolded her for dawdling. She must get dressed. There was no eagerness, no excitement. She felt awkward in her clothes. The dresses were those her mother had made. She was still a child then, but now that her body had started to develop into womanhood, she felt gawky and irregular in the passé apparel. Hagar had tried to let some of the dresses down, but the pale whitish mark where the hem had been was obvious and embarrassing. The waist of the dress rose up to meet her budding breasts. She looked in the mirror – as if for the first time, a stranger looked back at her.

After quickly making the bed, she sat down on the side of it. Now drained of tears, the emptiness took the place of her sadness. The confidence and eagerness of youth was a cocoon, shed for the reality of her bleak existence. Like her outdated dresses, her dreams and hope for the future no longer seemed to fit. She knew Mama would want her to make the best of it and be grateful. Of course, she would honor her memory by doing the expected. Lovingly she held the present again. It seemed to package some semblance of hope. After all, she mused, if it was unopened, God would reward her selflessness. She was cognizant of the flawed logic, but it seemed necessary to cling to some fragment of incentive. The small bit of expectation seemed somehow symbolic of the minuscule piece of hope that was still ingrained somewhere in the lost child, the child who lingered under the pretence and garments of adulthood.

I'll open it later, Martha told herself. It will be something to look forward to. She clung to the confidence they were in a good place and it would be a good year.

The clock in the living room struck. Twelve chimes rang through the house. Martha thought of Cinderella. The reality that her life was not a fairy tale was painfully evident. There was nowhere to run. Even if she could leave this place, there was no other place to go. No one else wanted them.

Since it was Saturday, Thomas was cloistered in his study preparing his Sunday sermon. He liked this time after Easter when there were no demanding liturgical symbols with which to deal. During Lent and Easter, it was easy to preach about suffering. He already dreaded the next important part of the liturgical year, Advent.

It was becoming harder, even with Constance, to

maintain the camouflage of autonomy he assumed with the congregation. Disguising his feelings was becoming more and more difficult. Even though he had not made Constance privy to the severity of his sadness, he suspected she knew. The pretense he often wore was a weighty yoke that was becoming more complicated to hide from her. The children would serve as a good distraction, he thought. She'll focus on them and be less likely to be conscious of my moods.

His study had become a place of safety where he could touch and judge the secret deception. He believed that examining it attentively would eventually expose its validity, or lack of it. Lately, uncovering it was proving to be a disheartening experience. There was a bottle in the locked drawer of his desk that helped him forget, helped him to numb the pain. He reminded himself that he needed to go to London to replenish the illicit nectar. A pastoral visit to Lydia would be a good reason to go to the city.

Today he felt impatient and unsympathetic towards his self-imposed seclusion. Through the window, he watched Jamie playing and envied his childish innocence. Why were children able to laugh even in the most trying of times? This child certainly had seen his share of suffering, yet he appeared untroubled and satisfied to set a new course for his life. He knew Jamie's friend, Marty. Until recently, he had regularly come to visit Constance. He loved her homemade cookies. Occasionally, she would watch him if his parents were away. When the boy's visits abruptly stopped, Constance was distraught.

"It's so odd. I don't understand why he hasn't been here," she had said to him. Even after Marty started to play with

Jamie, he refused all invitations to enter the house. It was something Constance could not understand.

"Yes, it's strange," he said, knowing he was the cause. He pushed away the reprehensible awareness of himself as a young boy. Was he damned to drag that reflection for a lifetime? For a time, after the war, there had been a remission of sorts. Eventually, the images resumed and he surrendered to its authority. He knew a powerful desire regularly controlled him; it overwhelmed his spirit and dragged him to a pit of despair. Yet, indulging in such commiserations, he chastened himself, was like wallowing in quick sand. With that certainty, he donned his clerical mask again. He was aggravated when he realized it was now well after noon and Constance hadn't summoned him to the table. He would have to talk to her again about maintaining the order in their lives.

Several times, he had already mentioned to Constance about intruding in his study. Last night when he had conveyed his concerns again, she hadn't taken the rebukes seriously and had seemed patronizing in her response. She promised to be more restrained in the future. It bothered him that she expressed so little regret for her actions. Although it was difficult to be displeased with her selfless motives, he made a mental note not to leave church papers lying on his desk. He realized he was hungry and he was bothered. The children had only been there for a day and already his wife was neglecting him.

Constance also heard the chimes and wondered whether to go and wake Martha. The outburst of the night before distressed her. From spending time with Jamie, she believed he would adjust quickly. He was young. He would heal. He could still be a child and she could mother him. Already he was playing happily outside with his new friend. Martha was different. She was already becoming a young woman; the challenge there was much greater. It was going to be difficult to shape their lives into being a family. She would have to work hard to convince Jamie and Martha that they belonged together. She resolved it would be her legacy to them. With her mind set on this intent, she remembered Thomas would be waiting for his lunch. Hurriedly, she set about to prepare it. It would not do to upset his routine.

17
Seeds

When the children arrived, Constance had immediately noticed Martha needed new clothes. She remembered how much Emily had enjoyed getting a new store-bought dress. Early in the week, while Martha and Jamie were at school, she went shopping. She would have liked to make a dress for Martha, but decided instead to buy her something more attractive. The Winkles store in Strathroyal had a good selection of children's clothing and it didn't take long to find exactly the right thing. Constance took great satisfaction in making the purchase.

Martha was overjoyed when Constance presented the new garment to her after school. It was soft, light blue cotton. The small cap sleeves and the daintily scooped neckline were edged with delicate lace. It was the most beautiful dress she had ever owned. There were no words to express her gratitude. Although she managed not to cry as she had on that first day, there were tears welling up. Constance pretended not to notice and insisted Martha try it on and model it for the family.

"You look all grown up," Jamie remarked proudly when he saw her.

Thomas smiled and said, "You'll be the best dressed girl in church, Martha."

Martha felt pretty and lighthearted and swirled around laughing. That was enough for Constance. It was a priceless purchase. She felt the sun had begun to shine for the girl thrust into the adult world long before her time. The dress had been expensive and she had needed to dip into her grocery money to buy it. This meant she would have to ask Thomas for more money, something she knew he hated, but she didn't care. The pleasure the dress brought into the dejected child's life was well worth the scolding her husband might inflict.

Later when Constance approached Thomas, she told him she needed money, rather than asking him for it. She was pleasantly surprised at how little he had commented about her spending. She planned it guardedly, entering his study while he was busy. He was irritated at the intrusion (as she knew he would be) but he opened his wallet and gave her fifty dollars.

"Here you are, Constance," he said. "Take care to spend it wisely." Although he was annoyed that she had barged into his study and demanded money, Thomas was pleased with himself. She didn't need to know that John Jacobs had given him the money for the children's care. His wife would be impressed that he was being so generous.

"Of course, dear," Constance replied meekly. His generosity surprised her. Since it was more than she had anticipated, she decided to take Martha shopping the following week for more clothes. She obviously needed new underwear and it was quite visible that the young woman should be wearing her first bra.

Neither Constance nor Thomas was aware of the web of pretense that they were spinning. They did not recognize that the carefully constructed, intricate lies were tenuous threads that would not hold the weight of deception. They could not discern that the silken threads could become fibers of steel that would bind them to a counterfeit relationship.

When Constance told Martha they were going shopping for new clothes, she was beyond grateful. It was the first time since the death of her mother that anyone had paid any close attention to what she wore. While living with Uncle John, she had outgrown her girlish dresses. No one seemed to notice or care. The shopping trip became a treasured memory. She felt guilty about feeling so elated, the way one does after raiding the cookie jar without being caught. She thought it was much more than she deserved. Constance completely ignored her protests and was jubilant at the reaction. She was hopeful the child would recover from the neglect she had endured. While they were walking the short distance home down Front Street, Constance gently reached for Martha's hand; she noticed Martha tense slightly but she didn't pull away. Constance was thrilled. Hand in hand, two women walked home that day, both unaware of what they had given each other.

Martha carefully cut off the tags of her new clothes. She handled them lovingly before hanging them in the wardrobe.

The Journey Home

Four new dresses hung there. It was hard to take the old dresses off the hangers. They were the last material reminder of her mother. She pressed them tightly to her heart, folded them thoughtfully and placed them in the bottom drawer of the dresser.

"I'll never part with them!" she vowed.

She had left the store wearing one of the two new bras. It felt uncomfortably taut around her chest. She stood and looked from side to side in the mirror feeling very adult. She realized that wearing the garment made her stand taller. Tears trickled down her cheeks. For the first time, she understood what her mother had often referred to as *tears of delight*. Thoughts of her mother overwhelmed her; she hoped and prayed she hadn't been disloyal to her today.

A soft breeze came in through the open window. It kissed her on the cheek and whispered in her ear, "Be happy, my precious one." Martha knew the words meant her mother approved. Gradually, the sadness that cramped and caged her strength was loosed enough to make happiness possible.

Her eyes moved to the brightly wrapped gift that still sat unopened on her dresser. Should she open in now? She wondered what was in it, but having it there created a unique sense of pleasurable anticipation. After a time, it became of symbol of hope. She felt a fresh sense of gladness, finally daring to remember and believe again her mother's teachings about faith and hope that had eluded her for a long time. When she became comfortable with her appearance, it also became easier to relax and find the sleep that soothed her saddened spirit.

The present was often the last thing she thought about before sleeping. She really was curious about its contents.

Fear that this new life would end as unexpectedly as it had begun, kept her from tearing off the paper. Uncle John had said this arrangement would be temporary. She often wondered how Aunt Lydia was doing. Martha thought about how her aunt's illness had given them an unexpected new life. Her joy seemed to have come at the expense of her aunt's health.

In the morning, when the gift sat in exactly the same spot, cheerful and unopened, there was an inexplicable assurance. Today, a person who truly cared would surround them with love. Since she had never been prone to being superstitious, this eccentric fantasy could be neither understood nor explained. She accepted it as a bequest, perhaps from her mother who was looking after them despite her absence. The less she tried to understand it, the more comfort it brought her. Although it would take more sunshine and rain to empower it to grow, the mustard seed of hope that Esther had embedded in her daughter's heart was not lost. It had taken root.

Constance wondered why the gift had remained unopened. She dared not ask Martha the reason. Even though the girl seemed to be adjusting and settling in, Constance feared it would take more time to soothe the heart of the child who already had lived too long as an adult. After the shopping trip, she was optimistic. Although she took no credit for it, she believed Martha was healing. She gave thanks to her God.

18
Spring Frost

As naturally as spring turns to summer, Jamie's knowledge that he was part of a family grew. Like a dry plant that hungers to soak up water, he guzzled the life-giving water of authentic charity. He flourished in the refuge of love. For a time, he selfishly lost sight of his sister's disposition.

Martha appeared to fit into her new routine with ease. After her initial catharsis, she emerged intent and deliberate in her demeanor. She assumed her new role with a willing passivity that resembled validation of her circumstances. Engaged in doing what was required, she incarcerated her loneliness in a locked chamber in the deep niches of her heart. Caged away, it could not intimidate her daily existence. It was only in the sanctity of her room that at times, the entrance forced itself open. Usually she was able to force the feelings to retreat; now, she chose to be happy. The sojourns with her identity were temporarily detoured by the adjustments and business of her new surroundings. In this place, living and even contentment were possible.

She was encouraged to invite school friends home. This was new to Martha and although she found it difficult, her caring personality won over peers who had previously shunned her. Naturally, she gravitated toward those, like herself, who seemed alienated from accepted circles. Regretfully her acquaintances didn't mature to friendship. It was too risky to build intimacy that might come crashing down at any time. Ultimately, the only person she could depend on for companionship was herself.

To outsiders who observed her, she seemed to have adjusted well to her new environment. It certainly appeared she was becoming familiar in her interactions with others. Constance was more than pleased to see how she seemed to be comfortable in her home; still, it bothered her that the young woman was incapable of building long-lasting closeness with her peers. She suspected underneath the composed disposition there still lurked lesions that required tending. In time, the torment will out and the festering wounds will be uncovered, she thought. Until then, she would give Martha the hiatus she needed and be there when the inevitable storm erupted.

Constance loved the children immediately and completely. She wrote long epics about them in her diary. She described their behavior and the progress she determined they were making. She detailed minute anecdotes about interesting things they said and did. She prayed that someday Jamie and Martha might read them and know how cherished they were.

Summer came and then fall. It appeared that the children were doing very well. They seemed to be happy. Although Thomas spent more and more time alone in his study, Constance was pleased they were building a family unit that was generally relaxed and secure. John had moved to London but regularly made brief visits to Strathroyal to inquire about Martha and Jamie and to leave money for their care. There was no discussion about resuming the custody of the children. Lydia's condition remained unchanged and she continued to be a patient in the asylum. Constance was torn between being happy for herself and grieving for Lydia's condition. She felt true compassion toward her, yet she dreaded the day she would come home.

With fall came Advent and the anticipation of Christmas. Thomas loathed the preparation, the waiting and then finally the celebration of Christmas. The self-imposed judgment that he was an impostor, preaching about joy when there was so little of it in his own soul, shamed him. It gnawed at his conscience. He preached hope, but knew only despair. He advocated peace, but didn't feel the promised tranquility. He knew the words of love, but felt he was unable to give or receive it unconditionally. All the while, he cloaked the awareness with the mask of gravity and dignity that his profession allowed.

Unlike Thomas, Constance thrived on the happiness and the activities of the holidays. She bathed in the enjoyment of creating a Christmas celebration totally focused and centered on her beloved adoptees. They made decorations and baked cookies. Late at night when the house was asleep, she knit mittens and scarves and created elaborate little gifts. There was delicate shell jewelry for Martha. The women, in the women's circle, were thrilled that Constance had finally taken an interest in their group.

For Jamie, she considered the watch he had admired in Woolworth's store window. Secretly she saved pennies from the grocery allowance that Thomas provided. Since he seemed less vigilant about monitoring the grocery receipts, she was able to glean enough change to purchase the watch with the fancy leather band Jamie had stared at until she had dragged him away. At first, there was a tinge of guilt. Never before had she done anything Thomas hadn't first sanctioned. She wasn't at all sure how she would explain it, but the excitement and pure gratification of being able to do it stifled any remorse that may have tried to squeeze its way into her conscience. The day she gathered pine cones to make a wreath, Thomas was noticeable agitated. He rattled about the house, muttering that the children should know the real meaning of Christmas and not be swallowed up by all the irrelevant trappings.

"You will ruin them," he said. "They should know more of the catechism."

The catechism classes had begun in the fall. When Thomas was busy with his parishioners, the sessions were less frequent. This pleased Constance; she was surprised Thomas felt it necessary to resume them at this busy time of year. At least Jamie has had some time to appreciate the traditions of the Christmas season, she thought. She was absorbed in the generosity so natural to her. She was bursting with the gratification of celebrating Christmas with her children.

In her heart she said, "Damn the catechism – he just needs

to be a child." Instead, she swallowed the words and said, "I know you do a good job teaching him, my darling."

"You're right, Constance," his voice sounded vacant. "He's such a slow learner." As an aside, he reminded her that it was her responsibility to instruct Martha. Constance nodded, knowing she did not intend to do any more about it until after Christmas.

Until that rainy day in September when he was first summoned to the minister's study, Jamie had forgotten Uncle John's words about the catechism. The hiatus of being a child again left little time to ponder the questions he'd considered in the apple tree. When love was real, there was less need to understand the mysteries of life. Already after the first lesson, Jamie decided Uncle John had been wrong about the catechism; it didn't clarify anything. He hated it.

Constance was aware that Jamie didn't like his religious instruction any more than he liked school. She also remembered clearly, the first time Thomas had summoned the boy to his office. When they had emerged after an hour, Jamie had quickly gone to his room. Thomas said that he needed to make a quick trip to London. Although she was pleased that Thomas was taking such an interest in Jamie, she had misgivings about the catechism lessons.

The routine was always the same. Today, when the *men* emerged from the office, Jamie was unusually subdued and silent. Dinner was on the table. Constance chattered about the fun they had making Christmas decorations and even Martha seemed genuinely happy. Conversely, Jamie was alternatively quiet. She missed his usual chatter. He seemed passive, even sullen. She would talk to Thomas about overdoing the catechism. He was such a little boy. Surely, there was lots of time for him to learn.

Martha noticed Jamie's mood as well. She wasn't fond of the catechism lessons either, but Mrs. Sluis had said not to worry as long as she read a bit of the catechism book now and again. If the minister asked, she was to tell him about the last thing she had read. She watched Jamie pushing his food around on his plate. When he timidly announced that his tummy was hurting, she offered to take him upstairs to bed. Before Thomas could deny Martha's request, Constance smiled and encouraged her to take Jamie to bed.

"He's probably overtired from having so much fun," she said.

Martha took his hand and led him upstairs.

Somehow, the energy of the day was gone. Like water draining from a bathtub, Constance felt it ebbing away. Thomas sensed it as well. It prompted him to announce he wasn't hungry either and needed to finish his sermon.

Constance was left in the empty kitchen. She sat as silent tears slipped down her face. How was it possible that suddenly it was so cold? Where had the warmth gone? Like a late spring frost, that kills the first spring blooms, the sprouts of joy were abruptly snuffed out by the icy wind blowing through the room.

19
The Key

Today the door was pink. Spring flowers covered it: bright red tulips, golden daffodils and fragrant hyacinths. They were alive and growing from the doorframe, almost obscuring the hinges and handle. Lydia stared at it, studying every minute detail. She still marveled at how the door could stand there alone, on its own, without any walls to hold it in place. Often she wondered what held it to the barren land on which it stood. Each day the door seemed different. Some days, like today, it was bright and cheerful, inviting her to open it. Others days, it was obscure and foreboding. One day it was dark sculptured wood, like the trunk of a fancy coffin she had once touched in a funeral home. Instinctively she knew the key that she kept firmly lodged in her closed hand, would fit all of the doors. Although she had no desire to leave the shelter of this strange sphere she now inhabited, the means was still there. She knew it was possible to escape through the door to the other side. But, there was no need because she was pleasantly euphoric in the peacefulness that swaddled her in this carefree, alternative place.

Strangers stood at the door. She watched them come and go. She ate the food they set out, but only if it was on her side. She feared even to put her hand through the opening. She listened to them talking, talking about her. They even came through the door to look in her eyes and place their cold hands intrusively and menacingly upon her. They shook their heads and said strange things she didn't understand. They put things in her mouth and her arms. At first, she would protest when they mauled her, but soon she learned if she sat very still without struggling, they would quickly disappear. Then she was free. Free to stray away from the door, following the road signs of unblemished memory that invited her to wander down the pleasant roads of reminiscence, stretching endlessly in front of her.

In the beginning, the door itself presented as a pleasant remembrance. The flowers were from her grandfather's garden. Profuse and diverse, they bloomed just as she had known them. The last of ten children, she was conceived and born in the sin of blatant drunkenness. In another time and place, it would have been a violation of matrimonial love. The seed, carried grudgingly to term, was delivered like a cumbersome burden and in haste deposited and left alone on the doorstep of life.

Initially sibling adolescents, named by number, handled and managed her days. When she was four, the aged patriarch arrived to live out his last days as unobtrusively as possible. Suddenly a troublesome child and a bothersome frail man both shooed away by caregivers who didn't care, found a kindred spirit – another soul to love. He sang lovely sweet lullabies to coax her to sleep. When all else failed, he was the one who could console and take her to dreamland. He loved and nurtured her. She gleaned the wisdom of age; he remembered and thrived in the pure simplicity and naturalness of youth. Together they created a world where it was possible for both of them to grow and blossom.

Each grew stronger. Their emotions and lives were intricately and singularly interwoven to form an attachment that shaped and defined their character. Their union released the otherwise occupied adults from their upkeep. Together they required little maintenance. Food and a place to sleep were expected and accepted. Their shared alliance kept the twosome out of harm's way. He protected her from the jeopardy of innocence and she shielded him from the restrictions of age. Their attachment kept them safe and complete.

The season he arrived, they created the garden. A plenitude of perennials was lovingly nurtured. There were different blooms that flowered just for the two of them. He told her a story for each flower, repeating it year after year until she knew them all. In spring, they planted the annuals. In the fall, he taught her how to gather their seeds carefully. They were stored and labeled in old envelopes to guarantee another season. At the end of winter, they were planted in rusty tin cans, ready to greet the promise of the warm sunshine of spring.

She always believed that the smallest of seeds produced the most magnificent blooms. The rainbow garden, they called it, when all the flowers were in their peak. A little part of heaven, the weathered old man explained. If you look very closely, you will see the face of God. Feigning wide-eyed wonder, she explored every crevice, assuring him she saw it, although she never really knew what it should look like. He knew and loved her more. Although he tutored her there should be no favorites in flowers, she loved the pansies best. Their rich, vibrant colors whispered her name. When she searched their brilliant faces, she thought they spoke of other worlds. He taught her pansies needed picking to thrive, so she culled them at their peak and pressed them in the old Bible that sat on the shelf in the kitchen, to enjoy again when the snow covered the garden.

It became their sanctuary. He taught her that gardens represent life. In their special place, each word her beloved Poppa spoke was appreciated and remembered. She tucked them away in her heart like pressed flowers, to be savored again during friendless, dreary, winter days.

Today as she rambled effortlessly through the summers of her youth, she searched for the meaning, detailed in the faces of the flowers. She saw bits of beauty but the essence of it seemed obscured, clouded by the murkiness of unknown uninvited snippets of life. This frustration initially did not deter her, but eventually made her feel the melancholy of later years. She would hold the key tightly and find her way back to the door, hoping, even praying the flowers would still be blooming. Often during these times, they hung limp and rotting, creating the rancid stench of death that clung menacingly to her nostrils.

When the door presented its dark side, she couldn't find the garden corridors at all. Those days, the pathways pulled her to places she didn't wish to visit. Enigmatic empty cavities void of feeling and color. They were hazy and held anxious echoes that resounded from obscured niches. Then it was much harder to return to the door. The way became littered with fault lines that were difficult to traverse. Only when she stopped and listened for the others to call her name was she able to weave her way back to the portal. On those days, she welcomed the aliens with their magic sleep elixir.

The last memory of her grandfather lingered. They had already started planting the seeds, when spring suddenly returned to wintry weather. Without warning, he was gone. As always, he kissed her good-bye when she went to school. Then he slept. She saw him next in the carved casket, a reserved expression pasted on his face. Staring at him, she wished she could snuggle up and warm his cold hands, the way he had done so many times for her. They all said he was in a better place now, freed from the pain and sadness of senility. Someone told her she should be happy for him. She was. Only because she knew he was free of the weight he had carried. The dismissal and rejection by his offspring had been a burden he had tried unsuccessfully to bury in his garden. In the coffin, she tucked their seeds, to plant on the other side.

"Remember me, she told him." She was content to know he would. The seeds were safe.

That year only the perennials bloomed.

The in-between years were devoid of season, chapters of her life written with invisible ink. She was inconspicuous. Talked at, but seldom observed or engaged in conversation. Strangers resided with her in the house, foreigners who existed together, but lived in different worlds. She was compliant and meek, remembering always her Poppa's example. His wisdom came as natural to her as the spring rain; she lived the life he had left behind, relying on the memory of his love to feel secure. After high school, she got a job as a secretary in an office. A rather boring job that people thought suited her.

Suddenly she was twenty. The risk of becoming an old maid brought the year sharply into focus. Then John noticed her. He smiled at her. She smiled back. One day he said hello, the next, he asked her to dinner. She baked him cookies. After an appropriate courtship, they were married.

When he spoke, she thought she heard her Poppa's voice, soft and assuring. She was pleased to be his wife. She loved him simply and completely. Like her, John had never learned how to love. He cared for her. They were like two children, trying to do right. Each was eagerly looking to the other for direction and completion. If there had been children, they may have become a family. When they did not conceive, each held the other secretly responsible. They were incapable of breaking the cycle of silence that had held them captive. Unwilling, they built a partition of privacy that was oddly comfortable in its familiarity. Leaning on it instead of each other, seemed to be adequate and soon became the norm.

When Esther and the children moved in, Lydia saw a ray of sunshine. She had been eager to welcome them, but trapped in her ineptitude, her actions were not a reflection of her feelings. The harder she tried the clumsier and more despicable her actions became. She would gladly have given her life to save Esther's. Her guilt sparked the first intense episode of desperate silence. Esther had been able to soothe and quiet her fearfulness. Lydia believed she had exploited her friend's goodness and when it was gone, any hope she would be rescued was buried with her caregiver.

When she moved to another bedroom to be able to rest, she felt the ultimate isolation. Sitting in the silence of her room, she became aware of the door and beyond it, she heard her name called. It seemed easy and natural to turn the key, cross the threshold and enter to the other side.

She was comfortable there, alone, unencumbered by the demands and needs of others. Sheltered from the reality of living, it was safe to wander through impossible dreams. After Esther died, John tried to be the husband she needed. At first, he could entice her to return from the other place. When she chose not to respond to him, his frustration turned to anger. She understood that he wanted more; she wanted more. Surely, there should be more to life. When the doctor offered little hope Lydia would recover, she accepted her life in the institution. She grasped the necessity and complied without any confrontation.

During his last visit, John remembered the first time he saw her. She seemed sweet and innocent, so different from the other women he knew. He wondered if he had ever really loved her. He had decided that this would be his final visit. It was just too difficult to see her in the comatose state. He stood tersely watching her. For a moment, John thought he saw a flicker of light in her eyes. Then it was gone. Her eyes were glazed – probably the drugs, he speculated. She saw his resentment; she heard him cursing. Cursing her. She screamed, but no sound came. Repeatedly, she tried. He didn't hear her.

"Take me home," she cried. "I want to try again. I want to love you. I want you to love me." She was too far away.

He only heard the screams of the demented echoing off the walls. Strangers locked in the confines and limitations of madness.

Where was she, John wondered? It didn't much matter now. She was gone. And Hagar was waiting for him at home. He sighed and realized his annoyance was waning. On some level, he sensed remorse; though, he refused to let himself feel it. He took a last look at the surreal figure slouched in the chair. Worse than dead, he thought.

"Goodbye, Lydia. I'm sorry." When he shut the door, he declared himself absolved of his matrimonial vows.

After that day, Lydia found it increasingly arduous to return to the door. Each day the blooms clinging to it were more disfigured and unnatural. She could no longer hear her Poppa's whispering words rustling through the garden. Instead, there were more inconspicuous, concealed memories. Apparitions hanging like wilted plants on the hinges. It was no longer a comforting place. The shadows of night seemed more welcoming than the stench of decaying memory. Aimlessly she wandered into the unknown region of darkness never before explored, searching for some release. When tired, she would find an obscure spot, pull her knees to her chest and curl up, praying for the night to assimilate her spirit. Even then, she could not – would not – relinquish her hold on the key.

She searched for the children's voices that were far, far away – a distant sound barely heard. She tried to return to the door, but each time it was more strenuous. Only there the whispers lingered. Killed by an early summer frost, the flowers now seemed to be only shadows clutching lifelessly to emptiness. For a time, there was only stillness, a cold numbness that impersonated peace.

Upon Thomas' insistence, Constance brought the children to see their aunt. It was his duty as her minister and their duty as her family. Not knowing what to expect, everyone was apprehensive. They brought cookies, sweet shortbreads that Martha remembered she liked. First, they stood in the doorway, overcome by the smell and sight of a woman they no longer recognized. Thomas made a hasty escape claiming he needed to speak to the doctor. Martha bravely approached her aunt.

Unaware of their presence, Lydia unexpectedly felt Martha's warm hand on her clammy skin. It was the first tenderness she had felt for a long time. Suddenly she was conscious of the boy and another woman she couldn't identify. She wanted to loosen her grip on the shadows, perhaps even open the door, but her fingers refused to move, refused awareness of the key. For the first time, panic swallowed her up. Without the key, there was no way to open the door; there was no way home. When she began flailing her arms, Martha quickly backed away. Distress surrounded the boldness smothering the bit of uncovered courage. Constance, ignorant of what was happening, was frightened and hurried the children out of the room to find Thomas.

The key lay unsecured in Lydia's limp hand; it threatened to slip from her grasp. It was the last visit she remembered for a long time.

20
Chalk Dust

Life settled into a comfortable routine. Martha and Jamie went to school. Martha excelled; Jamie barely survived. In their own way, they thrived in Constance Sluis' care. Martha had acquaintances at church and school. Jamie had Marty, his friend and kindred spirit.

School was a mountain for Jamie. A mountain he tried unsuccessfully to climb. He attempted repeatedly to scale the rocks that protruded in his path. Usually he stumbled and fell. Often the others laughed. There were emotional bruises that were displayed in the way he slouched in his desk and the sad look in his eyes. At first, his courage was indomitable. He refused to give up; he always did his best for his Mama. In spite of his valiant efforts, he failed. Eventually, his only option was to stop trying. It was painful but there were fewer bruises than those created by constant failure.

School finally became a safe place for Jamie in the third grade. Her name was Joy. He wondered how a name could be so perfect. Had her parents known that she would exude a special feeling of optimism in people? Names interested him. He remembered his friend Samson. He was strong and impressive, just the way a Samson should be. He imagined choosing an identity for someone not yet born. It seemed an awesome trust. He knew some people who didn't fit their name. He thought of the Mary in his class, who should have been meek and mild like the mother of Jesus. But she was deceptive and shrewd. Nothing at all like a Mary should be.

Joy had moved to Strathroyal with her family. Her father was the bank manager at the Royal Bank, the only financial institution in town. He approved the loans to struggling farmers and aspiring young businessmen. This made him an esteemed individual in the small town. His wife never shopped in town, but went to London to purchase her carefully tailored clothes. Her two daughters were dressed as replicas of her. The entire family was different. Not very small town, some folks said. Still, most of the townspeople acknowledged that they were generous and considerate. In spite of the fact they were well-to-do strangers, they fit into the community quite graciously and effortlessly.

Jamie was in the third grade for the second time. He had failed and was now officially known as being *slow*. Joy was in the same grade. She gathered friends as naturally and normally as a bee collects pollen. It was not just because she was the prettiest and best-dressed girl in the class, or because of her parents' status in the community. She was different in a singular manner. She exemplified a genuine kindness.

In her circle, there was always room for another person. No one challenged her when she asked the most neglected child to play. If Joy wanted to include someone, it was done. The teachers marveled at her persona. They watched her as she built bridges that had seemed impossible to construct. They discerned that she had a gift for doing the impossible for some of the most victimized children.

During a social studies class, the teacher taught a lesson about Indians. She brought in bows and arrows, feathered headdresses, a pair of moccasins and arrowheads. The class sat around a make-believe fire pretending to be native Canadians. Miss Mann said that she wanted them to experience how the Indians lived. Each person was asked to say something that might have been said while sitting around the nightly campfire. There were many stereotypical comments common to western dramas. When it came Jamie's turn, he sat and looked into the fire, unable to utter any meaningful comment. The fire had become real. He was a quiet courageous Indian boy contemplating his circumstances.

The teacher attempted to help him by asking, "Tell us what you might be thinking while you are looking into that fire, Jamie?"

Without taking his eyes from the flames, Jamie, spoke dauntlessly, "I don't like it that white men are here. I want them to leave."

"They were just dumb Indians, Jamie," Mary blurted out. "They wouldn't care."

The class giggled. Jamie felt himself turning as red as the make-believe fire. He was used to being considered dumb and didn't really mind it much, but he hated it when they laughed at him. Any bravery he had acquired would now take weeks to reappear.

"I think Jamie's right," Joy declared passionately. "I wouldn't like it if someone came to my house and told me what to do."

A silence echoed through the room. It was inconceivable that Joy could be mistaken. Everyone knew she was the smartest one. They considered the possibility that Jamie might have stumbled onto an idea most of them had never considered. Only Mary refused to believe this likelihood was feasible. Her jealousy of Joy created a cynicism that tainted her views. Nevertheless, she knew when she was defeated; it wouldn't do to alienate her rival, much less the rest of the class.

"Well, maybe I wouldn't like that either," she recanted apologetically.

Miss Mann smiled, "I agree boys and girls that Jamie has brought our attention to a very interesting point."

She told them about the struggle of native people for identity and freedom from the oppression of the Europeans. She wondered herself how much of what she was saying was being understood or even true, but it didn't matter. Jamie had been as heroic as any Indian boy who had ever stood up and boldly died to protect his family. He had spoken out for the first time and thanks to Joy, he had earned the respect of his peers.

That day at recess when teams were picked, Joy chose him first. It was more happiness than he had ever felt at school. When he hit two runners home, they cheered, even though he was tagged out. After school, he wanted desperately to thank her, but her mother was waiting to pick her up.

She hurried past him, smiled and remarked, "See you tomorrow, Jamie."

"See ya," he replied beaming. As he and Marty walked home, Jamie told his friend all about Joy. Marty hoped that she could become his friend as well.

That night, Jamie tucked the image away next to those of his mother and Samson. He replayed them repeatedly. Each time he summoned them, he smiled with joy at the feeling of acceptance. The gratitude he felt was passionate and earnest; he knew he owed Joy an immense debt. He made a pledge: someday, he would come to *her* rescue. He would be a strong, brave Indian and stand up for her. He would repay her the way a true Indian would.

The teacher knew she had witnessed a miracle that day. It was extraordinary; the simple kindness of a small child had intensely influenced another child's life. She prayed the endorsement Jamie had received would mean a new beginning for the pensive, shy boy. She had talked to him when they walked alone at recess and knew he often had intelligent, reflective views far beyond the understanding of most children his age. Often she wondered how to bring out this hidden ability in the boy, but his timidity had made it difficult. His fear of being ostracized and the belief he was stupid had gagged him. She considered the possibility that Joy had loosened the tether that jammed his mouth and heart.

Miss Mann was different from other teachers Jamie had known. She certainly was strict. There were many rules to follow and plenty of work to do. She was very tall but when he looked up, he saw something warm and inviting about her eyes. He saw the same look in Martha's eyes. He vaguely remembered the angel at the hospital; she had had it too. In the fading recollections of his mother, her eyes were also bright and clear like his teacher's eyes. This knowledge and her gentle caring questions finally allowed him to confide in her. He told her about his life – his mother, the apple tree, Martha, Mrs. Sluis and Samson. She never doubted his sincerity or suspected his integrity. He could ask his questions without the fear of retaliation or rejection. Always she responded with gentleness. There were no pat answers; many of his questions remained unanswered, but there was comfort in being able to voice them. He walked with her to protect himself from the bullies on the playground. He had seldom realized such safety. More importantly, there was affirmation for his soul. He knew she would understand about the minister and thought of telling her about the dreaded catechism lessons. Rev. Sluis had said very sternly that he was learning about special *man* things, things he wasn't to tell anyone, not even Martha. He suspected that meant he shouldn't talk to Miss Mann about them either. He often wondered why Uncle John had said that learning the catechism would help him understand about love.

It bothered him that Miss Mann didn't smile much. Some of the students called her crabby, but he knew differently. He sensed she had her own dark places. Places she couldn't let anyone enter. He even contemplated asking her about them, but the questions were hard to put into words and the resolve to do so never materialized before the recess bell ended their dialogue.

Shortly after the day of acceptance for Jamie, Miss Mann created her own milestone for him. She asked him to stay after school, quickly assuring him he had done nothing wrong. When the other students had gone, Jamie stood nervously at her desk.

She smiled at him, "Sit down Jamie; I just want to talk to you."

He didn't think she was angry or upset with him, so he was able to relax. Being good in class was easy for him; he knew she understood him better than almost anyone else did.

"Jamie, I think you are a very smart boy." Even her eyes smiled as she looked at him.

He didn't know what to say. The only other people who thought he was the least bit clever were Martha and Marty. She was his sister who loved him. He believed she said it to make him feel better. Maybe he thought, Miss Mann was just saying this because she liked him. He looked at her.

"Yes, Jamie, I really mean it." She responded as if reading his mind, "you have amazing ideas and you understand many things even some adults don't. I remember that you told me that your friend Marty thinks you're smart. And he's right you are very smart."

He didn't know how to react to her comments. This was his second year in grade three. Last year his teacher had said he was behind in his reading and needed to catch up. She told him he failed because he wasn't smart enough to go to grade four. How was it possible to be smart and still fail a grade?

"I think because you have difficulty reading, some other teachers may have thought you weren't very smart," she continued, again appearing to know what he was thinking. "But I know you can learn how to read better. I'd like to help you to do that if it's all right with you. Would you be willing to stay after school to let me help you?"

It seemed like a dream to Jamie. She was one of the few special people in his life. Spending time with her would be a welcome diversion, especially from learning the catechism. The idea that it was possible to learn how to read, brought tears to his eyes. He had tried so hard so many times, always with the same dismal results.

"I'll have to ask Mrs. Sluis about staying after school," he said knowing how she would worry if he was late coming home.

"Don't worry about that either Jamie; I've already talked to her and she thinks it's just fine for you to stay. So it's settled then," she stated matter-of-factly.

They worked together two or three days a week. At first, Jamie was embarrassed about his lack of ability. Miss Mann was always patient and she used some new methods she had read about for people who she said were just like him. She said the name for what he had was dyslexia. It meant the words were mixed up or looked backwards to him. She told him about a Dr. Orton, who understood why this happened and was helping people with this problem. The material he had written was helping her learn to be a better teacher. She explained that there were many people who had trouble reading. It was because of the way their brain worked. This doctor said it didn't mean that they weren't smart or couldn't learn. Jamie was surprised to hear there were many smart people who couldn't read very well.

It seemed like a strange thing and an even stranger word to Jamie, but he trusted her completely. He would have done anything she asked of him. Some of the exercises she gave him were tedious, but he never complained. She had him do things he'd never done before. He traced words with his fingers; he pictured them in his head and he wrote them over and over again. His favorite part of the lesson was *the collection*. There were long list of words she called sight words that they practiced repeatedly. They were written on cards she flashed for him to read. He even took them home and happily studied them every night. Every time he got the word right, she put a gold star on the back of the card. When he was able to read the word ten times, Miss Mann took it out of the stack and said it was now his to keep. Then she added a new word. In school, there had never been any gold stars for him. They were reserved for work that was perfect. Receiving more than one was beyond his expectations. His collection of owned words grew and with it his confidence and ability to read.

At home, everyone helped him practice the words. They were all proud of him when he ran in the door with new words to learn. Martha flashed them and Mrs. Sluis helped him just before she tucked him into bed. He even practiced with Marty when they were together.

He went to sleep telling himself, "I can read." When he began to believe the certainty of it, the word *dumb* was gradually erased from his forehead.

After several months of working with Miss Mann, he put up his hand in class when she asked a volunteer to read aloud from the reader. It was a story that he had practiced with her. Usually the teacher stopped after a page and let someone else read, but that day she let him continue uninterrupted. Confidently he read it to the class. Even the new words that some others didn't know yet, were familiar to him. "Brother

Rabbit and Tar Baby" was a fable about a rabbit that was tricked by a sly fox. The rabbit outsmarted the fox. He schemed his way out of a dangerous situation.

Jamie sighed deeply. He mustered all the expression he could and with a great deal of satisfaction, he read the last paragraph. "Off to his home went Brother Rabbit. As he hopped along, he was laughing about the way he had fooled Brother Fox. He certainly was enjoying himself."

For the first time in his school career, Jamie also enjoyed himself. It was clear he had taken great pride in reading aloud. The room was silent; the class stared in disbelief. For the rest of that year, his label was officially relinquished. The insignificant fable stayed with him for many years. Whenever he wavered about being able to accomplish something, he recalled his extraordinary grade three reading experience. Always it gave him boldness to attack seemingly impossible tasks.

After Jamie finished reading the story, Miss Mann turned to the blackboard and fumbled with the chalk. Joy thought it was very strange that the teacher seemed to be wiping away tears. She surmised Miss Mann must have chalk dust in her eyes.

Jamie sat down in his seat. He believed he was a moth that had eaten its way out of its casing and shed its cocoon. A new creature emerged full of sunshine and expectation. Slowly, carefully he spread his newfound wings; he was ready to fly. He was prepared to taste the sweet nectar of success. Learning to read became his emancipation.

Soon after the reading, Joy moved back to London. Tragedy struck the family when the dreaded polio virus invaded their home. Joy's sister was hospitalized, confined to an iron lung. There were no goodbyes. The sadness hung in the classroom like a fog. Their Joy was missing.

Jamie wondered why the people he loved always left him so abruptly. He rejoiced in the release she had given him from his perception of himself. He regretted he hadn't been able to do anything to show her how much she meant to him. Maybe, he mused, someday she'll come back. He added her memory to the most special of places in his heart. A place of Joy.

Although life settled into its habitual routine, it was never again quite the same. A brave little Indian lad had taken the place of a nervous little boy.

21
Cold Lunch

This time when she knocked on the door, Constance waited until he issued the "enter" command. It amused her that he insisted on this formality but she didn't question it. She understood the weight of his pastoral role was increasingly heavy; he brooded about the well-being of his flock and his perceived inadequacy to lead it. Less and less, he came to her for solace. Although she worked hard to be available and approachable, she sensed something was changing, not only in him, but also in their relationship. The responsibility of motherhood helped to soften the void, but the sadness that he had drifted away from her, like a ship without an anchor, intruded on her peace of mind.

There was no response. Constance smiled, understanding it was his way of letting her know that she was interrupting his work. She understood his need for control. After she had interrupted him the last time, he had sternly reminded her again to wait at the door. She knew better than to try the same tactic twice.

"Lunch is ready when you are dear," she announced.

Thomas heard the knock but could not answer. A sudden intense headache had made him reel backwards. He turned, thinking someone or something had hit him on the head; the room spun around uncontrollably. He tried to call out to her but no words would come. He tried to stand but could feel nothing in his legs. He slumped on his desk. His head landed on the open Bible. His text for Sunday's sermon was underlined: "Be still and know that I am God."

He had struggled more than usual about the selection of the text. The deception he had woven around his life was becoming increasingly oppressive. He felt it choking him. It was becoming an impregnable grip that bound his troubled spirit with fetters of deceit. Initially he convinced himself his unrest was a lingering residual of the horrors of the war. He acknowledged the war might have been the fagot that started the fire deep within himself. He was also aware that there were other embers smoldering and threatening to flare up uncontrollably. Only his work created a pseudo solace of sorts. He did his job very well. The community saw him as an upright, stalwart, paragon of leadership. Although there was little excitement or fervor in the Sunday services, there were no conflicts either. Dutifully they permitted him to resolve the routine troubles they brought him. Like Solomon, he adjudicated equity and stability to his flock. Even though it was boring in its predictability, they felt secure in the guidance he provided.

As time passed, it was not enough for Thomas. His sense

of purposelessness became more persistent. As it grew, he channeled his passion to oust his own demons into his sermons. He preached the words he perceived God was speaking directly to him. The sermons about an angry, judgmental God, who abhorred evil, seemed to meet the needs of his passive congregation. They could not grasp the personal, private rebuke, in which their preacher routinely engaged them. The loving God, who he had once gladly followed, became an enigma that he was unable to touch. His words of reprimand were directed more at himself and his flawed existence, than at the parishioners he served. It was painfully ironic to him that the words he spoke to lead his flock, were the same words that doomed his soul to eternal damnation. Because he could not bear the shame of unmasking his flawed self to Constance, he gradually withdrew from the protected haven she would gladly, without judgment have provided. He knew that alone he could not cope or survive, yet he dared not expose his true self to her. More and more, he yearned for peace. He hungered for absolution that would ease his guilty conscience.

Constance smiled. She knew the first knock would bring no response. Thomas often expounded the virtue of patience. She'd give him a few more minutes before knocking again. He was intensely aware of the second knock; he prayed she wouldn't stop knocking, as he had demanded so often. He tried to speak her name, but the heavy pain in his head stopped the sounds from becoming words. He asked for forgiveness from God and from her, for all the times he had barked commands at her. Where did I go wrong, God? You know I tried. What happened? Did I not believe enough? He remembered the old passion, the genuine desire to live a good life, the calling that he had heard; where had it all gone? He descended into hell as he recalled the details of his sins against Jamie and the other boys. He remembered preaching a sermon about the unwillingness to turn away from evil. He had called the refusal to repent, the unpardonable sin. After the service, several congregants had intently shaken his hand and congratulated him. They were proud of him for being so bold. In the modern, fast changing world, there needed to be more people like him who were loyal to the truth of old fashioned values. The weight of his transgressions sent new pains pounding through his head. Dear God, what have I done? He knew that soon there would be another knock on the door. Then it would open slowly and Constance would softly speak his name.

"Come along now dear," she would say, "lunch is getting cold."

Why this one time didn't she open the door?

Regret raced through his mind. There were so many times he had chided her with rough words of admonition. Why had she never snapped back at him? Why had she let him be so unfeeling? Why did she have the control he so desperately sought? Why had he resented her? In fact, the qualities he loved most about Constance were now the ones he railed against. The facade of his life lay at his feet. He could see it falling off and crumbling around him. Constance where are you? Why aren't you saving my life? Please do not let me die here, alone.

The words, "My God, my God, why have you forsaken me?" flashed across his mind, echoed through his heart and brought more pain than he thought he could bear. Desperately he searched for the lyrical phrases that he had so often offered up for the dying. Where was the comfort he had provided for so many as they took their last breath? Who would say the words for him? Who would comfort Constance and his beloved children? Surely, it was not too late. One more day, that's all I need to restore it all, he thought desperately. Hadn't he earned that right? After all he'd done for others, one day was not too much to ask. He tried to speak to his God but he could find no words. He had preached them and spoken them for others so many times. Now, they refused to be his. In the dark quiet of his abyss, he knew everything he had believed and sermonized about dying was a lie. All the clichés he had spoken were lost to him now when he needed them most.

He shuffled and realized his head was on his open Bible. The words of his text seemed to leap from the page to his turbulent soul. Stillness. His mind stopped. He knew the answers to the unanswerable questions. Nothing was different, except that it was his life dangling perilously at the door to eternity. Suddenly he gave himself permission to be still. The quiet fleetingly numbed the pain. He breathed deeply, grateful for the moment of relief.

The reprieve was brief. A thick foul fogginess seeped out from the unknown, enveloped him and made him gag. He tried to wipe it away, but it seemed to suck him into its center. He saw heinous effigies – things he couldn't identify except to know they were monstrous. They hung around him like skeletons at Halloween. The preacher had assured so many parishioners not to fear, but now he could taste the terror, rotten and sour. He had chided and challenged those who had yielded to fear. He had shamed them into denying their feelings. Now buried under the weight of the denial, he fought against the blackness, terrified it would swallow him. The words he tried to speak stuck like acidic vomit in his throat. He feared it was too late. The horror of his deeds devoured what was left of his spirit. The despicable scene played and replayed in his head. He had done to Jamie what his uncle had done to him.

"Sit on the chair, Jamie," he had ordered.

Jamie sat. He did as he had been taught. Obey. Without question, obey.

He sat and waited.

Thomas was impressed by the child's obedience. Every session was longer than the one before.

"Take off your clothes, Jamie," he ordered. What malignant power has possessed him, he wondered?

The look on the child's face almost made him stop. Despite what he saw, he had crossed the line and he knew from experience that retreat was no longer possible.

Jamie sat naked on the chair, shivering. Beads of cold fear trickled from his brow. The youngster wrapped his arms around himself. He blinked hard to stop the tears.

"Stop crying," Thomas snapped at him.

Obediently, he stopped the tears from falling.

"God has sent you here for me to teach you to be a man," Thomas pontificated. "Do you trust me, Jamie?"

Jamie knew the correct answer was yes, so he nodded.

"You're right, Jamie, to put your faith in me as God's servant."

Again, he nodded as Thomas began his exploit of the boy. For an hour, Jamie endured the unendurable. Then, there had been a knock on the door.

"Jamie, what goes on in this room is only for us men. You

The Journey Home

must not ever talk about it with anyone, not even Martha. We are learning about the catechism. Do you understand?"

Again, Jamie nodded.

"Do you have any questions, Jamie? Don't be afraid to ask me. No, well better get dressed. Remember that with very lesson, you will learn a little more. Right?"

Jamie nodded again. He quickly pulled on his clothes.

In his mind's eye, he saw his wife as she opened the door. The sweet, dear woman he had betrayed.

He had taken Jamie's hand and led him to the kitchen for dinner. He knew Constance would notice the gesture. Although she didn't believe the catechism was very important for the youngster, she had been thrilled that Thomas seemed to be developing a rapport with Jamie. That first day, she had commented on how reserved and quiet *the men* were. Thomas said he hadn't noticed; maybe he was thinking about their catechism lesson.

"He's slow learner," he had commented nonchalantly. He remembered Jamie had not eaten and gone to bed early.

If only the boy had questioned him or complained, he reasoned, I would have stopped. Jamie didn't speak; he didn't stop. The boy's innocence was sacrificed on the altar of lechery. The knife cut deep. Surely, God could have called out to me as he did to Abraham, Thomas argued. God could have stopped me. God should have stopped me, he reasoned indignantly. Why didn't you stop me God, his mind screamed in anger. In the dark chasm, he was certain he saw the gates to eternity. He was convinced he heard the angel of death laughing, welcoming him home.

"Open the door!" he screamed, but nothing came out of

his mouth. He questioned if either God or Constance heard him.

After waiting for an unusually long time, Constance reluctantly entered her husband's office.

"Come now dear, your soup is getting cold," she said as she cautiously opened the door.

Although it had only been moments, it seemed like an eternity had passed until he heard Constance's voice. Finally, she was there. He felt himself slipping away. I need to find the light he told himself. There has to be a light. He was aware of Constance's presence, could hear the frantic calling of his name. Could smell the soup she had made for lunch. Gratitude rose up in him. Still he saw only a blackness that seemed to mirror the darkness of his reality. The remorse for his despicable deeds was his only awareness. He feared the certainty of an eternity, languishing in hell.

Constance knew at once that something was very wrong when she saw him sprawled across his desk. When she was unable to rouse him, she immediately telephoned Dr. Smit.

When he arrived and examined Thomas, he became very apprehensive.

"I think he's had a stroke, Constance. We need to get him to the hospital."

She helped carry Thomas to the doctor's car. He warned Constance it didn't look good. Constance was concerned about the children coming home from school to an empty house. Dr. Smit suggested that his wife, a nurse, accompany him to London instead. He promised he would telephone Constance as soon as there was any news about Thomas' condition. Silently, they drove to the city to learn the fate of the Reverend Thomas Sluis.

Reprimanding herself for not entering the office sooner, Constance sat at the kitchen table in Thomas' chair. She stared into his cold soup, searching for some sort of understanding about what had happened. Unwelcome stalkers: regret, remorse, apprehension and angst, pulled up chairs and circled around her. She screamed at them in an irrational attempt to leave her be. They mocked her even more, taking her hands and her heart in their own, embracing her until she couldn't breathe.

She ran through the house trying to free herself of them, wishing she could turn back the clock, waiting for time to move a little faster, wanting to believe her husband would survive, wondering why the telephone in the hall didn't ring.

When Martha and Jamie ran in the door after school, she greeted them with her eyes and her arms. Instead of her usual cheerful welcome, she said, "Rev. Sluis is sick. The doctor has taken him to the hospital in London."

Mutely she clung to them so tightly, they feared she would smoother them. Jamie had a thousand questions but embraced his feelings; he knew about the hospital. Intuitively, knowing she needed them, they comforted her wordlessly. An audible silence enclosed them. Just as she had done for them, they did for her. She had no words. Suspended in the surreal circumstance, the orphans acknowledged her unspeakable pain.

When the telephone rang, she smiled at them; slowly she let go of their hands to answer it. They heard her muffled voice. They heard her weeping. Jamie looked at his sister and saw the tears in her eyes. He wanted to run; he wanted to hide. The promise he had made to his sister wedged him captive in the chair.

When Constance returned, she spoke in a soft, detached voice, "It was Dr. Smit. Thomas has had a stroke. It's very bad. We have to pray that he'll be OK. I'll go to see him tomorrow. We'll know more then."

Martha tenderly hugged the dejected woman and lovingly guided her to a chair. Looking around the kitchen, she saw that there was a pot of soup on the stove. She quickly turned it on. Something to eat would be good for all of them.

"Let's have some soup for supper," was all she could say.

Jamie quickly jumped up, "I'll set the table, Martha."

Constance looked up and lovingly gazed at the children. She didn't tell them she didn't want to eat. Finally, she glared at the unwelcome villains who had tried so tenaciously to hold her hostage. She stared them down believing they could only control her if she let them. She would not allow them to shackle her. Reluctantly they loosened their grip and slinked away. Unbolting the entrance, she warmly welcomed hope into the kitchen. It joined hands with faith. They held fast to the tangible love they saw there. The fog lifted and her path was clear.

Thomas knew his wife would be sitting at the kitchen table not knowing what to do. He could see her. She would be lost without him. The sudden awareness that a bright light was shining in his eyes, made him blink. The searing pain had abated but a strange numbness had taken its place. Unfamiliar voices and hands bordered his consciousness.

It would be days before he would grasp and comprehend the scale of his body's damage due to the massive stroke that had entirely disabled him. The doctors said he was fortunate to be alive. Thomas was unable to tell them he wished he had died. Before the day ended, he knew that being trapped in his own body was a circumstance much, much worse than death.

22
Decisions

In the month since his stroke, Thomas had made some recovery; however, it was clear he would never resume a normal life. His ability to walk and talk was cruelly affected. The best he could hope for was to be a housebound invalid, cared for by loved ones. He wanted to go home, but the doctor thought it was much too early. For the first time in his adult life, he was powerless. He was now unable to manage the circumstances that had seized him.

Constance was preoccupied with thoughts of her husband during the Sunday morning service. She heard little of the meditation by the enthusiastic young preacher. His comforting tone lulled her into speculating about plans for the future. It had taken only a few weeks for the anticipated visit by the deacons. It was time for her to move out of the manse. Since there was no hope that Thomas would

The Journey Home

recuperate enough to resume his duties, it was obvious he must be replaced as soon as possible. A new young minister, who was willing to begin his duties immediately, would soon require the residence.

There had been lots of talk about alternatives for Constance and her adopted family, but given her fiscal circumstances, the consensus was that there was really only one option. She could rent a small house owned by a parishioner. Thomas' token pension would pay the rent. To relieve the financial constraints, the deacons, with condescending wisdom, had suggested she should find another home for the children. She should spend her time caring for her husband. She immediately and obstinately rejected this proposal. She would certainly take care of her husband but she would also work, beg and even steal to keep the children she now claimed as her own. She was adamant. She would not displace them again.

Constance was keenly aware there was lots of talk behind her back about her perceived unreasonable stubbornness. Without Thomas to influence and subdue her, the stellar fiber of her character eagerly emerged. Dressed in the cloak of courage, she was ready to fight for her family. As she sat in the pew feigning attention, she decided she would go and see Thomas today.

After church, the cloudy morning transformed itself into a glorious fall Sunday afternoon. She felt prepared to inform Thomas of her decision. She had secured the rental of the house and she would move there with the children. When he was well enough, he would join them.

First, arrangements needed to be made for Thomas' transfer to the new county nursing home where he would receive the most modern care. The cost was minimal due to their status and she had been able to acquire a job in their kitchen. She had deliberately worked out all the details. She would earn enough to support her children and she could visit Thomas regularly. When he was ready, she would care for him at home.

Constance was very pleased with herself. She was quite proud of her new independence. The knowledge that there would be no blessing from Thomas, mattered not to her. She had discovered the tip of Thomas' sordid indiscretion, in his office desk. When she found the filth, she tore the disgusting magazines into tiny pieces and flushed them down the toilet. The remainder of the bottle of gin went with it. With the vile images went the marital promise to "honor and obey." Although she would never abandon him, he would no longer determine the course of her life. Deliberately she removed the yoke of promise strapped to her when they were married. Her wounded ego rebelled at all she had been taught and all she thought she knew. She wondered how long Thomas had been involved in this impulsiveness. She could not fathom why he had turned to this rubbish instead of to her.

She surmised that this must be the secret, which had come between them. Although she was indefinite about the details of his infidelity, she knew with every fiber of her being that he had sinned against his God and against her. Initially it had devastated and impoverished her spirit. After much soul-searching, she determined she was not to blame. When she had resolved the inconceivable hurt, she emerged free and untouchable from any further domination he might attempt to impose on her. She reasoned this would have to be his penance. To ransom his reputation and their marriage, she would regulate and define the future. She had been and would continue to be his devoted wife, committed to their marriage vow: "in sickness and in health."

Paradoxically, she believed Thomas' only redeeming quality was the kinship he had developed with her beloved Jamie. Even though she thought he overdid the catechism, she believed Thomas had developed a genuine affection for him. At times, Thomas had been tender and kind especially when he had helped Jamie with his homework. His caring attention to the fatherless boy was his deliverance from her total reprehension of him.

After Thomas was hospitalized, she began to realize that the demanding reins of those she served, completely harnessed her world. From her childhood home, she had moved to a life with Thomas. Restrained as a child by strict parents, dominance by Thomas had seemed natural because she had been accustomed to being submissive. His rule was camouflaged by the affection he genuinely felt and often expressed. Rebellion was never considered. The birth of her twins had been her deliverance. In retrospect, Thomas had spent little time fathering them. Although he appeared to love them and spent time playing with them when they were well behaved, she had been able to nurture them without much interference from him. As long as they were quiet at the appropriate times, he was satisfied to let her raise them.

Although there were moments of fleeting rebellion, she chose to be thankful for the life she had. She was a good minister's wife. Her home was always hospitable. She spent much of her time tending needy parishioners. Warm meals and a shoulder to cry on, were only a few of the comforts she constantly, cheerfully offered without any resentment.

Her own needs were seldom considered and always the last to be met.

After Thomas was disabled, she initially found it difficult to make decisions; often she sought the council of the elders of the church. Little by little, she began to realize she was more than competent to make her own choices, especially when it came to the best interests of her children.

Her beloved Daniel had come home from school and supported the decision to put his father in the new lodge in Strathroyal, until he was well enough to be home. Knowing her son supported her decision, empowered her to stay the course. She was disappointed he had stayed only a few days but understood his need to return to his studies. The joy of seeing him was undiminished by the tragic circumstances. He left promising to return to help her when Thomas was able to come home. It would only be a year until he graduated from medical school and she was optimistic he would then take a position in London.

During the morning worship service, she had meticulously reviewed all the details of the plan. Armed with the courage of an aloof lioness protecting her cubs, she determined they would visit Thomas in London. A brief visit to Lydia would make it a worthwhile outing on this beautiful Sunday.

Although she had her license, she had rarely driven the car. Thomas had not encouraged it. The first trip to London was challenging, but she persisted. She drove to the hospital every other day; the more she drove, the more she enjoyed it. Today she was looking forward to the excursion. Each new venture she attempted made her more confident.

Duty had been her master; now, she resolved love would define her responsibilities.

23
The Picture

Constance had decided they must try to visit Lydia again. She had heard John had given up visiting his wife. The poor woman had no one. Apparently, Lydia was still in a comatose state but was, in general, much calmer. She felt confident that a short visit would be a kind act of charity. During the drive to London, she talked to the children about their aunt's state of mind.

"Do we have to go and see her?" Jamie quizzed. Many times, he had wished she had died instead of his mother.

"We have to try harder this time not be frightened. Aunt Lydia is very sick, but she still needs us," she informed Jamie. As she looked in the rear view mirror, she could see his apprehension as she talked about her plans for the day.

Martha held his hand and squeezed it tenderly. "It's going to be good to see Aunt Lydia and Rev. Sluis," she said graciously. "And remember Jamie, we can ride up in the elevator."

Jamie was silent, thinking about the day ahead. Going to see Aunt Lydia scared him. She was so odd. Because life was much less stressful without the trauma of the catechism lessons, he didn't miss the minister at all. His stomach felt like it was doing summersaults. He wasn't sure why. He told himself it was probably the excitement. He loved the elevator ride.

Martha noticed the change in his demeanor immediately. It disturbed her. She understood his lack of interest but was disappointed he wasn't making more effort to be appreciative of Mrs. Sluis' thoughtfulness. His apparent selfishness reminded her he was still a little boy.

They entered the psychiatric hospital in silence. Jamie's delight about riding in the elevator withered when he noticed the locked doors and strange people staring at them. Some, tied to their chairs, pointed and appeared to sneer as they walked by. The unknown atmosphere upset him but there was nowhere to go. He felt Constance and Martha's hold tighten on his hand. Each stepped in tune to memories and feelings too intimate to voice. After a flight of stairs, the anticipated elevator ride and another secured door, they entered Lydia's room.

She was sitting upright, slumped over, supported by a number of pillows. Constance immediately set about straightening the bed sheets and propping her up. She prattled to her about the unusually beautiful autumn weather. There was no apparent response.

Jamie sat down on a chair close to the door. He looked

intently at his aunt. "What's the matter with her?" he whispered. "Why doesn't she talk to us? Can she hear us?"

"She's still sick, Jamie – her body is here, but she's far away right now," Martha explained patiently.

"Like being dead?"

"No, silly, not dead, just not really here." It was hard to explain something she didn't understand.

He nodded, trying to make sense of it. He sat and looked thoughtfully at her. How could she have her eyes open and not hear or see them? Recollections of the stern unhappy person enveloped him. The sweet songs Mama had sung to him were the same lullabies he had heard her sing to Aunt Lydia. Now all that remained of the comforting songs were faint strains that repeated themselves in delicate whisperings of remembrance. After her death, Maratha had tried to console him and Aunt Lydia in the same way. At times, he had resented sharing his Mama's songs, believing that somehow they belonged entirely to him. When he saw something of himself in her, he regretted the envy.

Although the remembrances of those days were becoming more and more clouded, he clearly recognized the feelings of isolation. Sitting in the apple tree, he had grappled with understanding his seclusion. When feelings of loneliness and sadness enclosed him, he was able to retreat to that sheltered secure place. First, it had been the tree but now he was able to find the breathing space in himself. As he studied his aunt, he wondered where she was hiding. Was she doing the same thing he had done so often?

Then he understood. This was not the same person who had terrified and intimidated him. This someone would not, could not, judge or reject him. Empathetic tears welled in his eyes. The woman who sat lifelessly in front of him confiscated the last innocence of his youth. Without explanation, he saw and understood what his mother had known and what she had done. Inexplicably, he knew it was now his turn. Immediately his mother's smile became his.

Without ceremony or celebration, he savored his coming of age. He breathed deeply and allowed his mother's mantle of wisdom to settle on his young shoulders. The weight of it left him breathless for a moment. It was heavy and somewhat cumbersome but it took only a moment to conform to his slender frame. His mind was too young to understand, but his soul knew what had taken place. She had been Moses. Now, he was Aaron. All vestiges of childhood must now be left behind.

Constance's hushed voice brought him back to the room.

"Why don't you tell Aunt Lydia about how well you are doing in school, Jamie?" she suggested. "Maybe she can hear you. Come, stand next to her and tell her about your last spelling test."

Spelling was not something Jamie could get very excited about even though he was very pleased with the nine out of ten that he had received on his last test.

"This week I got the word 'believe' wrong," he started obediently, "I always forget *the i before e rule*."

That was all he had to say about school. It seemed pointless to chatter on about the teacher or his friends. Why would it matter to her? Yet, he sensed more was expected. He stood up, moved in front of her, looked into her eyes and followed their blank stare to the picture on the wall. The tranquil beach scene intrigued him. It looked peculiarly familiar.

"Are you on the beach, Aunt Lydia? I went to the beach once this summer. It was nice. The sky was so blue. There were birds and the sand felt really soft and warm on my feet. I liked the water best when we played and jumped in the waves. Martha helped me make a great big sand castle, didn't you Martha?" As he spoke, he moved closer and gently took her hand.

Constance and Martha stood in stunned silence. Considering their last visit, they were amazed Jamie was making such an effort. Martha could only smile and nod. Why is he talking about the beach, she wondered. She listened as he described the afternoon they had spent at Lake Huron. At the time, he hadn't seemed to enjoy it that much, but listening to him now, she realized this light-hearted child was one she had not seen since before her mother's death.

Similar thoughts were going through Constance's mind. The pensive, restrained child had abruptly been transformed into an individual she didn't recognize. She marveled at the caring tone in his voice and the ease with which he spoke. It occurred to her that he was talking to Lydia instead of at her. She could see Lydia detected it as well. She's in there somewhere, Constance realized and she hears him. She wondered if Jamie knew what he was doing.

Lydia *was* affected. Somewhere in the distance, far, far away, she recognized her name. Someone she knew was talking to her. At first it was a faint echo, perhaps a bird singing somewhere in past times, she mused. The sound was lovely and sweet, one she thought she had forgotten. It had been a long time since she had ventured to the door. After the repeated rapture of the drugs took effect, the exertion had not seemed worth the effort needed to navigate her soundless world. She had become accustomed, even content, to let sleep carry her effortlessly in and out of consciousness to the silent shadows where she was immune to feeling. There she entered memory, alone. Desperate to find solace for her imprisoned self, she wandered through the badlands of the past. She found no peace, only remorse for knots tied too tightly to be loosened. When Jamie spoke, a glimmer of light was unpredictably exposed. Was it possible that the door, whose entrance held her in the past, could still be unlocked? Was there a future beyond this empty meaningless place in which she merely existed?

Gradually, she recalled a key. She felt for it, unaware she had dropped it. For the first time a sense of terror washed over her; without a key, there was no option but to remain in her god-forsaken abyss. She would die and live forever in the murky underworld that had become her life. The door must be unlocked for the threshold to be crossed. It occurred to her to panic, but some distant remembrance stilled the apprehension. Waves soundlessly lapping the shore soothed her crushed character. As the fog of narcotics slightly loosened its grip, she could feel the cool solace of the water. She had always loved the seashore, felt the peace and security its timelessness offered to anyone who would reach out a hand to accept it. As the water washed over her darkened spirit, her hand moved to grasp the key. The touch of Jamie's hand and his caring words connected to a distant time and place. It linked to him. This was Esther's child; the child she wanted to love but had unwillingly estranged. Surely this was Esther incarnated. She felt suffocated by guilt. It astounded her. If only she could go back. If only, there was another chance. She looked and saw the authenticity in the picture for the first time; inexplicably she heard Esther's reassuring voice speaking her name. When she saw Esther's eyes in the child, her tears spilled silently.

"Forgive me, Esther," she moaned.

The unperceived sounds were the first meaningful utterances since her committal.

"She squeezed my hand, Aunt Constance," Jamie stated meekly.

Constance nodded and smiled; there seemed no need to disillusion him. The doctor had made it clear that only a miracle could bring Lydia back. She would, no doubt, live out her life in the seemingly, self-imposed semi-comatose state. The staff had attempted every remedy known to modern medicine. She had been medicated, prodded and poked. Even the electric shock therapy, successful for others in her deprived state, had been futile. The physician had comforted the family with a distant hope that there might be new drugs, which might succeed in the future. Although he didn't believe it, he thought it cruel to leave the family without at least a little optimism. He was pleased that she was passive. The medication seemed to alleviate her agitation. For now, it was the best they could hope for.

Lydia's eyes focused on the picture for a brief moment. Why hadn't she notice it before? Although she couldn't decipher or hear Jamie's exact words, her mind connected to the place. In an attempt to shake off the lethargy, she tightened her grip on Jamie's hand. Then without warning, her body began to tremble uncontrollably. Although he was surprised and suddenly silent, Jamie remained composed during the outburst and did not attempt to move away or withdraw his hand from hers. Constance immediately went to call a nurse. Martha sensing the urgency, tried to hurry Jamie out of the room, but he stubbornly and unexpectedly refused to let go of Lydia's hand.

A nurse in a starched white uniform, quickly and efficiently, injected a fluid in her arm. As Lydia relaxed her grip on Jamie and began the retreat back to the darkness that had momentarily loosened its hold, she heard Esther's voice. "Come back to us," she whispered, before the waves of drugged euphoria unwillingly engulfed her.

"There, there Lydia," the nurse prattled, "there's no need to be upset. You just have a good little sleep and you'll soon feel better."

It was the first time in several months Lydia did not want to retreat to the dark place that held her captive. As the haze began to settle in around her, she grasped the key, determined not to let it go again. Only then did she release her hold on Jamie's hand. It was enough for now; she could rest for the arduous journey that lay ahead.

Jamie silently watched the incident unfold. His remembered encounters with Lydia were of a stern, unapproachable person whom he had feared. Today, there was something about her he recognized. He would never know his clandestine forgiveness was the catalyst, the miracle, which would eventually unlock the emptiness that held her hostage. He didn't believe what Constance and Martha had said. Intuitively he knew she had heard him. More importantly, he heard her unspoken prayer for release and was innocently able to give her back the key, the means to escape.

In a strange and complex way, Lydia had also touched a part of him asleep since his mother's death. She had listened and understood him. Unlike the others that had been lovingly overprotective, he recognized part of himself in her. There would never be words to describe what had happened. The moment was too intimate to share or even understand. Because his fragile, numb emotions had been paralyzed for so long, he didn't discern the freedom of being able to practice absolute kindness. Now he knew and tasted the quiet peace it offered. He savored its mysterious sweetness. Somehow, in the inexplicable moment, he was able to distinguish and acknowledge his mother and she had reconnected to his alienated self. It was enough to set him free.

As Constance and Martha led him from the room, he stopped and turned to smile sweetly at Lydia. Martha and Constance tautly held his hands. They pulled him in silence from the surreal scenario. Each caught in thought, tried to grasp the relevance of what had happened in the room. The person who lay staring into space was not the Lydia they remembered. Had she really responded to Jamie? Constance understood that in an extraordinary way it was a defining moment. Jamie's manner had abruptly reminded them of Esther. Was it possible that she had actually been in the room? What was it his mother's strength that had transformed the boy into an angel of mercy?

Thoughts of her mother flooded Martha's awareness, consumed her, bringing unexpected tears to her eyes. It was as if she had been there. She felt flustered and fought back the desire to cry out for her. Something important had happened there. It filled her with emotions she was unable to discern or grasp. For a moment, she turned and looked back at Lydia and then she looked into the mystical picture. She longed to talk to her mother. Jamie smiled thoughtfully at his sister and squeezed her hand as they left the room.

24
Eruptions

They drove wordlessly to Victoria General Hospital. Constance's main purpose for going to the city had been to see Thomas. The visit to Lydia had been an add-on. Although it had been very strange to see Lydia in such a depressed state, it had gone better than she expected. She regretted that they had upset her but was relieved that the children, especially Jamie, had handled it so well. She was relieved it was over. She understood why Dr. Smit had recommended she not take the children, especially Jamie, to the psychiatric hospital. She had dismissed his advice, because she believed the visit would help Lydia. It was obvious she hadn't realized the degree and intensity of Lydia's condition. Surely, there could be nothing worse than her depraved existence. She didn't understand what had happened with

Jamie, but she did know in some incredible way he had he had been able to make contact with Lydia.

Constance was confident that the visit to Thomas would be much easier than the peculiar exchange with Lydia. She was certainly grateful his illness was physical and not mental. At least, there was hope he could recuperate enough to come home. She was convinced seeing the children would do him good. When Daniel was home, he had suggested having them with her would make it easier to talk to him about the future. She put the episode with Lydia behind her and focused on her meeting with her husband.

Although the stroke had left his right side almost completely paralyzed, the doctor said Thomas was making progress. He had great difficulty swallowing even very soft foods and his speech was blurred and garbled. The frustration of being dependant on others was very apparent to anyone who saw him. Constance believed seeing the children, especially Jamie, would lift his spirits. She had deliberated that it would be a good time to present her plans for their future.

Constance tried talking to Martha about the visit with Lydia, but she could see the child had thoughts she was not able or willing to share. We'll talk later she told herself. Jamie sat alone in the back seat of the car subdued and silent. The encounter with his aunt had left him pensive and introspective. Somehow, he knew he was different. Although his young mind was disoriented and confused about the events, there was an unfamiliar serenity and sense of pride. Thoughts of his mother overflowed within him.

Her presence had been real and reassuring; he knew her voice had said, "I'm so proud of you, Jamie." The occurrence left him exhausted and he curled up and nodded off to sleep.

Martha's voice from the front seat was unusually sharp and brought him abruptly back to the present, "Wake up, Jamie, we're here."

Startled, he hastily sat up. The autumn day had changed. A sudden storm had come up. Water gushed from the sky, a substitute for the tears he would not allow himself to shed. Hurriedly, he followed his protectors through the puddles to the front entrance. He didn't want to see the minister, especially after the singular experience in the mental hospital. He shivered.

Martha noticed and folded her arms around him, "It's OK, Jamie, we'll be inside in a minute," she reassured him.

Jamie didn't want to go inside. He wanted to run to free himself from the ice that seemed to be forming around his heart. He wanted to embrace the paradoxical tranquility that had wrapped itself around him during the visit with Lydia. He groped for air as they entered the large ominous front doors of the hospital. His spirit, which had felt so liberated only a short time ago, now felt confined and chaotic.

"We can ride the elevator to the fourth floor, Jamie," Constance said as she took his hand, "that will be fun won't it? Have you ever been in an elevator three times in one day?"

Jamie didn't answer. Instead, he pulled back as she pushed him toward the door.

"Fourth floor, please," Constance spoke politely to the lift operator.

She felt Jamie's resistance and wondered why he was frightened of the elevator when he had been so excited by it just a short time ago. They rode up in silence, looking up at the numbers creeping by above the doors.

"Here we are," quipped the operator as she pulled open the sliding doors. "Watch your step."

Martha also felt the tense hesitation in Jamie's stride. The strange change in his conduct confused her.

"Jamie," she said somewhat impatiently, "hurry up."

He didn't look up, didn't hear her words. The antiseptic smell coupled with his fear, had suddenly made him nauseated. He swallowed hard to rid himself of the sour, bitter taste in the back of his throat.

Constance entered the room first. She kissed her husband and spoke softly to him as she fussed with his bedclothes.

"Look who's come to visit you dear," she spoke in a superficially cheerful voice.

"You look well, Pastor Thomas," Martha lied politely.

Jamie froze. He hardly recognized this man. He looks awful, he thought. His face was distorted and there was slobber sliding from the side of his mouth. Bottles hung connected to his arm.

Their eyes met and immediately glued to each other. Neither could speak. The man knew what he had done. The disoriented boy knew only that he felt sick.

"Jamie, tell pastor about school and the beach just as you did with Aunt Lydia," Constance encouraged him.

Jamie was afraid to open his mouth, fearing what might come out of it. He stiffened as Martha almost dragged him to Thomas' bedside. He knew disobeying was not an option so he stepped obediently toward the bed, trying not to breathe the repugnant stench that filled his nostrils. As he opened his mouth to greet the depraved remnant of the man who had stolen his childhood, he could not control his somersaulting stomach. The vile liquid that had been lurking at the back of his throat burst out like a primal scream. It spewed forth like the lava of an erupting volcano that had been stored in the core of his being since his first intimate encounter with Thomas. Jamie had no knowledge or control of what happened. As Thomas tried desperately to extend his hand to the child, his neat bedclothes and his upper torso were covered with putrid vomit that exploded from the victimized child.

Thomas was the only person in the room who fully understood what had happened. Long ago, he had been Jamie. His childhood suffering at the hands of his uncle had been his motive for becoming a minister. He thought he could make it stop.

When Thomas turned fourteen, somehow he found the courage to say to the uncle, "Go to hell!"

The satisfaction of saying it filled him with an audacious awareness. Sending his abuser to hell gave him a wonderful sense of power. He saw the effect on the man, who backed away from him in an uncharacteristic compliant manner. The statement, at the same time, released him from the physical bondage of the fiend and began his fascination with the authority of words.

When he went to university and studied philosophy, he became convinced his vocation was to endorse good and expose immorality. Rhetoric would be his weapon. He became a minister who righteously moralized to depraved sinners. His childhood suffering would empower him to make the world a better place. He believed it absolutely.

When he went to war, it cruelly distorted his beliefs.

The Journey Home

The beauty of language didn't matter much when the racket of exploding bombs was drowning it out. Moreover, he realized and reluctantly gave in to a dreadful awareness that the cycle, established in his youth, still shackled his existence and threatened his survival.

The sin brought an ambiguous comfort in the callous shadows of the battlefield; giving in to it sent him to a deep sinister hole. He blamed no one but himself and carried the shame home in his suitcase. He struggled, wanting desperately to confide in Constance. Unable to find the words that might salvage his marriage, regret spun itself around him, creating a cocoon that detained him in a halfway house of dejection.

When he saw Jamie enter the room, for a moment, he thought redemption might be possible. If the child could forgive him, he might be spared an eternity of suffering. When Jamie resisted coming near him, he knew. He tried reaching out his hand, in an effort to ask for forgiveness, although he had already determined his deeds were unforgivable. He took complete responsibility. He should never have assumed Jamie would understand, much less absolve. As he sucked the torrid stench of the vomit into his nostrils, he implored God it would be enough to rid the child of the pain he had imposed. He wholly understood what he had done. He recognized the cross he had created for the child to bear. It was identical to the one he dragged through his depraved, broken life.

A sudden pain seared through his head. Blackness swallowed him. He knew his life was over. He submissively accepted God's punishment for his sins, believing he would spend eternity in the scorching fire of hell. He remembered again all of his fire and brimstone sermons. The God he had attempted to serve would refuse to forgive the atrocities of his holocaust.

As the lights went dark, he prayed, "Mary, Mother of God pray for me."

He was curiously cognizant of what he was saying and would often wonder why it was to the mother of God that he reached out in that ominous moment.

They carried Jamie, still heaving uncontrollably, to another room. Gentle hands bathed his limp body. When an injection did its work, the crude eruption was tamed and he drifted into a restless sleep. Constance and Martha cried, trying to understand and cope with the scenario they had witnessed. Defeated by the day's unusual events, they clung to each other for comfort.

The doctors who examined Thomas confirmed he had almost certainly suffered another stoke. Another blood clot had bombarded his brain. He was not optimistic about Thomas' prospects. He might not awake until the following day or he might not awake at all. It was too soon to tell. Although he was willing to keep Jamie in the hospital, the doctor thought it wiser to take him home.

"Prepare yourself for the worst. Call your children home," he advised her.

After Jamie's strange seizure, Constance was aware there could be no discussion with Thomas. This second stoke would certainly make any possibility of going home inconceivable. The doctor was quick to tell Constance any hope of recovery now appeared to be gone. If he lived, he would no doubt be an invalid who would need constant care. It shocked Constance when the doctor implied his demise might be better than his life. Never! She would never acknowledge that verdict. Regardless of what he had done, she wanted him to live.

Although Constance was wholly distraught when she heard the news, she was relieved and surprisingly disappointed. She had wanted to look into his eyes and confront him. A part of her wanted to hear his confession about the things she had found in his desk. Now she knew there would be no questioning; there would be no answers. Constance seldom gave in to self-indulgent feelings. Her tears fell silently but they couldn't wash away the apprehension shrouding her spirit. It left her breathless and drained. Could it be that everything her life had been staged? Had the curtain fallen? Was the play was over? It seemed grossly unfair. She had always abided by the rules, had done everything that was expected and more. Surely, her life was meant to be more than just an unpleasant drama.

As they drove home, a strained silence was crammed in the vehicle. It held each person confined in a taut, sad package of disarray and despair. In the back seat, Martha sat placidly with Jamie asleep on her lap. Constance drove hypnotically to the place that had been her home. She struggled to shake off the day's disillusions and forced herself to focus on the two poignant people sitting behind her. Gradually her love for them made it possible for a new kernel of positive resolve to plant itself within the hopelessness of the moment.

When they arrived, Martha scooped up Jamie, carried him to his bedroom and tenderly tucked him into bed. Constance walked about the house. Like a robot, she locked it up. It was the first time in her life she left a cup sitting on the table. She disliked clutter; she always cleaned up. Tonight it was moot. Like so many things now, it seemed inconsequential. She went to check on the children, the only thing that genuinely mattered.

25
The Music Box

The strains of music that were barely audible met Constance on her way up the stairs. She froze. Was it possible? The muffled resonance of the sound roused and then revived a deep memory. She was a child again.

The box sat on the night table. It was warm, brown mahogany, darkened with age. The top was inlaid with gold aluminous mother of pearl stars. The tune was lyrical and sweet, embedded in the alcove of her first memory. Every night it played its meditative song for the old woman who lay in the bed, waiting to die. When she motioned to it at the end of the day, Constance knew it was time to wind up the box and open the lid. The melody was the sedative that lulled the woman to sleep.

Although the doctor said there was no physical reason for her illness, she seldom left her bed, complaining of phantom pain that would not allow her to walk even the shortest distance. There was an old cumbersome commode next to the bed. The room smelled stale. The odor of urine and unwashed hair hung like a thick, obscure fog in the air. At times Constance felt she could see it drifting about the room; at times, she felt she could touch it and taste it.

Before school and after supper, it was Constance's responsibility to sit with her grandmother. She scratched her nose, rubbed her back, helped her to the commode but mostly she listened to the blabber of the old woman who lay wanting and waiting to die. She blathered on about the hardships of her life, seldom having a positive word to say. It seemed she had never experienced any authentic happiness. She bemoaned the fact that her husband had left her a widow, that her children never visited and her grandchildren were spoiled and ungrateful for their affluent, comfortable lives. In a curious way, Constance felt drawn to her. She related to the isolation and loneliness of the old woman. The barrenness in her character spoke to her about her own apparent insignificance.

When she talked, Constance listened and nodded the anticipated agreement. Most of what the old woman said made little sense. Yet at a very young age, she knew what her grandmother expected from her. She sat and listened, providing a respite for the family who was waiting for the matriarch to take her last breath. Finally, an angel of mercy silently came during a harsh winter night and carried her to a better place.

When Constance arrived for her morning vigil, the woman's eyes stared vacantly at her. Instinctively, she held her hand and felt the coldness that had already settled on the flesh of the corpse. Then Constance stood and with a knowledge and wisdom beyond her ten years, she gently closed her eyes, kissed her cheek and bid her farewell. It was her first experience with the uncluttered finality of death.

Rid of the troublesome woman who burdened their lives, the family felt only relief. Constance mourned her passing. Her bedside send-off was her only farewell. They told her she was too young to attend the funeral. Before she left the room that day, she closed the music box and held it to her breast. She saw no need to ask permission because she was the only one who would even come close to missing the cantankerous old woman. She concealed it amateurishly in her dresser drawer. She remembered her grandmother on lonely nights when she held the unique box. She prayed all was well with her soul. For reasons she didn't understand, she dared not open it to play the familiar song. Perhaps, she reasoned, there was some demonic power that might be released if she enjoyed the pilfered treasure.

When Martha entered her life, she inherently knew the long-ago confiscated music box was to be hers. Constance had imagined she would pass it to her daughter. That might have happened if Emily had not left for faraway places. Although she had given her daughter unconditional love, they had never been close. It was to her father she went for comfort and understanding. Even though he was often distant with her, only he could dry her tears and make her laugh. Always there was an untouchable distance between them so there had never been a right moment to bequeath her daughter the small box, which enfolded so much of her past and so much of herself.

Martha's arrival had awakened her deep seeded need

to mother children. She knew immediately that this child was the only person worthy of the unique object that held so much of her lonely childhood. The memories would not encumber Martha. Perhaps it would give her the serenity it had offered her dying grandmother. Maybe it would restore some peace. There was no doubt that in her short dejected existence, life had cheated her. She grasped that underneath Martha's reserved endearing facade there was a forlorn, anxious child – a little girl forced to leave behind childhood for grownup responsibilities.

When she accidently noticed the children's baptismal records on Thomas' desk, it appeared to be a providential omen. Martha would arrive shortly after her birthday. It occurred to Constance that the music box would be the perfect gift for the orphaned girl who probably owned very few special things. Constance had lovingly wrapped the box in pretty tissue paper before the children arrived. When the present remained unopened, Constance speculated it was a curse instead of a blessing to the child. Why would Martha not acknowledge the gift? Had she been right all along? Did the box hold the bane of the old woman's life? Or was it perhaps tainted because it had been pilfered? Constance had dismissed the aggravation of trying to understand. It was an enigma, like the life of her grandmother.

When they arrived back from their visit with Thomas, Martha got Jamie ready for bed. He didn't waken as she put on his pajamas and lovingly tucked him in. It was easy to forgive him for his inexplicable behavior during their visit to Lydia. She couldn't remain angry with him for any reason and she reprimanded herself for doing so. Most of the day's events were beyond her ability to understand. He was so much younger; he must be even more perplexed than she was. He was still such an innocent little boy. She kissed him and promised him she would spend time tomorrow doing the things he liked.

She heard Constance fusing about in the kitchen and went down to bid her goodnight.

"Don't worry, Martha. Everything's going to be just fine," Constance tried to reassure her.

Martha heard the unusual heaviness in her voice. She hugged her and nodded in agreement.

"Mama said things always look better in the morning," she commented, trying hard to sound cheerfully optimistic.

"Yes, yes they do. Now go on up to bed, you must be exhausted," Constance smiled, thankful for the endearing support of this precious child.

Martha crept up the stairs wanting to believe her mother's words. She *was* tired, more tired than she had ever felt. There was unfinished homework she should do. Usually she spent time reading before going to sleep, but tonight all she wanted to do was to crawl under the covers and forget this awful day. Loneliness clung to her. The misplaced child longed to be held and rocked to sleep.

She had altruistically chosen not to cultivate friendships because there was always the self-imposed obligation to tend to Jamie's needs. Constance had tried repeatedly to encourage her to invite girls from school to visit. There had been a few visits from classmates, but she had still resisted the temptation to develop close friendships. It was easier to be alone than risk further rejection or loss. Moreover, she wanted to be there for Jamie. She deluded herself into believing he was all she needed to be home. The weight of the responsibility cheated her and embezzled her adolescence. Her spirit was too aged and weary for the young body that held it.

As she was about to turn out the light in her room, her eyes rested on the unopened birthday gift. Why haven't I opened it, she wondered. She picked it up as she had done so many times and held it lightly in her lap, admiring the beauty of the package. This day instead of putting it back on the dresser, she took the present Constance had adoringly wrapped, untied the ribbon and carefully examined it. She felt the warm wood, traced her fingers over the intricate design of the mother of pearl inlay and savored its chaste beauty. When she finally opened the box, the sweet melodious refrain of "Amazing Grace" greeted her tired heart. It was the most beautiful thing she had ever heard. Several times, she carefully rewound it, all the while holding it and letting the melody soothe her weary self. Her mother held her and rocked her to sleep; she heard her singing the sweet beautiful song as only she could do.

After she had checked on Jamie and softly kissed him goodnight, Constance stood outside Martha's door, ready to knock. This time she was certain. She recognized the familiar refrain. Although it had been many years since she had last heard it, the melody was etched in the deepest recesses of her heart. She knew it. Martha had finally released the treasure inside the music box. She eavesdropped at the door, surprised and pleased. Finally, she tiptoed to her room. Exhaustion folded its arms around her and transported her to another place and time. She slept. It was grace. It was amazing.

She was a child again, alone and anxiously standing on the sideline, watching a feuding family decide who would receive the matriarch's effects. She was altogether confused. The family members who had scorned her most were the ones who lamented her the loudest. Their negligence had held her Nana ransomed, alone in her room. The old woman had little of value, but like soldiers at the foot of the cross, they squabbled over her meager legacy. They ripped each other apart with words of greedy accusations, bickering over the valueless, earthly remnants of the old woman's life.

As she listened, Constance realized her music box was the most pressing matter. Who had taken it they questioned? Each suspected the other. Had anyone asked her, she would have confessed to the theft. Like the old woman, she was not considered significant. She voicelessly retreated to her room and wrapped the box in paper torn from a notebook. Then she tucked it inside the shoebox underneath her life's treasures. There were dried pressed flowers, report cards, a birthday note from a kind teacher, her tattered old teddy and other assorted, irreplaceable bits of her life. Her young imagination had labeled the box, "Bury me with these."

When she married Thomas, she hid the container in the closet knowing he would find it trivial and misconstrue its relevance. For years she left it behind, opening it only occasionally on special days to hold and touch the lingering memoirs of her life. She caressed each item, reliving the intimacy of it, making sure all the essential details were intact.

When Martha entered her life, she took the shoebox from its secret place in her closet. Carefully she stroked the items to appreciate each one. She fingered the music box and let the sentiments wash over her. She felt no distress, only a strange nostalgia. The tattered bear, who knew all her childhood secrets and fears, had aged. She hugged him as she had done so many times over the years. He commiserated with her, took all of her anger and frustration and tucked them away in his inner storehouse of youthful narratives. She cradled him, finding comfort in the innocence of childish aspirations, allowing herself the rare decadent extravagance of self-indulgence. How was it possible? Her entire childhood sat stuffed and crowded in this tattered shoebox.

Constance promised herself that someday she would divulge the intimate particulars of the music box to Martha. She would understand. She would be the daughter Emily was not able to be. Martha's joy was copious compensation for the lonesome time spent with the old woman. She believed her grandmother would delight in the knowledge that the music box had a home.

Martha lay in her bed clutching the melody of the box to her heart. Its gentle sound calmed her and lulled her to the release of sleep. She dreamt she was a child. It was Christmastime again. The sound of her father's voice telling the story of the Baby Jesus blended with her mother's clear sweet voice singing, "Away in a Manger." There was a tree with flickering candles. She saw her mother's tears and her father's uniform. She put on his cap and saluted him.

He gently kissed the palm of her hand, folded it closed and pressed it to her heart, "My sweet pretty one, I love you now and always." She hadn't seen the tears in his eyes.

Although the memory was murky and dimmed by time, once again, she knew why she always slept with her hand on her heart. The music box finally stopped playing.

In the silence, sleep tiptoed into the rooms of the big house and carried away the heaviness of the day. A new tranquility embraced the dwelling.

26

The Sound of Silence

After Thomas' second stoke, he died, but continued to survive in a completely helpless state. As soon as the doctors agreed that he was well enough to travel, Constance had him transferred and confined to the new nursing home in Strathroyal.

At first, Thomas received regular visitors from his congregation. They read scripture; others sat and criticized the flawed new minister who appeared to condone the modern beliefs and fads of post-war Canada. Still others, bothered by his voiceless existence, prattled on about politics and other news items, completely irrelevant to him. Their tone was condescending and distant. He listened to it all, but heard none of it. He resented their patronizing manner. He tried to speak, tried to convey his thoughts but it left him exhausted and entirely defeated. Communication became near impossible. Without words, he was impotent. Even the most sympathetic of his flock found it tedious to maintain any pretense of compassion. Eventually they deserted their helpless shepherd, moving wordlessly to graze in greener pastures.

Thomas eventually decided that the only two things left were the best and worst elements of his life. The only good thing was Constance. She cared for him in ways he didn't deserve. Every day after her work in the kitchen was finished, she came; she bathed him; she changed his diaper and gently rubbed his limp limbs. Although he felt her love, she never made eye contact with him. He tried to tell her not to come. Tried to explain the indignity he felt as she looked after him, rationalizing he wasn't worthy of the kindness she lavished on him. Although her visits were the only thing of value in his life, he felt disquieted and belittled by her care. He truly wanted to be grateful. Sadly, both his hands and his heart were incapable of telling her what he felt and wanted her to know.

The worst of his life came during the night. When he tried to sleep, when the room was dark and quiet, the boxes of memory stuffed and stored in the attic of his mind opened enigmatically. The concealed events of his youth stepped out, crept down the stairway, then chanted and danced around his bed. Sometimes during the most sinister times, when he felt very courageous and dared to look at them, they slinked away. Usually when the shadows of the night diminished to the dawn, they withdrew to their containers. It made him crazy. It made sleep inaccessible.

Although the nursing home claimed to be the most modern of facilities, in reality, it gave the inmates the most meager leftovers of human dignity. When the doors closed to visitors, those inside the walls were often tied down, bound hand and foot to chairs that didn't move. Malicious drugs quickly silenced those well enough to protest. Like a poisonous snakebite, it left them paralyzed. They were diapered morning, noon and night. Heavy disinfectants only temporally foiled the stench of human excrement. Every morning the staff lifted Thomas to his chair where he sat unattended for most of the day. Before his wife came for her daily visit, they washed his face, changed his bib and propped him up on the pillows. They knew Constance would change his diaper and were happy to let her do it. Although the facility was new, the methods were time-honored.

Thoughtfully, Constance brought him a radio to break the monotony of his days. She set the station to the one she knew he listened to in the car. She thought he'd like to know what was going on in the world. He tried to smile to show his appreciation. He hoped it would tune out the voices in the shadows. Every day she turned it on. Every day as soon as she left, it was quickly turned off – a waste of electricity for a paralyzed creature who couldn't appreciate the extravagance.

No one seemed to recognize or care that his mind was very aware of the happenings of his austere world. To most of them, he was just another inconsequential patient, blessed to have at least one visitor a day. Unseen, unknown to them was a prisoner locked in an obscure chamber of remorse. Day in and day out, he sat listening to the sound of footsteps in the hall, listening to the rain falling against the window, listening to the cries of the helpless individuals who had lost all remnants of humanity and self-esteem. He sat watching the waif, who shared his room. The odds and ends of a soul lost in loneliness. Constance stopped and spoke to him every day. Her genuine kindness humbled him. Occasionally the new minister, Rev. Collins came. The repertoire of comments was always the same.

"Hello Thomas. Everyone sends greetings," was the first remark.

There were uninspiring news updates about parishioners. The questions, to which he could give no answers, disturbed him the most.

"Are you being treated well? How's the food? Aren't you glad Constance is working here in the kitchen? I'm sure she saves the best food for you." His attempt at humor was wasted on Thomas.

Unable to answer, Thomas would close his eyes.

This was the reverend's prompt to say, "Well, I can see that you're tired. I'll be on my way."

"Is there anything you need, Reverend?" was always the last question at the end of the short visit.

If he had been able, Thomas would have told him precisely what he needed. Since that wasn't an option, he tried to shake his head.

After a speedy prayer for healing, he would take his leave. "Good, well don't go anywhere." Always the same joke, the same laugh, the same quick exit.

When the minister left, Thomas was both relieved and agitated. He remembered his former life, ministering in comparable ways. He prayed ceaselessly for forgiveness and for one brief opportunity to make amends, especially to Jamie, even though he discerned it would never happen. He accepted that the children would never visit again.

He retrieved the good times only occasionally. The wretchedness of his deeds like a night stalker, refused to let him rest. The few times he was able to filter out all the dissonance of his environment, when there was nothing else, all the Sunday sermons he had ever preached replayed themselves in mournful memory. He heard every word and saw every person who had heeded those words. There was no stopping it. If he was able to sleep, he awoke and heard more. Unlike the silent radio, there was no switch to turn it off, no dial to change the station. He named it purgatory, a lifeless limbo that would not let him go. Surely, he thought, hell could not be worse than this existence.

In a pathetic attempt to die, he refused to swallow the daily concoction of semi liquid slop they spoon-fed him. Then to his dismay, they put a needle in his arm. Sustenance, so he would live. Constance didn't think to question the wisdom of it.

Only Constance seemed to interpret his deepest despair. On their anniversary, she sat with him and for the first time looked deep into his eyes. He saw the woman he had married. What had happened to their love? He knew the answer. Suddenly it was all very clear to him. Desperately, he tried to verbalize his remorse, but the words wouldn't come. Only slobber dribbled from the side of his mouth. She wiped it away. Again, he tried desperately to speak.

She saw his tears. They dripped down his cheeks like raindrops on the window, soundlessly exposing what he was powerless to say. Constance could no longer hold on to the wall of resentment she had built in her heart. She wept with him, washing away the dam of bitterness. They were young lovers again, awkward and shy not knowing what to say.

Every ounce of strength left in his broken body forced his hand to touch hers. She took it and held it affectionately.

"Rest now my love. You are forgiven. You are loved," she whispered.

It was inconceivable; how could she know? How could she possibly forgive? Her love exposed the arrogance of his life. For the first time, he was able to be truly introspective. Like a flash of lightning, the epiphany showed itself. The truth stood naked before him. His heart gave utterance to the words he couldn't speak. He knew it was God, but not the God he had served. He saw no corporal features, only a magnificent radiating love that defied understanding. Then in one mystifying, miraculous moment, rebirth was possible as he recognized the command. It was love; it had never been about retribution. He had been wrong, had seen it all backwards. He saw it, felt it, for the first time he discerned its relevance.

Love – nothing less, nothing else.

Like the rising of the sun, like the first flower of spring, everything could be new again. Like standing in the fresh warm spring rain, humility rinsed off the stench of his arrogant pride. He knew it was much, much more than he deserved.

It was enough; his prayer had been answered. When he closed his eyes, the soothing sound of silence kissed him on the cheek. He knew. He slept.

27

Beans and Toast

When it came time to leave the manse, the deacons said they would help Constance move to the small cottage on North Street. She was grateful Thomas' pension would cover the rent. When Constance and the children went to view it, they walked through the small rooms in silence. There were few chattels and little affluence compared to the large rectory. On the main floor was a small bright kitchen that looked out over an unattended garden; an ornate arch connected it to a dining room. The living room was a good size and had an old fireplace on the outside wall. It had a warm comfortable feeling. From the hallway, two other doors led to a bedroom and a bathroom. There was a sterile clean smell, which reminded Jamie of the hospital.

At the top of a narrow staircase, on the second floor there were two miniature bedrooms. The ceiling sloped so there was little room for an adult to walk upright. Constance thought the rooms were very small and dingy. She would be sure to hang the children's pictures, to make it at least look familiar.

Jamie was the first to comment. "This house will be a lot less work to keep clean. It's not far from our old house so I can still go and play with Marty. Right?" He wouldn't like this new house if it meant losing his friend.

"Yes Jamie, you'll still be able to walk home from school and play with him just like always," Constance smiled. "You're right, Jamie. This house will be a lot less work for all of us." Indeed, it would take much less effort to maintain this home.

That was enough for Jamie. In his life, essentials could not be packed in a box or put on a shelf. The dimensions of his bedroom didn't matter as long as the people he knew and loved were close by.

"I like it. It's small but cozy," Martha stated emphatically. She didn't mention that the upstairs bedroom reminded her of the cryptic, shadowy attic in Uncle John's house.

"We can make it look nice," Jamie proclaimed ardently. He continued by running about excitedly and making suggestions about where to place furniture.

The helpful, conciliatory attitude of the children moved Constance. She didn't mind where they lived, as long as her children were happy. She looked out the window at the garden and frowned; it looked like an unmade bed but she'd remedy that in the spring.

When moving day came, Constance was amazed at the number of people who came to help. Several men moved the large furniture on their trucks. It was obvious not all of her belongings would fit into the cottage. She happily accepted the offer from a gracious parishioner to store some bigger things in his basement. She had thought about this dilemma, but hadn't known what to do. The thoughtfulness of her church community touched her. There had been so many details related to her husband's care, she had given little thought to the practical aspects of moving.

One younger woman who had no children offered to take Jamie off her hands.

"Thank you for your kind offer, Isabelle. The children need to be with me." Aware of the curt tone in her voice she added, "Perhaps you could look after him sometime for me if I need to go out and Martha isn't home."

The woman nodded. She thought she would be doing Constance a favor and had expected more appreciation for her charitable offer.

Rev. Collins asked if he could buy Thomas' office furniture. She was glad to be rid of it and could certainly use the extra money. She also gave him all the theological books; it would save her the trouble of storing them. On impulse, she lied and told him it was Thomas' idea. He was thrilled to take them and didn't ask any questions about how her husband had been able to communicate his wishes. Constance was relieved; it would have been difficult to explain.

The women were genuinely concerned for Constance and returned the goodwill she had bestowed upon them over the years. Her love had come full circle. They cheerfully helped unpack boxes and put things away. They even brought soup and fresh baking for lunch. Although Constance was overwhelmed with appreciation for the kindheartedness of her friends, she had no appetite for soup.

By mid afternoon, the house looked tidy and livable. There were still a few boxes to unpack but they were unimportant and could wait. Martha and Jamie had arranged their own bedrooms and all of their meager belongings were thoughtfully placed in the small spaces. Martha had even made the beds, leaving Constance time to organize the kitchen. The house was quickly beginning to feel settled.

As each person left, Constance warmly kissed and hugged them. It was the first time in her life she had been the recipient of such genuine thoughtfulness. She recognized her pride might have too quickly discounted her friends. Despite the dire circumstances of her life, the day's events now seemed to make everything much more manageable. It was an unanticipated singular keepsake of the day. She tucked the token of love in her shoebox of memory.

Later in the day when they sat at the kitchen table discussing the day, Jamie honestly and innocently commented to Constance, "It was good soup, but it was kind of watery. It wasn't nearly as good as yours."

The women looked at each other and smiled, each for different reasons.

Jamie understood the nuances and added his own devious little smile, "Can we have beans and toast for dinner? Please? Then it will really feel like home!"

Although it was his favorite, he knew neither Constance nor Martha liked this dinner option. He also astutely detected both of them were in an unusually relaxed mood, one in which they were likely to humor him. Constance nodded her head. She was tired. It was an easy meal to prepare. They could unpack some more boxes tomorrow after church.

"You little rascal!" Martha exclaimed, laughing. *He knows exactly what he's doing*, she thought.

Even though he often has a perspective and maturity of a much older child, in so many ways he's still a very naive young boy, thought Constance. She raised an unvoiced prayer that he be spared any more pain in his life. *May he always be able to have beans and toast*, she thought.

"That was delicious!" Jamie wiped the last bean off his chin. He was completely content.

"Well, it's been a long day. What do you think?" Constance asked after they had cleared the table and washed the dishes. "Shall we all go to bed and get a good night's sleep?"

Jamie was quick to respond, "I think it was a great day. Maybe we could remember it by having beans and toast every Saturday."

It had been a long time since Martha and Constance had both laughed so loud and so long.

"What's so funny?" he asked earnestly.

Constance could only say, "We'll see. Now off to bed with you." She wondered how such a small indulgence could provide such enormous pleasure.

Life took on a veneer of normality. Every day Constance went to work in the kitchen at the nursing home. Her competence was evident and it wasn't long until the job of managing the kitchen was hers. It meant she was able to have regular shifts. Barring an emergency, she usually had Saturday and Sunday off. This gave her time to tend to the cottage and spend time with her children. She always found time to visit Thomas, even on the weekends. Occasionally, Martha would ask how he was doing.

"He's fine. I think it's hard for him to be alone," was the usual response. Given Jamie's reaction to him in Victoria Hospital, she had determined it was best they not visit. Clandestinely, she hoped they might ask to see him, especially Jamie, since he and Thomas had seemed close. But she didn't know Jamie was trying to erase all memory of Thomas. Constance was thrilled that Jamie appeared to be doing so well. He often spent time at Marty's house. The boys had a unique close friendship now.

The companionship was also good for Marty, an only child who was extremely intelligent and well spoken. People often considered him a miniature adult, a replica of his pharmacist father who owned the only drug store in Strathroyal. In school, he had skipped a grade. His teachers referred to him as a cerebral little man. He had a hunger for understanding anything scientific and was effortlessly able to explain complex problems. His teachers and peers considered him one of the smartest students in school. He would, no doubt, go to university and take over his father's business.

Because he grew up in a world of adults, he had little contact with children his own age. As a result, he lacked most social skills. Although he could effortlessly carry on an intellectual conversation with an adult, conversing with other children was awkward. He became tongue-tied and could only manage to sputter trivial anecdotes, which others often didn't understand. They laughed at him and he became a misunderstood misfit and eventually a loner. Like Jamie, he learned to entertain himself and was normally content to read books and play chess with his father.

Although they were two grades apart, the boys were the same age. From the first day they met, they bonded. Most of the people who knew them thought they were a strange pair. Few saw how similar they were. Both had specific distinctions imposed by their peers that set them apart from their social group. Because of their unusual individuality, few people understood their need for acceptance and companionship. They connected because they were able to give this to each other unreservedly, unconditionally. Jamie understood what Marty was feeling and unable to say. Marty understood and clarified the questions Jamie was unable to put into words.

Every day, the two walked to and from school together. Sometimes they talked; sometimes they sauntered in silence. Often they discussed concerns about school. When one told of a distressing incident, the other nodded with absolute authentication. Like conjoined twins, they identified each other's thoughts and feelings. Marginalized in dissimilar yet parallel ways, they were kindred spirits, allied and attached. It made them inseparable.

Jamie often went to Marty's house. He learned to play chess and word games. It surprised Marty that for someone deemed slow, Jamie learned quickly. When he knew the games, he often legitimately won. Effortlessly, he recognized and affirmed Jamie's intellect.

"You're pretty smart, Jamie," he would say. His friend would only smile and shake his head. The boys never verbally contradicted each other. It was an implicit, unspoken rule of their relationship.

Early in the friendship, Marty informed Jamie that his parents didn't allow him to go to the minister's house. Jamie didn't ask him for an explanation, although he wondered why Marty's mother and father didn't like the minister. When the weather was good, sometimes he would come over to play outside. Constance would bring drinks and snacks; that seemed to be permissible. Jamie accepted the situation because he was thrilled to have a friend.

One day on the way home from school, Jamie was deep in thought and unusually quiet. It had been a day that hadn't gone well. He had been in a fight in the playground with another boy who had bullied him relentlessly. Usually he was able to walk the other way but today the remark was too personal to ignore. Anthony had made fun of his family. He had mocked Martha and Mrs. Sluis. This time, the *sticks and stones* cliché didn't do its work. There was nothing left to do; he surprised even himself and hit the boy in the face. Anthony's nose started bleeding profusely.

The stunned boy fell down crying. "Help! Help! Jamie hit me!"

The other children were flabbergasted. Although most of them were glad that someone had finally stood up to the bully, they were completely astounded it was Jamie. They acknowledged him with newfound respect.

Unfortunately, they couldn't deny what they'd seen when the teacher asked, "Did Jamie hit Anthony?"

Crying uncontrollably, Anthony was escorted to the nurse's office. A perplexed teacher marched Jamie to the principal's office where he was strapped five times on each hand. He was informed that Mrs. Sluis would be contacted. His penance was to write, *I must not hit other people* a thousand times, a task that would take hours. He could already see the sad look on Mrs. Sluis' face when she received the telephone call. He was completely humiliated and reminded of the way he had so often felt in the minister's office.

On the walk home, Jamie was unusually quiet.

Marty respected Jamie's dejected mood but finally asked, "Do you want to talk about it, Jamie?" It hadn't taken long for the account of Jamie's deed to spread through the school. As a result, Marty had already heard about the playground scuffle.

Jamie gave Marty a grateful look. "Anthony said that my sister was ugly and stupid. He told me that Mrs. Sluis doesn't really love us. She just feels sorry for us." As the words tumbled out, Jamie kicked a stone on the sidewalk. "The principal said I should just ignore him, but I just wanted him to stop. I didn't even know I was going to hit him. It just happened."

Marty could see the tears in Jamie's eyes. "I'm sorry Jamie," was all he could say.

Jamie acknowledged the empathy with a smile and then he continued, "Then the worst thing was being in the principal's office. It made me think about learning the catechism. Did you ever have to study it?" Jamie spoke slowly and gave his friend a painful look.

"No!" was the emphatic response. The answer shocked him but also resonated to a deep obscure place.

"Good. It isn't much fun. I don't learn it anymore because Mr. Sluis doesn't live with us now. And Mrs. Sluis says there's lots of time to learn it when I get older."

"Will he teach it to you when he comes home?" quizzed Marty.

"No, he's always going to be in the nursing home. He's never coming back. He can't even talk anymore."

The Journey Home

There was silence. The boys looked intently at each other. Each was unable to acknowledge or release the constraint that suddenly loomed between them. It was an obstruction too massive to scale with language. When they came to the corner where they usually parted ways, Marty continued in the direction of North Street.

"I think I'll come to your house today. I can help you with your homework. Is that OK?" he asked nonchalantly.

"What about your mom and dad?" Jamie was taken aback and concerned, given Marty's parental restrictions.

"I'll telephone them and let them know I'm at your house. They won't mind," was the composed response.

"Good, if you stay for supper, maybe we can have beans and toast. It's my favorite." He didn't ask if this was something Marty liked and was unaware that his friend had never tasted this special meal.

Everyone was surprised. Marty's parents had often wondered why he wouldn't go back to the minister's house after his first few visits. They knew he loved the hot chocolate Constance made for him. When Jamie became Marty's friend, they were overjoyed he'd finally found a companion. His parents still thought it strange that he refused to enter the manse.

The adults had questions about Marty's change of heart, but no one wanted to intrude on a friendship that was as unique as the two boys themselves were. Like opposites on a color wheel, they complimented each other to create a compelling, spectacular work of art that defined the splendor of friendship. The people, who knew them, stood at a distance and admired the inexplicable masterpiece.

Marty stayed for supper. He didn't understand what was so special about beans and toast. All the same, he enjoyed it for Jamie. It was a gift that alleviated the pain in Jamie's hands and heart.

28
The Leaving

After the move to North Street, the next few years in Martha's life were relatively uneventful. High school was undemanding because she always expected more of herself than her teachers did. Every day, the walk to the big school on the hill was an undisturbed relaxing time to plan and rehearse the answers to academic questions that might arise in class. She worked hard to accomplish her mother's dream that she get an education. She would excel; she would make Mama proud. At times, the flame flickered, threatened by the unnatural events that composed her life, but it was never extinguished. When endangered, she would hide it carefully in a recess of her soul, protected at all costs from the reality of her life. To shelter its survival, she extended herself around it. Because nothing mattered more than keeping the spark lit, she often appeared aloof and unapproachable to outsiders. Her aspiration to be a teacher was the only dream that had substance and meaning; she clung to it believing her mother would somehow make it happen.

Every six months or so, John visited to show interest in his charges and to give Constance money for their care. When Martha turned sixteen, Constance would not consider John's suggestion she quit school and go to work. The day John came to visit, Constance quickly excused Martha from the room; she listened secretly behind the door.

"You will not stop this child from reaching her potential," she had informed him.

"She doesn't need school," he retorted.

"She is in my care and I will decide what she needs," Constance had replied.

A long silence followed. Constance stared at him. No woman had ever spoken to John in this way; thus, he found it very intimidating. For the first time in his life, he backed down from a female. It unnerved him, making him uncomfortable and angry.

"We'll see," he managed to say, knowing unless he resumed total responsibility for Martha's care, Constance was right. Right now, it wasn't an option he wished to consider. He resisted slamming the door as he left.

"You can come out now, Martha." Constance said with complete composure.

Martha emerged in tears from behind the door. She hugged Constance.

"Thank you so much," was all she was able to say. "Thank you, Constance!"

Long ago, Martha had given up trying to understand the twists and turns of her life. Only acceptance made it possible to live. She seldom allowed feelings to show. When she was emotional, she felt fragile and breakable. It was much easier to pretend and hide behind a veil of composure. Today there was no need to hide. It was the first time she called Constance by her first name. Mrs. Sluis had said they could call her whatever they wanted. Jamie had often questioned Martha about what to call Mrs. Sluis. He wanted to call her mother but it just didn't seem right. In his heart, he believed that if he used the word, something of his mama would be lost. When he asked Martha what their mama would want them to do, she didn't know what to tell him. She assured him that it didn't really matter, their *real mother* would understand. She told him Mama was different than Mother. There were different names for special people. Jamie didn't know what to do so he just kept calling her Mrs. Sluis. Today, Martha finally believed what she had told Jamie, but she still couldn't call her mother. For Martha, calling her Constance seemed a good compromise. For Constance, the familiarity was an unforeseen gift; she was overjoyed and hugged her cherished daughter.

When she received the school award for being the top student, the flame that had flickered became a fire that burned brightly. With it came a scholarship that would allow her to go to Teachers' College. Even though she had long ago given up believing there was a God who cared, there were unvoiced prayers to her mother's God. Too much reality had disillusioned her beliefs and values. A loving God would not have left her and her brother stranded. In reverence to her mother's spirit, she thanked her, believing in some surrealistic way *She* must be responsible for making the dream happen. Somewhat begrudgingly, she opened the door and acknowledged God; she was very grateful.

In September, Constance had to go to work on the day Martha was to leave for college so she would be taking the train to London. Jamie and Constance stood silently in the warm sunshine outside the station. Each person held back tears. Words were unnecessary. Their hearts laced together, intertwined with cords of experience that would perpetually bind them to each other. Martha kissed Jamie and hugged Constance goodbye. She would be back on weekends but now at last she was free to let her heart be her home. Free to put aside the weighty responsibility of promise she had carried since her mother's death. She had anticipated that the leaving would bring a temporary sense of release from her duty to Jamie, but in reality, she had mixed emotions. She saw Jamie waving, knowing he would continue to do so until the train was out of sight. She already missed both of them.

The rhythmic movement of the train let her mind wander to the surprise party given the day before. Churchwomen and acquaintances from school had come to wish her well. She had tried hard to keep them at arm's length but their tangible kindness had dented the resolve to stay unapproachable. She fought back the dammed up wall of tears. Did these people really care? Had she misread their intention over the years? Could she have been so wrong about everything? She set the thoughts aside. It didn't matter now that she was leaving. This piece of the puzzle didn't fit into the dream she carried, so it was quickly discarded before it could clutter and cloud her single-mindedness.

After the party, Constance tried to have a *mother-daughter* talk. Martha was uncomfortable; she wanted to go to bed because she was tired. Constance's disappointment was so obvious that Martha quickly embraced her lovingly and thanked her for her years of caring.

"We needed each other," Constance said graciously.

Martha was annoyed with herself for not being able to tell Constance how important she was to her. Much later, it occurred to her that there had been no suggestion of going to say goodbye to Rev. Sluis. She wasn't sorry that he had been purposefully and permanently, erased from their daily lives.

When the evening ended, Martha tiptoed in to kiss Jamie goodnight; she realized he too had evolved. He was no longer the little boy she had tried so hard to nurture and protect. Lately she didn't understand his reserved nature; she assumed it was his age. Soon he would be in high school. Since his friendship with Marty, his need for her had changed. She smiled remembering how proud he was of her. The local newspaper had taken her picture at the graduation ceremony and he had cut it out of the paper to display on his dresser.

Jamie, the young impressionable child, hugged her, unwilling to let go.

"You're famous now, Martha," he had beamed at her proudly. "You're so lucky – you got all the brains in the family."

There was no point in trying to dispel this perception. Someday surely, he would realize he had gifts that were so much more important than being academic. Although she knew there were things she could have, should have done differently, the extravagance of emotion were again dismissed. Regret would only give way to sentiments that could not be resolved with logic. Someday when her life was hers, when she was free from the heaviness of experience, she would sort it all out.

Remorse for not telling Constance what was in her heart followed her to bed. It nudged and poked her and wouldn't let her sleep. Finally she got up, found a piece of bright yellow paper and wrote what was truly in her heart, what she had wanted to tell Constance earlier in the evening.

> Dear Constance,
> This yellow paper reminds me of the sunshine you've brought into my life. You're always there for me and I know as I'm writing this I'll miss you! I love you.
>
> Love Martha.

She left in on her dresser. When Constance found it, she wept and put it in her wallet; it remained there until she died.

When the train pulled into the London train station, Martha was determined to make them all proud of her. Attending Teachers' College meant leaving the only two people who mattered. She summoned the resolve needed to make the dream happen, believing it would empower her transformation. She would emerge and show the world her colors. This one thing, she would do for herself; then it would be possible for life to begin anew. She would be a teacher. She would be independent and able to look after Jamie.

At the boarding house, she was to share a room with

a girl from Woodstock named Anna. It was immediately apparent to Martha that they were complete opposites.

When they met, she hugged Martha, "We're going to be such good friends. Can't wait to be sisters." She went on to tell Martha all the particulars of her life.

Even if she had wanted to share her family information, there was no opportunity to do so. The landlady, who Martha had found through a friend of Marty's parents, called them for dinner. She seemed pleasant and straightforward as she explained her rules to the girls and wished them well at school. The most basic edict was concerning men. There would be absolutely no tolerance for entertaining men alone in their room. It might be possible to have visitors if she or her husband was home; they would have to discuss it and an appropriate decision would be made. She made it very clear that she considered looking after their well-being, a sacred trust. They were encouraged to come to her with any problems or concerns. They could call her Mother Jane or Mrs. Lehman, or Mrs. L. She preferred Mother Jane because she considered herself a substitute guardian for young women who were away from home for the first time and would no doubt need her expert maternal support.

She would make them breakfast, pack a lunch and make dinner. Of course, if they weren't going to be home they needed to inform her a day in advance. It had been a long time since anyone had made my breakfast or lunch, thought Martha. Mrs. Lehman's demands seemed reasonable and she determined to try hard to get along with Anna and make the best of her year at Teachers' College. She knew she would always call her Mrs. Lehman.

Later as they unpacked their clothes, Anna continued to

talk incessantly. Martha gathered she had a colossal interest in boys and had had a number of boyfriends in high school. Martha concluded that her roommate was very fickle because she couldn't wait to see how many men would be available at college. She was completely engrossed with being on her own, away from her parents. Finding a husband seemed to be her first priority.

Martha liked and was comfortable with silence. Anna's constant chatting was annoying but she took consolation in the realization she wouldn't have to talk a lot. She certainly wouldn't have to reveal much about herself. That was exactly the way she expected to keep it. To drown out the jabbering of her roommate, she carefully set her music box on the night table and opened the lid to release the melody.

29
The Promise

"Hello pretty princess."

She giggled. He put his head close to hers and again whispered it softly, lovingly in her ear.

Then she would throw her arms around her beloved daddy and ask, "Will you marry me Mr. Prince?"

"No precious princess, but someday I'll find you a prince," was the unchanging response.

Her mother, Esther, would smile and say, "First school, then a prince."

She'd laugh as he swept her up, hugging and throwing her at the same time. It was their game. Every day they played it; every day until he went away.

That day when he held her so close, she protested, "Daddy, you're hurting me."

The child sensed a difference. They played the game one

last time, but the familiar light heartedness was missing. The hug, the tears, the unwillingness to let her go and the strange clothes he was wearing were all mixed together now into a memory that needed to span a lifetime: his and hers.

When he went away, he waved and said, "You'll always be my pretty princess." He blew her a kiss and put his hand on his heart.

She caught it and put her hand on her heart. That too was part of the game. One last time they played it.

The voice came again, "Hello, pretty one."

Martha was in class trying to listen to the lecture about classroom management; she found it harder to dismiss the voice the second and third time she heard it. Professor Newton was giving an uninspiring talk about how to maintain order in a class with rowdy boys. The disinterested mood was evident by in the students who were fidgeting and disengaged in what he was saying. The lecturer was oblivious to his complete lack of effectiveness.

Martha did her best to take notes and listen to the instructor's monotone voice. In this class, there were times when even she was preoccupied. It was easy to slide into the comfort of memory. Normally, dwelling there was an extravagance Martha had long ago abandoned. In her youth, it had offered some consolation. The memories were interludes that were easy to slip on and off, like well-worn comfortable slippers that helped to warm the coldness of reality. Then there came the gradual realization that her feet had grown too large. When the slippers pinched, she left them behind. In the stern practicality of life, there was no consolation in the phantoms of the past. Yet in this class, it was easy to relinquish the resolve and rest in the protective arms of a father she had long ago lost and just barely remembered.

Martha's world did not include fairy tales. Unlike her brother, the story of Peter Pan did not entice or draw her in. The fantasies of childhood held no attraction for her. For too long she had lived in the grown-up world. Her innocence had died with her parents. Although she seldom complained, her vulnerability was hidden by stoic exterior attire that protected her from the pain of loss and permitted her to survive outside of Neverland. Eventually there resided in her an unacknowledged anxiety of remembering. Like a toxin, locked in a box, it was not to be touched lest it should somehow seep into the relative manageable existence of daily life.

The armor protected but also <u>marooned her. Often</u> it left her stranded, solitary in crowded places. She wandered alone, dodging attempted efforts by those who wanted to engage her in friendship. Eventually they stopped trying. Jamie and even Constance accepted her detached persona, loving her in spite of her apparent insensitivity.

Life in London, soon took on a comfortable routine. Mr. and Mrs. Lehmann were cordial but eventually gave up pressing her to be personal. She managed to draw away from Anna by not engaging in conversation and by continually studying. At school, she easily maintained her allusive manner. Since she made no attempts at friendship, her peers simply left her alone. Her only focus was learning how to be *the teacher*. The resolve to emerge and show herself was stifled by practices she had learned to survive. She needed someone to teach her there was another way.

"Hello, pretty one." The persistence and nearness of the

voice made her realize it was coming from Joe who was sitting behind her.

This time, a part of her center that had fallen into a deep sleep, stirred. She had successfully ignored all of his attempts to engage her in conversation. It was easy to see that Joe was not part of a culture she knew or wanted to know. Suave, cultivated and genteel were foreign and uncomfortable qualities to Martha. He was tall and well groomed, always wearing the required shirt and tie. She could see his clothes fit and were a cut above the ones that came from the Simpson Sears' catalogue. She had no desire to make a fool of herself by taking part in an exchange that could only serve to make her look like a small-town girl.

There were few men at the college. Teaching in elementary schools was largely the domain of women. Men, who attended Teachers' College instead of university, probably had not been able to make the grade. They were second best scholars who no doubt, would eventually aspire to become elementary school principals.

Women often buzzed like bees around the men who were there, hoping to snare one and emerge with a ring instead of a teaching career. Several indiscreetly tried to get his attention. Like adolescent schoolgirls, they exposed their eagerness, stripping themselves of any dignity. Anna was one of them. He played intriguing word games with them, obviously enjoying their advances. Even so, he always kept them at a distance by never divulging anything of himself.

Martha was annoyed with herself for having a certain admiration for the easy smoothness he used to deflect their advances. He was a master and he moved those around him like pieces on a chessboard. She wondered why the girls couldn't see they were pawns in his game. It was humiliating to watch how they near prostrated themselves at his feet to get his attention.

In most classes, seating was optional but always he seemed to be positioned behind her. Like a stone in her shoe, it rubbed and irritated her focus.

"Hello, pretty one," persistently his voice whispered again.

His tenacity annoyed her. Finally, she turned around, "Leave me alone," she snapped after many futile attempts to ignore his remarks.

For the first time, their eyes met. It startled her to see their intensity. She expected them to be cold and thoughtless, but instead they were warm and inviting, reflecting the color and warmth of enticing blue waters. For an instant, she imagined she saw his soul and more surprisingly a reflection of herself in the deep dark waters. It left her totally, visibly shaken and disordered.

"Ok, but only if you have coffee with me after school," was the casual response.

"No!"

"Then I'll just keep on asking."

"Don't bother – I won't change my mind. There are lots of girls who'd love to go out with you, why don't you go and bother them?"

"Because, you're the only one I'm interested in," he whispered.

The bell rang. She slammed her books shut and hurried past him out of the room, painfully aware of his eyes following her.

The next day, the first practicum placement began so

there was a reprieve from his advances. She expected him to move on.

That night as she lay in her bed, she saw his eyes again. She dismissed the memory, altogether rejecting the encounter and fell into a fitful sleep. Unknowingly she clung to a distant likeness. It was her father's voice whispering, "Hello, my pretty princess. Remember? I promised."

30
Time

When Thomas was institutionalized in Strathroyal, working, tending him and caring for the children, occupied all of Constance's time. Life took on the routines of normalcy even though nothing ever felt normal again. The responsibilities weighed heavily on her time and spirit. She worried about the children. She realized that in pragmatic ways, living had been much easier when Thomas had provided a life for them. Now she felt handcuffed to her varied responsibilities and with Martha at school in London, providing the stability Jamie needed, left her feeling stressed and tired. The life she had cultivated so precisely now seemed overgrown with tasks that were difficult to naturalize, like weeds that grew deep roots. The simple pleasures of daily living had turned to obligations demanding disciplined routines. Dark clouds settled in and obscured the warmth of the sun. It happened gradually like the fading of a loved garment. Only shadowy hues of her former life remained to be enjoyed. Life, overgrown with responsibilities, did not allow for enjoying the tranquility of the garden she had lovingly tended.

Now she treasured time. It was a precious commodity that was carefully packaged. There were days she felt cheated because there was so much to do and so little time. Time had become a reckless robber of her youthful dreams, trampling her content nature as it hurried past. Silently she rebelled. Secretly she was annoyed that the benefits of position and prestige were no longer hers. The contradiction of it did not escape her. The desire for independence, so often her dream, was now an incubus from which she longed to break free.

The children felt it. Martha seemed to understand and effortlessly embraced the posture of adulthood. She did more at every opportunity to assist with the demands of daily living. On the weekends she was home, she became a steady, unshakeable strength. She did what she had seen her mother do. Constance saw it, accepted it and thanked God that the child she had loved was strong enough to return that love so selflessly. She believed Martha was a precious gift, a God-given solace sent to sustain her during this demanding, punishing time.

Jamie, now a young man, continued to be well behaved at school and at home, although he now carried a dreariness that often left him sullen and forlorn. Because Marty was now in high school, he walked back and forth to school alone. His classroom had once again become a lonely, miserable place. He began to slip more and more into a dream world, created to deal with his changing reality. He liked pretending he was invisible. Sometimes he tied a towel around his eyes so tightly that stars appeared. He imagined drifting from star to star trying to find the mother he barely remembered. Her face was now a blur that was nearly impossible to distinguish. Sometimes on a good day, he could hear her whisper her name. Nothing else remained. Like the last leaf, clinging to the tree in winter it waited, waited to fall from memory.

When Martha was home, he saw how she was changing. After she went away to school, a subtle distance came between them. He dared not try to cross it, fearing she too would disappear from his life. In the mundane routines of daily living, there was some safety. When everything remained regulated, when there was no space for disorder, he could breathe. Marty still came over regularly and helped him with his homework and now they even talked on the telephone. The satisfaction of being with him was cloaked by an inexplicable fear that eventually he too would be gone. Although he wouldn't allow himself to think about this possibility, the apprehension stubbornly intruded its way into his peace of mind. As always, Marty understood. He did consider the possibly their friendship wouldn't survive their separation. This time, he was able to put it into words.

"Jamie, we are always going to be friends, aren't we?" he asked on a day that Jamie seemed dejected. "Please promise me you'll always be my friend, my best friend." He trusted, believed with all his heart that their relationship was mutual. He needed to know Jamie believed it too.

Jamie had no idea how Marty always knew what he was thinking. He didn't let him see the tears in his eyes.

"OK, I promise." He managed to say, then added, "Let's shake on it then." The uneasiness slid from his body as the two young men shook hands. An unexpected hug sealed the covenant.

Initially Jamie mutely rejoiced in Thomas' absence, not really understanding why. When Martha and Constance had discussed the minister's condition over dinner, his appetite would disappear and a hard knot formed deep inside his stomach. He imagined strange sensations: a touch, a whisper, a taste, all of which were revolting. At first, he would excuse himself and go to the bathroom where he tried putting his fingers down his throat to rid himself of *the thing* that seemed to be stuck there. Soon he realized that throwing up caused Constance and Martha so much concern, that he stopped. They fused and fumed like mother hens until he felt smothered by the attention. He was unable to explain it to himself let alone to anyone else, not even Marty. Eventually, doing something that caused the two people he loved pain, was too caustic to continue.

To shield himself during the conversations about Rev. Sluis, he learned to use invisibility as his cover. If he sat very, very quietly, pushing the food on his plate around, Constance seemed not to notice. He could block out anything he didn't want to hear. Most of the time, the knot loosened. Sometimes it simply refused to budge and then he would escape to the refuge of the obscure place where he felt nothing.

It worked so well at home, that it became common to retreat to the place of unseen shelter whenever he felt threatened. When his peers at school taunted him as a *dummy*, when the teacher kept him in at recess to finish his work, he donned the angelic protective apparel. He saw and heard no one. It became a safe, comfortable existence.

Church was the same. Jamie didn't like church. He went

The Journey Home

and sat in silence, giving the appearance of a sweet child, engrossed in the rituals of religion. Other women regularly asked Constance what she did to get him to show such exemplary behavior. Mothers used him as an example for restless prodigies who in turn, resented him for his proper demeanor. They could not know he was seldom really in church. The God he chose to serve did not reside in the tall building with the beautiful windows. He rejected the words that captivated the worshippers. He saw past the pretty pretence there.

At first, he studied people; each week he picked a different subject. Each detail was noted. Clothing, gestures, hair, singing and all the little oddities were examined. Mrs. Maxwell was always sweaty and her clothes smelled of mothballs. She was a big woman who wore clothes that were too small. He wondered why she didn't know her tight clothes made her look big and probably made her smell. She smiled a lot but she didn't look happy. There was sadness in her eyes that looked familiar but defied explanation. He wondered if she was like him, pretending to be there but really, she was somewhere else. Only when she sang did he sense joy in her. He liked her, but didn't think that too many others did. When it became too much for his young mind to process, his thoughts turned elsewhere.

On occasion, he slipped into the picture on Aunt Lydia's wall. It became an irregular shelter, a place where he was protected from the raw realities of his life. He went there when he wanted to be alone. It didn't matter where he was in church, in school, anywhere he felt estranged from his surrounding, anywhere he felt hemmed in by authority, anywhere, or anytime he felt defenseless and alone. There he was sheltered, wrapped again in his mother's shawl.

The visit to the beach was a memory, a joy that lingered, like a security blanket, cuddled and embraced for comfort. He imagined his mother had been there with him. There he listened to the secretiveness of silent waves lapping the shore, breathing in the tranquility. There he let the sand flow through his fingers; he collected interesting stones like he had done with Samson; he shared his secrets with the birds, telling them about the people who sat in church, explaining to them he wanted to remember to love God, to be good and to work hard. There were wordless conversations that demanded wisdom beyond his years. Sitting at the water's edge, he was able to retrieve the lost embraces and comforts of innocence. He could be the person he was, with no disguise. There was no need to camouflage the wounds festering beneath the surface of his youth. The escape became the closet in which he hid when his world was too alien and lonely to endure.

After his visit to Lydia, he often thought of her. The picture had taken him aback. How was it possible that his beach, his place, was on her wall? He took as a sign, of what he didn't know, but he was penetratingly aware of its significance. At times, he imagined Aunt Lydia met him in the picture. There she was very different from the person he remembered. She laughed and told him stories. She answered his questions and held his hand. Sometimes the surreal image merged miraculously with an apparition of his mama.

So life continued. Time silently, effectively stole the robust physique of the family. Each was left separated from the source of its collective power. Its strength ebbed soundlessly into memory, soothed into silence with the absence of knowing what was happening. They labored to protect each other from any form of anxiety. Each unknowingly built a wall that kept the others outside of the familiar intimacy that had formerly framed their lives. Each wanted to believe that in time, all would be well again. All their deeds were the people they became. Like lessons on a chalkboard, time dulled and erased the memories. Only anemic markings remained, etched into the alcoves of their lives. Protected, like fine china behind locked doors, taken out and savored perhaps on special occasions.

Eventually, Jamie's bond with Marty became the unwavering stability in his reality. Everything else changed. Martha, now a grownup, was away at school. Constance worked and was always busy when she was home. Their friendship was the constant that sheltered him from circumstances, emotions and memory that persistently intruded on his confidence and independence. With Marty, there was contentment. With Marty, he could just be himself. In the awful instant when Jamie's life was suddenly, tragically, distorted again, Marty was there. It was with Marty that he could grieve.

It was completely unexpected. Buried deep in thought and the business of her life, a car from nowhere struck her as she hurried across the street to run one more errand. Constance died instantly. Like her dreams, time took her to itself, laughing at the merciless malice it once again inflicted on innocent bystanders.

31
Again

This time it was the funeral home. An old home, transformed to make death more palatable. Pretty pictures of pretty places adorned the walls. It was the pretence of peace. The smell of perfumed flowers hung heavy in the air. The casket, stark and open, exposed the facade. Dressed in her finest, Constance slept.

The mourners came, stared and shook their heads – such a waste, such a loss, so meaningless, such a good woman. These truisms explicated and touched nothing. They were comfortless words that washed over Martha as she politely shook their hands and endured their embraces. These sorry acquaintances unwittingly added insult to an injured spirit by seeking comfort from the inconsolable.

"Thank you for coming," was the only response she could muster.

Repeatedly she said it. At her side, she heard Jamie saying it. Although some faces, like Constance's friends and people from church, were familiar, she saw only obscured features, clouded remembrances of times past.

Daniel had made all the arrangements. She felt his presence beside her – strong and silent. Martha knew Constance would be proud of her son. Emily was unable to come. Thomas was not well enough to attend.

Suddenly amid the blur, Martha was aware of gentle hands and eyes that sought her out. A tender touch respected her pain. It was a selfless caress lovingly offered and gently given without demanding anything for itself. His eyes met hers and spoke silent, caring thoughts. His hands earnestly, genuinely acknowledged her hurt. Without words, he knew. He understood. There was absolute solace in his presence. It shook her stark, stayed demeanor and threatened the defensive partition, consciously constructed to contain the well-meaning trespassers who came to offer consolation and in turn expected reciprocal clichés of comfort.

Emotion obscured her vision. Tears threatened to erupt until determined resolve rose again. She looked once more for his eyes, but he was gone. Perhaps an illusion, she thought, but felt the object he had pressed into her hand. She clung to it, could feel his touch burning in it. Like the comfort of a fire on a cold night, it warmed the brittle reality of the day. For a fleeting moment, she was no longer deserted in the sea of people, still not connected to them, but suddenly not forsaken nor abandoned in their midst.

The young minister expounded Constance's virtues. He canonized her absolutely in glowing details. She was the epitome of selfless compassion. Pointing directly at Martha and Jamie, he alluded to all she had accomplished. She was a saint who had dealt with catastrophic loss. Lots of words Martha thought, lots of empty words. Constance would not have wanted the platitudes of praise heaped upon her. That's why she's a saint, argued Martha silently. She searched the audience for the eyes that would understand.

She dared not open her hand, fearing reason would expose the imagined illusion. A profound relief lifted her up above the crowd. She could see the sorrow there; it was tangible as it clung to those who had truly loved Constance. The realization that her isolation was self-imposed began to dawn. The palisade that had fenced her in cracked, exposing the vulnerability of a long lost child.

The formalities came and went. They moved to the cemetery. She knew the words: *from dust to dust*. The preacher said that only in death, does life has meaning. It is only after we have become memory that our life story becomes genuine and truly appreciated.

"When we are gone," he claimed, "our true picture is developed. In the end, nothing comes to nothing; only the essence of the honorable remains."

Martha tried to understand what he meant. Constance would not leave them – the resurrection of the body and life ever after. The expressions were hollow; they meant nothing as she tried to grasp the magnitude of their loss.

Jamie was totally lost. Only Marty's hug had offered any solace. The minister had so many words, he thought, so many useless words. Why couldn't he just say what her death really meant? Like all the others, she was gone. Once again, he was an orphan. The hollow language could not placate the emptiness that held him tightly in its grip. The beginning and end of the eulogy all sounded the same. He didn't know or care what it meant. The words were not enough. He closed his eyes and focused on her face; he clutched firmly to her love.

Once again, he wanted to be invisible, shielded from the loss that mirrored all the abject alienation he had endured in his short life. When Martha let go of his hand to say her farewells to the mourners, he felt defeated; he heard nothing. He was numb to the lyrics and gestures of those trying to reconcile their own feelings of inadequacy by illuminating her character. Drained of pride and purpose, he slipped away from the internment, utterly alone.

Martha sensed his absence even before she realized he was missing. Experience led her to Esther's grave. Dear God, she whispered, please let him be there.

Seemingly asleep, once again he lay prostrated, his arms outstretched hugging his mama's marker. Martha gathered him up and wrapped him in her arms. His emerging manhood, at first proudly resisted her touch; then wordlessly it slipped away. She rocked him as she had done so many times and through her own tears, comforted him with unspoken assurances of her love. Their unbreakable pain, unending sadness, unbending regret, flowed together like rivers that overflowed their banks and threatened to drown both their spirits in their imploding currents.

Anger and remorse, that she had not been enough for him over the years, filled her heart. She had failed him. She had promised her mother and she had failed. School will wait, she vowed silently. She would not let him be alone again; she would be home to him.

John found them. Silently he stood and watched. The tears

he had held back stoically for so many years now cascaded silently from an unknown secret cistern inside himself. He remembered his words to Jamie at Esther's funeral. How could he have believed that the man-child did not need to cry? Unexpectedly, he saw his former self. The futility of the life he had cultivated stared at him. The horrific epiphany shamed and humiliated him. Constance was gone, but now in a singular, providential way, he saw an opening for redemption. This time he vowed, I will not fail them or myself.

For a time, he stood back, not wanting to intrude on their grief, on their relationship. Finding a focus in his new promise, his strong, steady hands finally wrapped themselves around the orphans.

"It's going to OK. I promise it going to be OK," he murmured.

With all the niceties shattered, surprised and too drained to resist, they sat huddled together resting for a moment in the unexpected sunshine that broke through the clouds.

When the silence was the only sound left, he let them go. He moved back, respecting the resistance that emerged from their disbelief.

"Forgive me," he pleaded, "forgive me for everything. I hurt you; I wronged you. You are my family. I love you and hope you can learn to love me."

It was difficult to trust, even more difficult to believe. Yet they felt the authenticity of his words; his mouth spoke them and his eyes conveyed their truth.

There were so many details, so much to learn and so much to know. It grew dark, but in the small circle, there was a flame ignited by hope, kindling for the possibility of a new beginning. Perhaps too much to grasp, but enough at least, to know that love might make the future possible.

Martha remembered the object in her hand. Opening it, she saw a tiny angel engraved exquisitely on a translucent crystal. She fixed her eyes on it and then held it to her heart. Once more, she felt his reassuring touch.

32
The Journey Home

After he had relinquished the care of the orphans to Thomas and Constance, John had run from truth, from himself, from everything familiar. He ran deep into the shadows of the unknown. The faceless apparition of his dreams became his friend. It was always there hiding in the shadows, lurking behind the trees, running behind him, pursuing him. It became a game. Like a child's diversion of hide and seek, he engaged it. At first he was afraid, suspicious of its intent and then there was some comfort in its steady presence. It was constant, never wavering from the chase. Perpetual permutations that perplexed, yet in the peculiar pattern it took, there was some reassurance in the chaos. In the confusion, the focus and purpose for life was lost. It eluded him, concealed behind apprehension, obscured by desire; it seemed to be there only to tantalize his confused senses.

The perceived yoke of obligation that had been thrust on him appeared to be shed when Lydia was hospitalized. Like the skin of a snake, he squirmed and twisted his way free of it. Gone, he reasoned. He disowned his heritage, rented the farm and moved to London with Hagar. He shook off the cultural obligation of his youth. His tedious factory job in the city, for a time dulled his yearning for meaning.

Believe, he told himself. Believe that it is possible to escape the rigor of duty imposed by generations of the past. Believe. For a time, it seemed life was plausible until he realized there was a price to pay. Hagar deflected the ambiguous despondency that began to consume him. She soothed his troubled heart with unimagined primal pleasures, which for a time became his opiate. He needed more and more to satisfy his appetite. He took everything, unable to give anything until she was spent, taken hostage by her own demon. When both were empty shells, no longer able to fill the void in each other's heart, he sent her away. The satisfaction had worn off, replaced by futility. There was a hole where his soul had been – a deep cavity he tried to fill first with Hagar, then alcohol and other assorted sins. For a time, it dulled his senses but always the end was the same purposeless living; it left him sad, angry and terribly alone.

After the years of desperation, he went to visit Lydia. He realized her total depravity in some way mirrored his own. The doctor assured him there was no fault. He was not responsible for her predisposed illness. He knew differently. If only, he thought, he had made different choices, they might have avoided their journey to hell. He talked to her, even though the doctor told him it was useless. He grasped what he had done, what he had lost. At last, he prayed, begging for a possibly. A chance to untangle the hideous chaos he had created.

He changed. He prepared. He read. He devoured every book in the library that dealt with catatonic psychosis. He went to the university library and poured over every medical journal he could find on mental illness. Slowly he began to understand the search for meaning in life. In the process, he found himself. He found the boy who had tried for so long and so hard to please his father. It was the father whose rules and expectations were clear and obeyed without question. The realization he had become the person he loathed sent him to the brink of despair. He stood on its mountaintop and surveyed the decimated backdrop of his life.

He found the child his mother had clandestinely nurtured and loved. He dug out the root of deep seeded expectations he couldn't meet and he embraced the shrouded recollections that lay buried beneath the guilt of his brother's death. The brother he should have loved but only scorned. The brother who had sacrificed everything.

When he saw the panorama of his life, he wondered at his self-centered stupidity. The certainty of the revelation led him to a horrific scream, so long and loud that when it was finished he was spent in body and mind. It was a purging of sorts, far beyond his interpretation. He slept for days, unaware of the time or season. He allowed the process to happen and with it came a metamorphosis. When he awoke, it was as if he were a child again. He noticed the spring sunshine. He saw flowers blooming. He heard birds singing. A transformation although not understood, inspired and filled him with a sense of innocent, guiltless awe and longing. It was a hunger to live again. It was a yearning to love again. It was longing to be loved again. It was driven by his need to make restitution. He understood that his commission was to right the wrongs of his past. This belief now dominated his existence.

In the process, he met God. It was not the angry, vindictive God of his ancestors, who screamed of vengeance and hell, but a loving God who was kind, gentle and accepting. The God, who in her own way, his mother had worshipped. Her gentle words, once mocked and seen as weakness by the males who surrounded her, now came into a clearly formed focus. She knew this God, but the chains of her traditions had also shackled her; they were manacles that bound her to the preconceived notions of an irate creator. They became restraints, which twisted her strength and her life. She had had no means to free herself. She had no expectations except the ones predetermined for her. There were no options; her ethnicity tightly cemented her choices.

Despite the limits imposed on her, he also retrieved bits and pieces of precious moments she had bequeathed him. A soft caress silently given on cheerless days, a poem, a song long lost to timelessness were all snippets of salvation that might have offered some deliverance if release from the rules had been possible. Even though she could not travel it, she had showed him an alternate path. One where there was joy, one where there was love. He realized that he had seen it again in Esther. Was that why her presence had agitated him? Had he been trying to run away from truth all this time? Running from the one thing that he should have embraced?

The one thing that was so natural, so valid that it could make all things possible.

Words, he searched for words and wrote long letters of mental notes. Then words of explanation were written to abandoned family and forsaken friends. Finally, he wrote Lydia. It mattered not that she would not read it. Only that he confess and free himself of the transgressions that he had committed against her. He prayed that somehow, someday, she would be able to understand. Her forgiveness, he believed, was too much to ask. How could she forgive when he found it impossible to forgive himself? He hoped and prayed that at least she would be able to rid herself of any blame for the course of their lives and thereby be able to find herself.

When the answer to his prayer came, he was more humiliated than he thought possible. Dr. Smit telephoned him. Constance was dead. If he'd behaved differently, the tragedy might have been avoided. The tone in the doctor's voice confirmed his thoughts.

"Time to own up, John," he stated curtly as he hung up the telephone.

After Constance's funeral, he went again to see his wife. He tried to explain his catharsis, determined to undo the past. Her gaze never met his, still he thought he saw a spark; something of the woman he had loved was still there. He believed that if he could find the key to unlock her person, his own redemption might be possible and complete. He was convinced that somewhere there had to be a path that would release both their spirits. Long hours were spent rewriting his letter to her. It had to say everything; she had to know.

My dearest Lydia,

    Your forgiveness, I know, is not possible, but it is my hope and prayer someday you will be able to read this letter and you will then be able to understand, if not forgive me, for all the ways that I have sinned against you. God has forgiven me and I am learning to forgive myself. Your forgiveness, let alone your love, is something I don't deserve. I sincerely ask that you read this letter so at the very least, you will know nothing that has happened is in any way your fault. I humbly ask that you allow me these few moments and then you may rid yourself of me. You have paid too high a price for my sins. I give you my solemn oath that after these words, you will be free of me. I ask this only as a last obligation to our wedding vows from which I release you totally and completely.

    You must know that our marriage at the onset was real, although I confess that I was a hypocrite. Our life was not always pretence. When the call came to enlist, my father implored me to use my age as an excuse not to go to war. James, he argued, was much more suited for any sacrifice that our country might need. It was my job to produce an heir for our family. He believed I was stronger and more needed at home to secure our future. The knowledge that he was wrong haunts me. Please understand that I do not condemn him. He too, was shaped by his upbringing and understanding. I accepted without question his dictates, thereby giving up responsibly for my choices.

    James accepted his fate without argument or question. Willingly, he gave his life. I watched and knew it was wrong, but I chose to be a coward and sacrifice all of our lives. Now I know my pride and arrogance grew to repress the weight of the guilt. It was as if I watched another person take over my life. A person I hated. Moreover, as I became that person, I punished you. You, the only person who knew me and loved me. I confess I ignored your needs, focusing only on my own. I made myself the victim of fate. I should have considered our life a gift; instead, I resented it and you. I believe that is why you suffer so now. I punished you for my sins, for my shameful, cowardly choices.

Every day I live with the regret. It may be meaningless to tell you this, but perhaps someday, at the very least, you will know that it's not your fault. Dearest Lydia, the blame is mine, all mine.

When Esther and the children came to live with us, my bitterness grew. A sickness took over me. Her loving nature should have inspired me, but instead I resented it. I gave into weakness again. Together we could have made a life for them, but my selfishness didn't allow it. I thank God that the children found a loving home when Esther passed.

For my unfaithfulness with Hagar, I fear there is no redemption. I do not expect forgiveness from you or her. I wronged her as well. I know now my rebellion against you, against our marriage, was only a feeble attempt to bury the burden of James' death. It should have been me who died. You should have been free of me so many years ago. Even so, that doesn't change the present. Now because of my failings, my impotence, all of you are gone.

You must believe that all of the choices were

mine. You, like so many that I touched, were my victims. The only consolation for me is that the God has set me free of the past, allowing me to live this day. I no longer run from what has happened but humbly acknowledge my stake in it. The rest of my life, I will spend trying to make amends to those I exploited.

Constance has died tragically. Now, Martha and Jamie will again be in my care. There is an opportunity for me to make things right for them. How I wish you could also be part of their lives.

Now I live in the certainty of grace. The past is unalterable, but I believe that the future is ours to cherish, to live. I pledge to you my support for the rest of our lives. I will do all in my power to bring you back to living.

Dear Lydia, if you are reading this letter, I give thanks you have found yourself. It is my greatest wish that your life will also be restored and happiness will be possible. Your courage in the face of my ill-treatment gives me hope someday you will emerge a stronger person. Despite what I am told, I believe that you are still here. You are much too strong to stay forever locked up inside yourself. Fight my dearest, fight to come back.

Your loving husband,
John.

He read, wrote and rewrote it. Finally, after intensely scrutinizing every word, it was finished. He held it lovingly it, hoping and praying that somehow the words would find their way to Lydia's heart. If it had been possible, he would have sacrificed his own soul to redeem hers. He placed the letter in a pocket over his heart, fully aware of the sentimental silliness of his actions. It mattered not. This act of love was more important that anything he had ever attempted to do. It might well be too little too late. He was certain that any authentic happiness, any contentment that might be possible to resurrect, depended on it.

The fog had lifted. The demons that had taunted and engaged him hid and then retreated when the light of love met their gaze. Now eagerly clothed in resolute devotion, he set out. His course was clear. The journey home had begun on a "road less traveled."

33
Possibilities

In the five years since the death of his sister-in-law, John had not attended to the legal paperwork that would have formally transferred the children's parentage to Constance and Thomas. As a matter of principle and conscience, he had given Constance money for their care. Although he had been upset that Martha had stayed in school, he had resigned himself, believing he had absolved himself of her care.

The new possibility of having to father Jamie was terrifying. There was much he needed to learn about parenting. Martha was nineteen, so she was responsible for herself; he knew she was at school in London. In hindsight, he reflected, it was a very good thing; he was grateful Constance had stubbornly stood up to him. He thought it out as he drove to Strathroyal to see them. He was adamant he would provide for his charges. Jamie would live with him;

of course, Martha would finish college. First, he would have to convince them that he was a changed person.

Carefully, he devised a plan. The tenants had recently given up farming. He had thought he might sell the farm but now it was clear that moving home with Jamie would be a much better solution. He would be the father that Jamie had never had. He knew it wouldn't be easy, remembering his own sense of rebellion when he was going on thirteen. He acknowledged that his first endeavor at parenting had been a dismal failure but now he owed it to Jamie, to his brother and most of all to himself, to try. Recovery might indeed be possible.

The obstacles seemed somewhat daunting, but now he saw them as unexpected opportunities to make small meaningful restitution. It was providential, he thought, how Constance's death had opened doors for him. It was a heartbreaking tragedy; even so, his new autonomy allowed him to be thankful for this singularly unexpected prospect. It was far beyond what he deserved. He seized the moment and let himself hope. Somewhere deep inside his sanctified self, a small seed of faith was planted and sprouting. The mountainous turmoil that had enclosed his life had begun to shift, just enough to make it attainable.

His exchange with Martha and Jamie after the cemetery service, made him confident that his goals were achievable. He had taken the children home and left them in Constance's house with Daniel. There were few words spoken. He didn't know what the outcome would be, but at least the children hadn't rejected him entirely. That was an opening. The country life would be good for Jamie. He seemed to be a pensive, rather lonesome child. Since he had begun to understand his family dynamics, he believed going back to their roots would be healing for all of them.

Sleep eluded him that night. There were so many details to consider. The rent from the farm and a frugal lifestyle during the last few years, had allowed him to save a bit of money. Since he had already quit his job, he could now prepare to return to the country. He would need some help, but it all seemed doable now.

Like an old movie, he played the day's events repeatedly in his mind's eye. So much had happened; it would take time and hard work to make the changes. Like a gardener, he prioritized the affairs that needed tending and planning; he would cultivate and sow new crops. The laborers might be few, the labor would be difficult, but the harvest would be worth it.

There was one more thing he needed to do before he could think about sleep. He got up and examined his old worn wallet. Good thing I've been too cheap to buy a new one, he thought, as he inspected it. Deep inside its folds, he found the slip. He supposed it was the guilt of his former self that had cached it away, like a buried secret that could now be uncovered and perhaps even released. The numbers and writing were only vaguely visible. Perhaps, he thought, an omen of future events. Then he slept.

The following day he went back to the house on North Street. He had a long talk with Daniel and Martha at the kitchen table. John outlined his plan, being careful to include Martha in the discussion. Martha perceived he was unlike the uncle she had known. Still she felt anxious about trusting his words. She had already begun to make plans to look after Jamie herself. The events of the previous day had left her drained and now there was even more to consider. Unraveled emotions made it difficult to think. The lifeline Uncle John was offering dangled in front of her dreams.

Jamie, surprisingly, wanted to go to school. The reality that he had lost yet another mother totally overwhelmed him. School would be normal and there he would have less time to think about his loss. Marty had asked him to come to his house after school. He knew his friend would help him understand what was happening. Yesterday was a blur. Uncle John's promises were still a blur. It was too much for Jamie to process; he needed the protection of friendship.

For a time after John's proposal, Daniel and Martha sat silently, each one trying to discern what to say and do. John understood. He explained that he needed to make arrangements so he could move back to the farm. He promised he would be back soon. Neither Daniel nor Martha doubted that John was determined to follow through on his plan.

For Daniel, it was a relief. Although he thought it might be possible to move to Strathroyal to tend to his invalid father, looking after Jamie would be very problematic. Of course, Martha would finish her year at college, but Jamie needed a home. Although he didn't know all the details, he still had some concerns that John might not be the best parental choice. Right now, there were not a lot of options. John was, after all, the child's legal guardian. After Daniel's residency in Toronto was finished, he had wanted to stay there or perhaps move to London. Now that the care of his father was his responsibility, he intended to open a family practice in Strathroyal. He had sent his sister a telegram but it was impossible to know if she had even received it. He was also aware that he resented her absence. Even so, he knew what he had to do and wholly accepted his duty.

As he drove back to London, John looked at his list. The first stop was the abysmal pawnshop. Not much had changed except the air smelled sweeter and denser. John knew the aroma. There was much more stuff than he remembered. Lamps without shades, armless chairs, legless tables, assorted bottles, knickknacks and boxes of all kinds were still crowded haphazardly into the small space. The chaos did not bode well for his mission. John quickly surveyed the room looking for the owner, remembering he was a strange old fellow. A younger, less energetic man, openly engaged in smoking a small joint, now occupied the shop. When John entered, he made little effort to stir from his reading or to conceal his illegal habit. He waited patiently. Like a new pair of shoes, patience was a virtue that still agitated and caused blisters of rebellion for John.

Finally, he said, "Ah, excuse me."

"Sorry, good book."

"Sure. Just wondering if you would check if you still have some things I pawned about seven years ago?"

"That was before my time; there's not much chance of that, my friend. That was in the old man's day. He died a few weeks ago and now I have a huge mess to sort out. His bookkeeping left a lot to be desired. Last few years, he only worked when he needed money. Seems that wasn't very often, given the mess he left. Got a slip?" The man spoke in a monotone voice.

John produced the scrap of paper that verified his claim.

The man eyed it incredibly, "You got to be kidding."

"No, no I'm not. It's important, can you try?"

"Might take a while; can you come back?"

"No," John quipped, "I'll wait." He was becoming aware of his impending impatience,

"Suit yourself. Have a seat," he motioned to an old chair in the corner of the dimly lit store. "I'll have to go to the back and find the book."

John looked at the cases of jewelry displayed under the glass counter. He scoured the contents, but was disappointed that his treasures were absent. After what seemed like a long time, the young man returned. He carried a large, tattered, accounting book.

"These are the old man's records. With any luck, should be able to tell ya what happened to the items."

Another ten minutes passed as he went through pages.

"OK, found your receipt number. Now if the old man had had any smarts, he would have recorded where he put things. Says they're still here but don't mean much as he often didn't record a sale. Little extra spending money, ya know. Such an old Jew."

John didn't know or care, but he smiled at the paradox of the comment. He allowed himself to hope, just a little, that the items could still be found.

"Hum, silver. There's a chance that the silver might still be here. He had a habit of putting good silver pieces away from the light, to keep the tarnish from settling. Trouble is if people don't see it, they don't buy it. Some drawers under the counter I can check."

He rummaged under the counter and produced a large drawer filled with small black velvet bags. One by one, he opened them to reveal the treasured possessions abandoned by the dictates of unknown necessities.

"Lot of good stuff here," he mused to himself, "been gonna get at this for a while. Maybe a good thing you came in."

John saw the locket even before the man identified the number on the small tag attached to it.

"That's it! That's the locket."

He opened it and was surprised that even the pictures of Martha and Jamie were intact.

Hidden in the darkness, the filigreed silver locket and earrings that Esther had worn so often had retained their shine. Her serene, beautiful face flashed itself across his memory. His brother had given them to her that last Christmas Day. He remembered not only her face, but also the face of his wife when she had admired them. His gift to Lydia that year had been a new washing machine. At the time, he had not believed in splurging on luxuries and had resented his brother's generosity to Esther. It made him look bad. If Lydia ever came back to him, he would show her that he loved her. More and more he understood the brother he had for so long resented. The young man's voice brought him back to the shop.

"Guess it's your lucky day," he quipped.

"It will be, if you can find the other things."

"Hmm, cameos – think he had another ledger for gold pieces. Lemme see if I can find it. Still wanna wait?"

John nodded.

"OK, well, if ya wanna go through this tray of rings, ya can try to find the wedding ring you're looking for. The old guy never bothered to put tags on them so you'll have to know what you're looking for. And here's a bag of gold stuff that's marked *SELL*. Think he usually sold them to a jeweler for old gold after a few years," he said. "I can trust you, right?"

"On my honor," John smiled.

Again, the irony of the question did not escape him. Yes, he told himself, today you can trust me. Today, I am even able to trust myself.

The tray held about fifty gold bands, strewn about with no apparent order. He examined each one carefully for the inscription that would identify the ring. It wasn't there. The larger canvas bag contained an assortment of gold, necklaces, bracelets, rings, all seemingly in a state of disrepair. He rummaged through the mess; angst was beginning to set in. There was uncomfortable awareness that each item he touched was a tiny fragment of some person's life. He wondered at the story each piece could tell. Would the tales be as despicable as his own? So many more things mattered now. Like a grain of sand irritating his conscience, the surreal imagined implications of the surroundings began to agitate him. Time to go, he decided, as he sorted out another wedding ring in the heap.

Love always, James 01-01-36

A drop of perspiration that had begun to form on his brow fell on the recovered band. Love always!

"That's it!" he exclaimed, putting the ring on his pinkie finger, "that's it!"

The young man returned, "Sorry, couldn't find the

cameo – probably sold. Leave me a telephone number and if it shows up in some other drawer, I'll give ya a call."

It was sufficient for now. John was gratified to have found at least two of the items. Some things lost may never be recovered, he reflected. The implications of the truth had not escaped him. Like his shadow, it had followed him as he had begun his journey to healing. Keep the faith, he told himself as he shook off the relapse into memory.

"OK, how much?" John asked.

"Hundred and fifty, cash. That's a deal for you."

Obviously, this young man was related to the original owner, John speculated, but never mind, it would be worth it to see the look on Martha and Jamie's face when he surprised them with the treasures.

John opened his wallet; it was as good thing he had stopped at the bank before he came.

"I only have a hundred and twenty-five with me, but I'll come back and give you the rest," he promised.

The young entrepreneur could see the contents of John's wallet. Since he had expected to negotiate the price, he agreed. It was going to be a good day.

"OK, you look honest," he said, as he greedily stuffed the money into his pocket.

Must be the old guy's son, John smiled, as he hurried out of the establishment into the daylight.

He felt invincible. The next stop was the jewelry store on Dundas Street. He wanted something beautiful for his wife. When she was ready to resume living, ready to come home, she would know she was loved.

34
Natural Causes

The doctor talked to her as he did on every visit.

"The truth of the matter is, dear Lydia, that you are already dead. You don't know it but your friend, Constance died unexpectedly. She was such a good woman, such a waste. She tried to be your friend, you know. She visited you and even brought the children here to see you. Like the rest of us, you rejected her love. It might have been better if you had died instead of her. We have tried, Lydia, tried to bring you back. Since you've refused, it's time to let you go. I know you really don't want to live anymore. I am truly sorry."

The old doctor spoke as much to himself as to her, as he swabbed her arm. The death rate in this ward had always been high. No one questioned it. Sick minds with no awareness or purpose often just gave up and died, letting their bodies succumb to what their minds had already done.

He sealed and then signed their fate. *Natural Causes* the death certificates read.

This month he had been a bit more cautious. There was an up-and-coming young doctor who wanted to try newer, more modern methods. He'd even had the audacity to query some of his diagnostics and treatments. Just like me when I was young, he theorized. No matter, his motives were always good and since there were no autopsies done, there could be no consequences. Most families were relieved when a loved one no longer had to suffer the stressful stigma of having one of their own locked up in the psychiatric hospital. He believed that his cause was entirely in keeping with his *first do no harm* oath.

At the same time, he was more deliberate in his actions and even thought briefly about retiring. Over the years, his practice had been very comfortable. The pay was good and he'd set aside a fine nest egg that was waiting to be spent. On the other hand, he still liked the control he had and the esteem in which he was held. The established doctor had free reign to do whatever he saw fit. He laughed aloud. He was King of the Crazy Castle. He smiled knowing some of the nurses used the term. He had never questioned the notion. It was a compliment and had its own benefits. Over the years, he had spun the delusion into a network of beliefs that suited his purpose very well. Now so entangled in the dogma, it would have been inconceivable, even impossible, to be free of the fine steel-like threads that held the web together.

Although his course was clearly set, he did have some regret about Lydia. For a time he had had hopes for her recovery. There had been small indicators she might be responding. A response to touch, some light in her eyes, had been markings of a return to the living. It truly saddened the doctor that her progress had not continued. When he felt sure her mind could not be revived, her fate was sealed.

Lydia had been sitting with her back to him. For the last few days, she had been able for brief moments to cross the threshold of her world into reality. When John had come to visit last week, she was vaguely aware of his presence far in the distance, near the door. It took all of her energy but she was beginning to think it might be possible to escape the darkness. She sensed a difference in him, but was unable to determine what it was. Those who cared for her seldom saw her, tending only to her physical needs. Feeding, grooming, toileting her in the shortest possible time was the goal. There were some who cared but because the extravagance of time was unavailable, they too came and went promptly, grateful that she had been calm and quiet, complying with their demands.

When the doctor began his soliloquy, she was at first confused. She liked him because he reminded her of her grandfather. Unbeknownst to him, she had looked forward to his visits. Unlike most, he spent time with her. He talked to her, telling her of other patients and bringing her news of the outside world. She had even begun to imagine that she might be able to communicate with him.

When she realized what he was about to do, it left her paralyzed with panic. Surely she had misunderstood. During her last visit, Constance had even talked to her about making a home with her when she was well. She had begun to envision that it would be a safe place. Now the news that her friend had died was like water on the small flame of hope that had begun to burn. Yet despite this setback, she didn't want to die. She turned to face him, but before she could meet his gaze, there was an unexpected intruder in the room. He was familiar, yet different.

"Hello, Lydia," he said quietly.

The doctor turned and saw him, "Well hello Mr. Jacobs. I didn't expect to see you today."

"Yes Doctor, I'm going to be a regular visitor from now on," John replied.

The doctor recovered quickly, "Glad you're here, Mr. Jacobs. I've was going to telephone you. Lydia is regressing. She's slipped farther and farther away."

Not true, Lydia wanted to protest, but the reality of her situation held her in its grip. Why was John here again she wondered. He had said he'd be back, but she hadn't really understood that he meant it.

John was sickened. He had been hopeful there would be a way out.

"She's lost all touch with reality, son. I've seen this type of illness many times. It doesn't usually end well. Realistically, release from her suffering might not be a bad thing."

"I came to try to talk to her and leave a letter," John stammered.

"Well, best you read it to her as soon as possible. I'm sorry to tell you, but her case seems hopeless. I'll let you alone with her and come back later."

Disappointment overcame him; he berated himself for waiting too long to make amends. He took the letter from his pocket.

"Lydia," he began, "I wanted so much to believe you could recover. So much has happened. I'm so very, very sorry."

He stopped, not knowing Lydia was hanging onto every word.

He put his hand on her shoulders and gently kissed the top of her head. It could have, should have been so much different. So engrossed was he in his own thoughts, his own guilt, he failed to notice the reaction of his seemingly comatose wife as he prepared to read her the letter. Her eyes became focused; she was aware of his words. She reached far, far back in memory.

The man she had married stood before her. She thought she had lost the memories, as she had lost him. He was tall and handsome. His dark hair was a sharp contrast to the fairness of his brother. Was it when James went off to war that a part of him had gone as well? Was that when the gentleness in him had died? It seemed he had refused to grieve, that he had hidden behind duty, compelled to choose alternatives that mirrored the darkest part of his character. She knew there had been no wisdom in either of their choices. Their road had split when they turned their backs to each other's grief. Was there a possibility that they could continue together?

John sat down and faced his wife. He took the letter and read the words that he had so carefully penned. When he looked at her, he was amazed to see the tears that seemed to be forming in her eyes.

"Lydia, Constance died and now the children are homeless again. Yesterday was the funeral. Martha is going to college and I am hoping that Jamie will agree to come and live with me on the farm. I have a second chance; we have a second chance. I'll be here every day," he promised. "Please, please come back to me."

He kissed her cheek and held her in the gentlest way. Then he put the letter on her table and rose to leave.

Cloistered for so long in the confines of her emptiness, she whispered the first words she had spoken for a long time, "John."

He was already at the door and thought he had imagined hearing his name.

"John," she managed again, this time with more determination.

They turned and met each other's gaze, fearfully. Lydia saw the truth he had spoken. John saw the woman he had married. He took her in his arms, rocked her back and forth. The pent up emotion of all the years flowed soundlessly from her eyes, washing away regret, flushing away the hurt. It was a divine song of lament that purged the malignancy. When she opened the door, hidden tears flowed and flooded the dark caverns, in which she had wandered. The regret of the past was washed away. She vowed never to return to that dark godforsaken place.

When it was finished, she took the key and locked the door behind her then tucked it in her heart. The realization it had been there all along, make her smile. Then deep from within, the smile turned to pure sweet joy. Then laughter started like a mountain spring, gurgling gently then gaining momentum until it splashed and splattered over the sides. Surprised by the unanticipated happening, John was caught up in the current. Together they floated in the clear pure waters, letting their hearts enjoy what their mouths could not put into words. Each one baptized, washed clean of past sins, they sat, hands and eyes clasped to each other.

"Take me home," she whispered. "Please John, take me home."

John was speechless. Yes, he wanted to take her home but given the doctor's diagnosis, just a few minutes ago, he wondered at the wisdom of her request. Was it really possible?

"I'll talk to the doctor," he said.

"No John – if you meant what you said, just take me home. You can help me be whole again. Help me, please, please help me."

It was the voice of the woman he had loved and wanted to love again. He had hoped and prayed for this moment but hadn't expected it so quickly. The idea so incredible, so impossible just moments ago, now seemed within reach.

Lydia attempted to stand. Her muscles were weak from lack of use. She steadied herself on him.

"John, be sure to let me know where I can get a hold of you." The doctor had returned to give John a final word of preparation for Lydia's impending demise. Never in his lengthy medical career had he been speechless. He was unable to utter a sound.

"She's alive," John exclaimed excitedly, "I'm taking her home." He was surprised to hear the words come from his mouth. Why not, he thought, why not?

The doctor recovered quickly, the thought of his earlier conversation ringing in his ears. Had she heard him? It wasn't possible; she had been too far away. What had happened? What had he missed? The self-made pedestal on which he had dispensed wisdom, split in half, exposing the lies at its core. He balanced himself on the door to keep from stumbling to the floor.

"Dear God," he stammered, "what have I done?"

His heart knew exactly what he had done. His arrogance had created a god who had dispensed judgment on minds too fragile to protest. He had become an angel of death who had spread its wings when he saw fit. He had been so sanctimonious, had been so sure that he was the answer to the suffering souls who he had terminated. The doctor steadied himself, moved to Lydia's chair and slumped into it. He put his face in his hands and wept tears of remorse.

Lydia and John were stunned. What could possibly have caused the doctor to react this way? John went to the door and called for a nurse to attend the distraught doctor, who was trying desperately to regain his composure.

"Yes, John, take her home. Take care of her," the doctor managed to say. He wondered how he would ever be able to make amends for his reprehensible deeds. He thought he had known everything there was to know about his patients. The reality that he knew nothing at all left him totally disheartened. "Go! Go now!" he hollered at the couple. They didn't know that his anger was directed at himself and not at them.

John and Lydia slowly they made their way out of the mausoleum into the sunshine. Lydia stood and looked at the forlorn edifice in which she had existed. She felt as if she had stepped out of a tragic novel. Now it was possible to close the book and start a new edition of living. In the distance, the unusual door came into view. Standing with John at her side holding her hand, the image was paradoxical to the passageway that had intrigued and invited her into its maze years ago. Now it appeared weathered and dirty. Beyond the entrance was a bleak, inhospitable panorama so unlike the enticing loveliness she had imagined seeing from her bedroom window that day long ago.

"I won't ever go back there," she said to herself.

John assumed she was referring to the hospital and replied, "Lydia, I promise you will never go there again. Let's go home."

She looked into his eyes and wondered how it was possible that he had changed so much. She wanted to believe they could start over, wanted to trust they could make a life together. She let John help her into the car. His hands were tender and loving. She felt in them, what she saw in his eyes.

As they drove to Strathroyal, Lydia listened as John explained how he had prepared for her homecoming. He had updated the farmhouse with a new stove and even a modern refrigerator. The room had been painted and papered in fresh bright colors. Most of the old furniture had been burned. He had planned to have all new furniture before she came home. He hoped she wouldn't mind that some rooms were a bit empty. When she felt up to it, they would go to the furniture store on Front Street and she could buy whatever she wanted. Lydia was overwhelmed by her husband's obvious care and planning.

"How did you know I would come home, John?" Lydia asked.

He looked at his wife wondering how to explain the inexplicable. "I learned love is able to make all things possible," was all he could say.

Although she had a multitude of questions, she decided to appreciate this moment silently. She totally savored the rebirth of their love.

The Journey Home

As they drove through the countryside, she was aware of unique transformation everywhere. Where there had once been farmland, new homes had sprung up. She especially noticed the colors. Intense greens, vibrant reds and energetic yellows, splashed across the landscape. The nightmare was over. She was awake. The world was real again.

The couple relished the soothing balm of serenity that was beginning to heal the abrasions of the past. It was so more than they had dared envision or anticipate.

35
Grace

It was Spring. The sun embraced the earth, breathing breath into barren ground. Crocuses exposed and unearthed hidden splendor buried beneath the frigid, sterile pallet. Robins wonderfully reappeared, resuming unfinished melodies. Rains caressed life back to the deep stillness, embroidering the canvas with color, ending winter's bleak reprieve. There had been poignant parting but death would not conquer; the finale greeted a prelude to a new overture of life. Spring, as much a credo as a season.

In front of her, Lydia sat in awe of the picture; no longer confined to the wall, it was now authentic. Perfect. The labor of lament had birthed a new truth. The sun shone; the water glistened. The summer crowds had not yet appeared. The beach was luxuriously empty. It reverberated with the faithfulness of waves lapping the shore, waiting for friends to come and share their secrets with her.

Like the flora of spring, Martha had blossomed. In Joe, she found acceptance and she found herself. He had persisted in his pursuit, this time not with words but with the language of kindness that asked nothing in return. He had done little things no one else had thought to do. On her desk appeared the notes for all the classes she had missed. He left a chocolate beside her lunch bag (she wondered how he knew it was her favorite kind). Then, a flower and a book appeared.

Finally, she looked into his blue, mesmerizing eyes and said, "Thank you."

He smiled then winked at her. It was enough to open the entrance to her heart. Like a bubbling spring, laughter spilled out permeating her pretense, washing away aloofness and sadness. When the barriers were rinsed away, she could no longer hide from herself or from him. The healing could begin. She gave him her hand. He held it tenderly, bandaged it gently and treated it with loving care. When Martha reached out her wounded hand to Joe, he knew it was actually her heart he had to treat.

Now able to forgive herself, the wounds of the past were healing. The salve of love was making it possible to let go of the lesions of grief. She could absolve fate. She could sanction a new season to emerge.

The lovers, Martha and Joe, found a piece of driftwood on the shore, smooth and worn by the embrace of countless waves. They would keep it, to touch, to remember, to celebrate this new beginning. Martha felt her mother's blessing as she fingered the silver locket that hung around her neck. She was content, savoring the day, permitting it to cleanse so many disappointments, preserving this memory to enjoy again on cold, dark days.

The blue in her antique sapphire ring reflected the brilliant blueness of the June sky. It was the color of Joe's eyes. They were the unforgettable eyes that had seen her and had not let her go. Joe had taken Martha to meet his beloved Gran. When he introduced her he said, "Gran, I haven't asked her yet, but this is Martha, the girl I'm going to marry. I think she's a lot like you."

Gran gave Martha a warm hug that let her know she was already part of her family. "If Joe loves you, then you must be a very special girl," she said. "Special people need special things." She took the exquisite ring off her finger and gave it to Joe. "I'll let you give it to her my precious boy. Your grandfather gave it to me many years ago. It's blessed with lifelong love."

Joe hugged his Gran and then got on his knees in front of Martha, "Will you marry me?" he asked simply. There were only smiles and tears as Joe put the ring on her finger. It was a promise, a symbol of his devotion and their life together. The memory was now as precious as the ring itself.

Jamie had also made a transition. At first, he had resisted, hiding behind a facade of apathy, afraid to be visible. Like the earth responding, rousing from its icy winter slumber to the renewal of warming rains and spring sunshine, the warmth of love also unlocked his twisted existence. In Lydia, he discerned a kindred spirit. They recognized themselves. The vulnerable child he had long ago left behind found his way back to the family who swaddled him in the comforting assurance of stability.

The quiet boy learned to drive a tractor and plant crops.

His spirit found solace and purpose in the cycle of the seasons. The land understood him and it was teaching him to appreciate and understand himself. Like the crops he tended, he began to grow confident and strong. When he looked at the sky now, he could hear his mother words. "Love as big as the sky," had new meaning.

Lydia and John sat, arms linked, on a blanket. They watched Martha, Joe, Jamie and Marty on the beach. They were a family.

Lydia admired the exquisite diamond ring on her finger. The day John brought her home, he had surprised her with it. The beauty and extravagance of it had amazed her. She cherished it not for what it was, but for what it meant. The stone was bright and clear like a mirror; it reflected the radiance of renewed commitment. She held the hand of the man who had come out of the past and walked with her to a new prospect of promise. Together they had found their misplaced dreams; now they were transplanting them to the future.

Joe was patiently explaining the procedure for skipping stones. "The water's just right," he said. "It's tranquil and smooth. We need to find small flat stones."

He showed the boys how to stand and hold the stones and flick them effortlessly across the water. The stones bounced smoothly over the water several times until they dropped into the shadowy depths.

"Wow! Can you explain why it works, Joe?" Marty asked seriously.

"Marty, everything doesn't need an explanation. Let's just learn how to do it," Jamie commented as he tried to skip the stones.

Marty laughed. His friendship with Jamie had remained vital to both the boys' happiness. He still wanted to understand it. He'd look it up in the encyclopedia, at home. The next time they came to the beach, he'd tell them why the stones skipped across the water. Then they would both enjoy and appreciate the beauty of it.

They had come to celebrate Martha and Joe's engagement and their graduation from teachers' college, but it was much, much more. Having found their estranged selves, they were free to laugh and love. Living was now possible.

They knew there were unfinished alcoves, whereabouts that needed cultivation, plants that needed tending, paths that needed wandering. There were unwritten melodies that needed words to be sung. There was untapped knowledge needing discovery. Yes, there were still peculiar impediments aching to be restored, braces that needed to be loosened. They were a work in progress, developing in the growing. Cultivating blooms in their seasons, not yet complete but enough for today. They were forgiven and forgiving, absolved of deficiency, released from shame and emancipated from guilt, now able to celebrate absolute affirmation.

They were composing a new melody, a new song of permanence. It was a motif of the rhythmic continuance of life. It was enough. Amazing grace had led them home.